MW01275475

Breakwater

Breakwater

Kate Duignan

VICTORIA UNIVERSITY PRESS

VICTORIA UNIVERSITY PRESS
Victoria University of Wellington
PO Box 600 Wellington

Copyright © Kate Duignan 2001

ISBN 0 86473 417 4

First published 2001

This book is copyright. Apart from any fair dealing
for the purpose of private study, research, criticism or review,
as permitted under the Copyright Act, no part may be
reproduced by any process without the permission
of the publishers

Published with the assistance of a grant from

Printed by PrintLink, Wellington

FOR NOELENE AND MICK,
MOLLY AND JACK

Consider this barbarian coast,
Traveller, you who have lost
Lover or friend.

James K. Baxter
'At Akitio'

ONE

'Ella, it's positive.'

The first thought: *I'll have to leave varsity.*

The second thought: *Fuck. God, fuck.*

The third thought: *It's okay. It will be all right.*

She lets her breath out slowly. The doctor remains quite still, peering at her over small green glasses, blonde hair startled all about the concerned professional face.

'Would you like me to refer you to someone you can talk this through with?'

The surgery carpet swims briefly up to her face. She focuses on her toenails, painted purple that morning, and steadies.

'No, I'm okay. It's okay.'

The doctor talks on, giving information, outlining various futures in careful, logical steps. Every now and then she asks a question. Ella glances out across the surgery carpark, and gives small answers, or none at all. Two teenage boys cut between the cars, unwrapping and eating hamburgers as they go.

Eventually the doctor sits back in the chair, considering her in silence.

'Perhaps that's enough for now. I can see you'll need some time, Ella. Shall we make an appointment for next week?'

'Yep, that would be fine.'

By then this will have become concrete fact, stored in the appropriate part of her mind, registered on official records. She will have considered it, and she will know what to think. For now, there is only the formless, engulfing thought, hitting against the simple day and changing the weather, the shape of the afternoon, everything.

As she stands to leave, there seems to be a certain awkwardness.

'Well. We'll see you in a week, okay? Get plenty of sleep.'

The doctor keeps looking at her, keeps a hand on her shoulder, until Ella smiles and shakes her off, stepping out from the surgery door to stand blinking in the bright waiting room.

*

Ella walks into the flat and checks the table for mail and the phone for messages. The afternoon sun slants over the kitchen floor, lighting up the set of red wine glasses lined up across the bench. It is warm and airless, and the glasses cast odd, elongated circles over Andy's piles of paper, his accounting books, and his bag full of gym gear left on the dining-room floor. The circles are pretty, but Andy's stuff is everywhere in this house; the house is pretty, but suffocating, and seems suddenly wrong.

They live at the base of Mount Victoria, which isn't a mountain at all. It is simply a hill slightly higher than the rest that circle the city. She walks up there occasionally. She likes to stand in the centre of the round lookout and scan the bowl of the harbour, picking out the sailboats, squinting to try to see the houses on the far hills. Then she paces back, resenting the point where the walkway drops sharply off the ridge and out of the wind, down into the shelter of the suburb.

Each month they find a real estate notice in the mail: *It has never been a better time to sell*. Andy laughs, and composes the description: Gracious, grand old lady, suntrap, a real delight. The house belongs to his second cousin, a doctor who has been removing cataracts in Mongolia for a decade now. They landed the safest, sunniest flat you could hope for.

Ella has lived here with Andy for six months, but maintains a stubborn preference for her first Wellington home, the two-room unit perched near the top of Houghton Bay with the window facing south to the ocean. Here she survived her first winter, thrived even on the daily battle with the wind, the occasional bird stunning itself on the sliding doors, and the fifty-seven steps down to the street. After some months she noticed tight balls of muscle developing in her calves. She thought of her father, calling her Skinny Lizzie and making her drink the creamy part of the milk at the top of the bottle. She wondered if he would ever visit her here, and laughed at the thought. Dad with a beaten-up suitcase in hand, coming over the hill on a rattling number twenty-two bus.

Back then, each day began with a view of the grey horizon. She would make a cup of tea and count the surfers who arrived at dawn. The black flecks fell and crashed with the swell, and the same utes and Holdens would be parked up again in the evening, when she came panting through the door and curled her body around the fins of the oil heater. She watched the boys, and every now and then a dark-haired girl, leap over the sand and up the wooden steps. They would shelter behind the rusty car doors, and strip down to red skin, tossing the wetsuits and boards in the back and roaring off around the corner. She imagined them rubbing at the white nubs of their feet and someone quietly saying, Hey, look, as they caught the last light over the Kaikouras.

All this existed before Andy. A time without the little interchanges that now mark out the day, without anyone in the whole city to catch her if it went wrong. Or slow her down if it went right. The house on the hill had been her best place yet.

Andy's mother had been shocked – nineteen, and living alone in such a place. She would get cold! hungry! lonely! She thought his mother sweet but sweetly refused to be drawn into the discussion. Until Andy picked her up from varsity one Tuesday afternoon in the spring and without explanation drove to Newtown and pulled up outside the villa. Let's flat together, he said. Let's flat here. They moved her battered pots, single bed, heater, books and collection of posters in a morning.

She wasn't quite sure about it, she wasn't sure it was the best idea at all, but Andy was certain, and he organised everything, and she let him, then, because she thought perhaps it might work.

Andy convinced his friend Peter, the saxophone player, to move in with them, signed the bond papers and returned late that afternoon with a pack of fluorescent pink pegs, a coffee plunger, a dishrack and two large rubbish bins.

Together, they learnt to live with the ongoing argument over food. She wanted only avocado on toast, or soup, or gingernuts, and he would hassle her about it, quote her passages from books about vitamins and iron, fuss over her like a worried mother. She learnt to live with it all and after some time no longer blinked twice on waking in the warmth of his bed, finding his pale arm flung across her breasts, his face pressed against her shoulder.

She opens the fridge door and pulls out a bottle of beer. As she opens it there is a small explosion in her stomach – but I can't (and she says the words aloud, astonished) I'm six weeks pregnant. She puts the bottle gently down in the sink, walks slowly into the dark bedroom, lies on the tangled sheets and shuts her eyes.

I don't want to do this with Andy, she thinks. There won't be any space for me. I won't be able to get out of it, she thinks. Ever. But then, perhaps she doesn't want to do this at all. Perhaps Andy doesn't even need to know. Because there are other options.

She thinks of Scully, the grey cat, thinner and slower than Snow, and remembers Dad carrying her inside one night, wet and bleeding. He had heard her crying and found her huddled at the back of the woodshed. She had been mauled by neighbourhood dogs, and her fur was clotted into lumps of grey, stiff with blood, mud and saliva. The front leg was bent impossibly backwards, and her eyes were puffed up and shut tight. Dad dipped his finger in water and dripped it into her mouth, and then he took her outside, and Ella heard the gunshot from the kitchen. Thinking about Scully, she realises she doesn't want to consider other options any more.

She lies on her back and stares at the ceiling. After half an hour she brushes her hair out of her face and gets up to put the kettle on. She begins work on two lists: 'Who to Tell' and 'Matters to Consider'. Writing things down in a logical order helps, and soon she is clear. The house seems wrong, and Andy seems wrong, and she decides that whatever she does about this situation she will do it alone. There will be nothing to discuss – not with Andy, not with his mother, not with anyone.

She raises her head from the page to look hard at the capsicum plant blooming out of season on the hot windowsill. Three flowers have budded today, and one green fruit is forming, curled in upon itself, an ear. For the final quarter hour before dusk the sun blazes hard against the glass, showing up the rain trails formed in the grime and dust.

*

There is a man lingering behind, an older man in a maroon jersey and charcoal pants. At first Ella thinks this is the next lecturer getting ready for his class, and she is embarrassed, afraid that he will notice her and call out. She is relieved when he checks his watch and turns to leave by the lower doors. Then she is alone. She puts her head down on the wooden bench and shuts her eyes.

After a few moments she stands and folds her notebook shut. She got down half a page of notes, and copied out one of the five dorsal fin diagrams. But she missed the Hector's dolphin on the overhead projector slide. *Cephalorhynchus hectori* is the one with an unusual fin, and this is the information she needs, but she missed that slide; she didn't get the diagram down and she doesn't know the shape, or the characteristic markings. There is no one she knows in this

13

class, no one to ask for notes. A wave of furious helplessness comes across her and she sits back down. They have just this week come on to the family *Delphinidae*. It's the dolphins that she is interested in – she's been waiting for this part but now she's losing track.

Today was the second lecture from a visiting expert in human interactions with dolphins. Bang on eleven o'clock the tall blonde woman charged into the room and started chatting in a nasal Australian accent to the handful of students who lunged to the front with questions from her Monday session. They reminded Ella of puppies at the farm, yelping and skittering, begging for attention.

This lecture was about mating rituals in artificial environments. The woman turned out the lights and flicked up a slide of a bottlenose dolphin sliding her belly against her mate's flank. In the dark, Ella felt rising nausea and put her pen down on the bench, watching the image swim in and out of focus as she tried to decide how urgent the problem was. It had almost been too late and outside the door she had to turn to the nearest rubbish bin, then felt disgusted and ashamed of the smell. She thought of her chicken sandwich and retched again.

Looking around, she saw there was no one on the landing and walked quickly down the stairs to the bathroom, washed her face and drank a mouthful of water. In the mirror she was so pale that the little scar on her nose stood out against her skin, and her hair was matted against her temples. It occurred to her then that it might be best to pack it in for the day and go home to the empty flat, and bed. But it seemed easier to face the afternoon lectures than that bed so she slid back into her seat, smiling weakly at the boy across the aisle who shot her a strange look. She would buy some fruit after the class and see out the day.

When the lights came on at the end of the lecture she hung back, waiting for the room to empty, wanting to avoid being caught in the crush of bags and rushing bodies in the narrow passageway leading out to the quad. If she had to walk down that crowded passageway she would probably throw up again.

'Hey.' There is a girl standing at the back calling out. She is tall with a freckled face, auburn hair hanging loose to her elbows, and she is grinning widely. She wears jeans, a blue parka and thick-soled boots, and she looks strong – the kind of capable, sporty girl who climbs mountains, or gets up before dawn for rowing practice. She is slightly familiar. Scrabbling through the faces of people from tutorials and parties produces no clues. There is only the sense that this is someone comfortable and easy, and perhaps they had talked about study, the ocean.

'Hey, it's Ella, right? I'm Tess. You helped me out with dissection in first year. Umpteen bloody cod organs. I didn't know you were still up here. I haven't seen you for ages.'

A sudden, disproportionate rush of gratitude. Ella looks back down at the graffiti on the bench.

'Yeah, it's good to see you.'

Tess clomps down the stairs and swings down the seat next to her.

'Is everything all right? You look kind of – bad.'

Later on it will surprise her that it happened this way. She has never done this, not even with Andy, or Dad. She is sobbing hugely, with this stranger's arm around her, the tears running off her chin and down the front of her shirt.

Of course then she has to say, about being pregnant, and telling Andy to go, and hearing the words spill out it all sounds pathetic. Tess puts her head to one side, and looks a little bit like a spaniel. She doesn't say much. Maybe you should stay with your mum for a while, she suggests. Ella explains about Mum and then Tess looks even more upset, and makes an offer, tells her to think it over, to keep it in mind if she ever

15

needs a place. Then they start to laugh about Professor Gregory and his obsession with Hooker sea lions. After a while they leave the theatre to go and drink coffee in the student union, sitting at one of the kidney-shaped tables where the sun pours in from the high glass roof. Ella feels herself heating up and drying off, sips at her sweet hot chocolate and realises with a strange lift that she is not even ashamed.

She comes home, walking in past the remaining boxes in the hallway, the empty bookshelves and the space on the desk where the computer belongs, and doesn't even slow down. Andy will come by at the weekend to pick up the last of his gear, but he's leaving the queensize bed. She knows he can't bring himself to make her shift back into the single bed, stored out in the garage, and she is not going to make that easier for him. In any case, there's no room for the big bed at his mother's place. And perhaps he reasons that it leaves something open.

There's a book lying on his desk, the book he brought back from Kaikoura last summer, and noticing it there she's tempted to take it, to hide it among her clothes. The book has fantastic underwater shots of the blue whale, taken from below, clearly showing the silver-yellow sheen of sulphur on the underbelly. She flicks directly to the page, the centre already deeply creased, and notices once again the way the changing light and angles have reflected different shades in each of the three photos. She wants the book but closes it firmly and leaves it there on the desk. Andy would find out – eventually he would realise, and then she would be left owing something.

Coming into the bedroom she sees that Peter, her flatmate, has put her mail on the dresser. He is being kind, separating out Andy's letters and forwarding them himself. Today, a statement from the bank, showing her account hovering at three hundred dollars overdrawn, and a note from Student Health reminding her about her next appointment. Also, a small brown envelope addressed in her father's uneven handwriting. His letter is on a page of lined Croxley. He must have gone out to buy that specially.

Dear Ellie

Hello love. Well John next door has gone to hospital. He's down in Gisborne getting an appendix taken out and he says he should get his insides cut out more often because he's never felt better. Hope you are good love and your mates being good to my girl. Say hello to the PM, bloody Mr Bolger, if you see him give him a kick from me. Couldn't believe it I went into town last Tuesday for a copy of the papers that were lost in the flood last winter, and the girl at the Court said I'm to send a cheque to Wellington for it. Ellie I tell mum every week about her smart girl when I take the flowers over. Snow and me are fine. She split her paw open last week but we've bandaged it up all right and she's back at the birds. Billie and Toss are also good, Billie getting slower now though. I have taken him off the run. Well this must be boring. You will be going to parties. Hope the city friends are treating you well and don't wear yourself out with study. We will see you in the winter.

Love Dad

PS Your Auntie Del says she's got some money for you how about you write her a letter.

She wonders if she should write back, or wait until she goes home in August. By August she might not need to say anything at all. It will be quite obvious. She's glad now that she never mentioned Andy because that is one less thing to explain.

She was surprised that Andy hadn't shouted at her when she told him. Often when they argued his neck would mottle and he would stamp off, yelling back down the hall, Well, maybe you should think about that, but this time he barely said anything. He didn't cry either, as she had feared he might, but just kissed her lightly on the forehead and said in a small voice that he would call her in the morning. It made her wonder whether he was desperately pleased to see the off-ramp. It is easy to believe this; it leaves an almost pleasant melancholy, and a certainty.

Now, eating steaming noodles and cheese in the early evening, with the lights coming on in the street below, she knows she has done well. She has told him, she has decided, she is alone and managing fine.

Three days later Peter stays out late at band practice, and the sounds of the house are everywhere around her. The radio plays classic hits. In the middle of the big bed she lies quite still, running her hand across her stomach, feeling taut muscles and the smooth curve down to the waist. It's difficult to imagine it happening. A *b*, growing there, just a beginning. Strange to want it like this. But she does; she is getting keen on the idea now, this baby being hers, wrapped tight inside. She wants it to be brown. She doesn't want it to be pale like Andy, or Dad. She wants it brown, like her and Mum and the aunties.

And then she's taken by surprise again, crying furiously, shaking her head in bewilderment at the suddenness of it, flooding through her from no particular place. They are an invasion, these unpredictable waves, the loss of control, and she would like to stamp them out. She will pull herself together – pull as hard as she needs to – because she needs to be together. In this state she will not be able to complete the things that must be done.

In the morning she finds her zoology notebook. The phone number is scribbled on the corner of the page, the name smudged by a splash of hot chocolate. But she hasn't forgotten her name anyway, or the way she said, Give us a call, perhaps you could come and stay for a while. She sounded as if she meant it, as though this were a reasonable idea, an everyday proposition.

Ella dials the number; then, as soon as it starts ringing, hangs up. It is raining hard today, the first autumn southerly lashing at the windows, and she stands hopping from one bare foot to the other on the lino. Maybe it's better not to bother. Better perhaps to go and have a smoke, the last one in the packet, the last one she's going to have. It would be better in fact to do almost anything at all except make this difficult call. But Peter has told her that he wants to move out soon – he wants to move in with his girlfriend. He says there's no particular rush, but the reality is they could find a place within weeks. You could advertise for new flatmates, Peter suggests, but the idea exhausts her, and besides she has no money to cover the rent if anything goes wrong.

Eventually she dials again and waits for someone to answer.

Louise stands in the shower and turns the dial clockwise until the water runs as hot as she can bear, holding her head directly under the thick stream so that her chest tightens and her skin flushes. She shuts her eyes, presses her hands in over her face, breathing into the darkness. Then she shakes out her hands, turns the dial sharply back around to blue and gasps as the first flood of cold pours over her scalp and down the backs of her legs, shocking her tight muscles into relaxation.

She has spent the morning working through the tax return for the café, and her shoulders, back and arms are clenched with the effort of concentration. The job is finally finished, and she's determined to relax and have the rest of the day to herself before Kevin arrives for dinner.

Stepping out of the shower she stretches her body back in an arch, and then reaches down to her toes, enjoying the sensation of release down through her vertebrae, and surprised to find that she is easily able to reach the ground. Steam slowly clears from the mirror and she is pleased, as always, by the outline of the figure reflected back – slim, if not toned: much the same body as twenty years ago, and this is astonishing really, considering her lack of exercise and less than careful diet.

She is rubbing violently at her hair when she hears the front door slam, a bag dropping to the ground, and the thump of footsteps down towards the far bedroom. Tess has decided to come home for tea then, but clearly her mood has not improved.

It is difficult to imagine how it will all work out this evening. Kevin is back from the sea and will turn up at six-thirty with a large package of twenty or thirty assorted fillets: tarakihi, kahawai, warehou, blue cod. Some people have brothers who come and help paint the house, or move furniture around, but Kevin has this one gift: fish. He has been away for a short five-day trip on this occasion, the first winter stint out to the Strait and back.

The freezer is still full from the last time he came in: neither Tess nor Jacob has been eating at home lately. They are out four or five nights out of seven, busy with university, part-time jobs and innumerable social events. Down at the café, lamb cutlets, rather than fish of the day, seems to have become the meal of choice. But still, she will graciously accept the gift, because Kevin, with his big hands and shoulders, will arrive at the door dressed in his only shirt and a pair of black jeans, and will stand there looking awkward and uncertain. Gidday, Louise, he will say, and the large package of newspaper wrapped fish in his hands will be his opening piece, his one passport and bridge into the frighteningly steady world of land and family.

After years of turning up at the door like this, every month or six weeks with tidal regularity, Kevin is as shy and uncertain as ever. Little brother, she wants to say to him at the door, are we so terrifying to you? What is it, Kevin, that makes you shuffle your feet on the doormat and skim your eyes around the kitchen like a nervy cat, restless until you have taken your third beer and lit a cigarette? Only when the red starts to show through the brown skin of his cheeks and his steel-capped boots come to rest on the lino does he finally cease scanning the room for the nearest emergency exit.

He last came for dinner in the middle of a storm, the wind bashing hard against the south window and the rain pouring down in furious squalls. As night fell, the wind picked up even more, and Louise had been concerned about him driving all the way back out to his bach on the Makara coast in the weather, down the deserted valley road with blind corners, steep grades and no street lights at all.

'Kevin, stay here if you like,' she had said casually, after they finished the chocolate cake. 'It's awful out there. We've got the spare room.'

He'd looked surprised, and uncomfortable. 'Thanks, ah, no, I'm right. In fact I might head off soon.' He'd looked around the kitchen for a clock. 'Got an early start tomorrow. I'm heading up to Auckland with a mate of mine.'

'It's past ten,' she said. 'I'm worried that you might have lost power out there – doesn't that happen in the southerly sometimes?'

'Yeah, nah, no problem. I've got a bit of a system rigged up for that. I'll be fine.' He was on his feet before she could continue. 'But thanks, Louise. That was a fantastic meal.'

'Are you sure?'

'Yeah, I'm right, thanks.' He bent down and kissed her goodbye, his stubble scratching briefly up against her cheek, and was out the door before she could say anything further.

So tonight there will be Kevin, needing careful cajoling to get any kind of conversation started, and Tess, fuming silently. If Louise's sensor is correct, Tess won't talk any more than is absolutely necessary with her mother and uncle this evening. She will eat with them because she has no cash and no choice, but will leave immediately afterwards, heading out into the dark to walk to the bus, following the string of lights up the valley road to a world of sympathetic friends. Louise imagines there will be an elaborate laying out of the sins of the mother, perhaps in a bedroom supplied and furnished by some other, more benign parent, or perhaps over gin and tonic in some dark bar in the city.

At times she finds it hard not to laugh at her daughter: so sensitive to slight insults, and wearing her wounds with such gravity. Today it was her comment on Tessa's new job at a second-hand clothes shop that had inflamed her daughter. Over breakfast this morning she had asked evenly whether the shop had given Tess a written contract, and whether she had discussed holiday pay and notice regarding shifts.

'No. I guess they'll figure it out. It'll be fine, Mum.'
Louise had decided to risk making a point.

'You know, you really have to learn to stand up for yourself.'
Simply that, and it was too much. Tess had stormed out.

She has picked up her new book, and read the first few
paragraphs of chapter one, when the phone starts ringing.

'Mum, it's for you!' Jacob calls from the hallway.

She lifts herself up from where she is lying on the couch
and takes a long sip of her tea before moving.

'Louise!' Margie sounds flustered, and it's noisy and
crowded in the background.

'Hi, Margie. What's happening?'

'Look, I'm *incredibly* sorry to ask this . . .'

'. . . but could I come down?'

'. . . just for an hour, I promise. It's your one Saturday off,
I know. I feel so mean, but it's gone completely mad down
here. The rugby's finished up at the park. They're pouring
through the door, and everyone's stroppy because we lost.
They're frozen and starving.'

'I'll be right there. How are the cakes lasting?'

'Almost gone.'

'I've got an orange and coconut in the fridge. And I think
there's a couple of cheesecakes at the very back of the main
freezer. Might be worth pulling them out. See you soon.' By
the time she is off the phone her mind is already racing, thinking
about what is likely to run out, wondering whether she ought
to take down extra milk.

Outside, she realises it is a warm day and crosses the road to
walk by the sea. The sky is hazy, overcast with fine white cloud.
The water is pallid blue and almost completely still. Small waves
lift in a slow, lazy rhythm, breaking over the rocks and rushing
up on the pebbles with a rough hiss. A truck loaded with gravel
roars past, kicking up dust all the way along the coastline.

———

When Kevin arrives, he brings beer instead of fish. Tess doesn't leave the house, but doesn't eat with the family either. She takes the phone into her room, and the muffled thud of the stereo sounds out all night. Louise has abandoned her plan to make chicken casserole because she was stuck down at the café until six. She opens a jar of pasta sauce instead and has a bowl of fettucine on the table in less than fifteen minutes.

'Sorry, Kevin,' she says, 'it's a bit basic. It's been a hectic day.'

'Looks bloody good to me,' he says, piling food on to his plate, 'specially after five days of cruddy food onboard.'

'Did the fishing go well this time?'

'Not so well. Nah.'

She asks a series of other questions: How many were crewing? How far did you go? But it's hard work keeping the conversation afloat, constantly rescuing it from the little lulls that threaten to sink it altogether and leave them both silent and uncomfortable, alone in the kitchen.

She doesn't object when Kevin decides to leave at nine.

'It's a shame Jacob was out,' she says. 'He'll be sorry to have missed you.'

'Well, I'll see him another time.'

'Another time. Bye then, Kevin.'

As soon as the front door shuts, Tess emerges. Without preliminaries, without any attempt to apologise or resolve the argument from earlier in the day, she starts making a request in an agitated tone. She won't give any details about the situation, but she is adamant that it is necessary, it is an emergency.

All right, Louise says eventually, all right, she can stay. But just for two weeks, and then we'll have to reassess. Tess rushes out of the kitchen, elated.

'Where are you going?'

'To call her,' she yells back from the bedroom.

'Right now? At least wait until tomorrow, Tess!' Give me tonight at least, she thinks, without having to plan for what comes next.

Ella pulls the curtain and lies back down in the bed to watch the light rising in bands across the sky. Gulls wheel past and the day is busy already. There are voices in the kitchen. It is frightening and difficult; she is groggy and does not quite remember why she came here, and she wants to stay in bed with the door shut. She does not want to deal with the voices in the kitchen. The sheets on the bed are made of something soft that makes her skin unusually warm, and the pillow smells vaguely of spices.

She sleeps again and is woken at eight by the sound of the toilet flushing. Pipes clunk through the thin bedroom wall. The front door slams and then there is quiet, except for classical music – violins – drifting from the lounge. This morning she has a lab test and there is no alternative but to get up. But between here and varsity there will be awkwardness and conversation: she will have to speak to somebody. She will have to speak to whoever it is that sits in the lounge and plays classical music. Get up, get going. She pulls on her jeans and yanks the top button closed across the bump. She wonders when she will start to feel movement. She would like to ask her mother when she first felt kicking. She would like to ask her mother quite a lot of things now, but instead she writes her questions down, and is keeping an eye out for a helpful book.

The music through the wall suddenly stops and she hears a door closing somewhere in the house, so she throws her books into her red backpack, pulling at the broken zip. She slips out the door and heads down the hallway, and is almost out the front door and safely into the day when she realises that her wallet is still in the kitchen, on the table, where she left it yesterday. She resigns herself to going back in, and to the high probability of having to talk to someone. It makes her nervous, trying to figure out how she is supposed to behave in this new situation, in this house where she doesn't belong. But, she thinks, at least this way I might be able to have breakfast, because she is starving, and her stomach churns in a way that she recognises, and resents.

What she really wants is a smoke, but she's not going to have one. She hasn't got any, anyway. She's given all that up now.

Louise's last job for the night is restocking the bar. It's down by two reds and half a bottle of Drambuie but at least the boys did the glasses this time. She'll mention that to Jacob. It can be a positive opening note for the next matter she wants to raise: his use of the car. Of his own volition he gave her fifty dollars for the alcohol that they drank last week. She looked at him, grateful and surprised. It made her feel competent, proud of how she had managed that difficult conversation. She had gone into his room, pulled back the curtains to let in the afternoon sun and stood over his bed, saying in a firm, clear voice that he was taking her for granted. It's just as well Margie trusts the private accounting that takes place between her business partner and her business partner's son, and doesn't ask too many questions.

On a Friday or a Saturday night the last slops are emptied and the mop bucket filled around midnight. If Louise is running the shift she'll usually let the last girls go around half past eleven, and finish up herself. The girls shoot her hopeful looks and gaze up at the clock, itching to head off to boyfriends or into town, and she finds that it takes too much energy to fight this clear-faced desire. It is altogether easier to be left alone, to put on a violin concerto and end the night quietly. And besides, it saves on wages. Despite a number of steady years, profit margins remain slim and they still need to watch the overheads.

Friday nights the bar is left unlocked and the dishwasher on, because Jacob and his friends have a regular fixture: drinks that start at one in the morning and finish – well, she's not sure when they finish, but often she'll wake back at home to find two or three bodies sprawled on the lounge floor. They stumble out of sleeping bags at midday and Jacob fries them

27

bacon. They make vague greetings in her direction, and drink their way through all the fresh coffee.

These friends are from university but seem no different to the adolescent boys that Jacob would bring home after school six or seven years ago, with uniform grey shorts to their knees and gangling limbs that did not know their own length. Sprawled out across the couch the boys would inevitably knock over a glass, a picture, a plant. Ducking and shuffling, one would come out to her in the kitchen, mumbling, Um, Mrs McMahon, um, I'm really sorry, have you got a cloth?

Except Chris, of course. Chris has been confidently addressing her as Louise since the age of eight. As a teenager, in contrast to the other, shadowy boys, he teased her shame-lessly. Working on that banana plantation again, Louise? he asked whenever he saw her emptying the compost bucket full of fruit peelings out onto the pile behind the shed, and bedding banana skins in among the scraggly rose bushes.

Chris would come out alone from the garage where the drum kit played all afternoon, pour himself a glass of lemonade and sit up at the table making pleasant conversation while she cooked. Seen any good movies lately, Louise? he would say, and there was something amusingly adult in his manner. One afternoon he asked her advice in a serious tone. Which did she think was more romantic: tickets to a play or a picnic at the beach? Her name is Monica, he said shyly, and she plays the cello. I think she'd be into theatre, don't you? After a moment's consideration Louise said, Well, Chris, you know, I think both would be equally romantic. A day at the beach could be perfect if you get the right kind of weather and take some nice food. She thought to herself, *lucky Monica*, because how many sixteen-year-old boys would consider plays, or picnics?

Chris and Jacob see less of each other now and he doesn't often come to the Friday night drinking sessions. It's a shame. Louise still thinks of Chris as the sunshine child: a welcome antidote to her often moody son. His parents moved away to the other side of town two years ago and his presence dwindled to an occasional drop-in to collect Jacob, a late-night meal once in a while. Sometimes she still says to Jacob, How's young Chris? Tell that boy to come round and visit sometime.

Saturday mornings, with the smell of bacon thick in the kitchen and the television blaring music videos, Louise gets out of the house. She walks around the bays, or takes books back to the central library and stops in to look at the art gallery. Lately there have been a lot of tapestries and sculptures. She takes longer over these exhibitions: she likes these forms that come out at you, the surfaces bubbled or smooth or hairy. Of course, there are good reasons for the lines of white tape on the floor around the shapes, and she would slap a child for such behaviour, but she finds it irresistible – checking for the guard, she runs her little finger quickly across each surface, walking out the heavy glass door tingling with quick impressions of copper, flax, feather and resin.

Last year they had an exhibition of pottery painted by Picasso. They kept those behind glass. She looked at the elongated noses on the vases and thought of the pottery class she took when Tess first started school.

Those days were marked by a startling, empty sensation, the hours until three o'clock stretching gloriously out in front of her. She stood at the wheel, mesmerised by the sense of control, the entire form submitting at the slightest pressure. Widening her hands into fat bowls, and knowing in that moment that the worst of it was past, and that she herself had achieved this. It was as though her life was cracking open with possibility: a new place and a second chance.

Tonight is a quiet Monday and she finishes, alone, by eleven. The restaurant lights are all out except for the row closest to the back wall. Outside the sliding door the ocean is black and invisible. The chairs are stacked onto the tables and the restaurant is warm with the woodburner burning low. It occurs to her that it would be pleasant to curl up and rest there, lie down on the rug and drift into the morning. Perhaps Margie will turn up tomorrow and cook bacon for her. But, she thinks, seriously, why not stay a while, make a final coffee and read a chapter here rather than back in the cold bedroom? It seems vaguely irresponsible, but who on earth would know and who would care – who would be affected by this, her staying behind to read her book by the fire?

Mr Ramsay stands before his wife and demands sympathy. Louise reads the passage again, trying to figure out whether the words are actually spoken or simply lie between husband and wife as a palpable thought. The son pulls at Mrs Ramsay's arm, wanting his story read, wanting to carry on with his mother, her arm around him, her voice uninterrupted. Someone, Lily the painter, has painted this as a purple triangle. The son wants to go to the lighthouse and the father says it won't happen, and the mother is given over to both of them, feeling their every sorrow as if it were her own.

An old friend from nursing days visited last week and told her she ought to try Virginia Woolf, handing her this book with a pastel sweep of sand and ocean on the cover.

'Ever read her?' the friend asked, and Louise shook her head, feeling slightly embarrassed, as though she had failed in some small way. Thanks, she said, and put it on top of the fridge, asking no questions.

But now she wants to ask Jacob a couple of questions about the author, because it is very interesting, this beautiful mother and the needy, brilliant father. Later they go walking in the evening and he is melancholic and does not look at the flowers.

She puts the book down and a string of small lights crosses past the centre of the window pane. It is the late ferry, coming in from the south. The room has become stuffy and airless;

it is difficult to breathe. It is past midnight and time to go home.

If nothing else, Tessa's friend might wake up in the night and need something urgently. She can't think exactly what she might need – what on earth a guest would wake a person up for in the middle of the night – but she is overcome by the sense that she ought to go home and ensure that she is all right. The girl is slight and small, with dark hair and very serious eyes. She slept on the couch this afternoon, with her bare knees tucked up into her stomach and one brown arm crooked around the back of her neck, flung over her face. Louise stood watching her for a few moments, and then searched through the cupboards to find a blanket.

'I'll do it, Tess said, taking the blanket from her and bringing it into the lounge, where she arranged it carefully over the sleeping body.

It has happened before. Tess forms intense friendships, often within days, with each new person becoming a consuming event for a week, or a month, or a year.

Once, in the fourth form, Tess came home on a Friday afternoon and spent the weekend pleading. She urgently wanted her friend Rebecca, Rebecca's younger twin brothers, and also the family dog, a labrador puppy, to come and stay for the May holidays. Rebecca's mum's going into hospital, Tess argued, trailing Louise around the house, and her dad has to go to Australia for work. She repeated the facts over and over again, stating and restating her case, becoming entrenched.

But is there no one else? Louise queried. Perhaps her mother could call me, she suggested. Do I know this Rebecca? I've never heard you mention her before. Tessa's face screwed up then, trying to ward off tears. You just don't care, she yelled, you don't give a shit!

Finally Louise relented, because the situation seemed so

31

dire. She thought, somewhat ridiculously, that she would have them all, muddle through two cold weeks with five children, an unreliable car and a yapping puppy. But when she phoned Rebecca's mother she was informed that there were grandparents in New Plymouth lined up to have the kids and the dog. There was no difficulty at all. There was simply Tess, distracted at the prospect of spending the holiday away from her friend.

Tessa's attachments are various and unpredictable. Last winter an elderly man began to appear regularly in the restaurant, coming in each Tuesday and Thursday afternoon, sitting quietly at the bench for hours, slowly drinking his way through a single pot of tea. Slight and well mannered, with a careful English accent, he was a derelict – unkempt, with wild hair, and, when you came close, the keen, tight stench of unwashed sweat. He consistently wore the same green sweater, and a dark suit jacket in an odd style, the elbows patched and repatched. Louise often wondered where he went when the restaurant closed and he shuffled out the door, but never spoke to him about anything beyond tea, and the weather.

But Tess was working occasional shifts at the time, and eventually it fell to her to deliver his drink. From behind the till Louise noticed her swinging through the kitchen door with the pot and the cup, and then some time later looked up to see Tess with her own cup, sitting up beside him at the bench. Mr Deebing, she told everyone later – his name is Mr Harry Deebing. Then Tess started working shifts every Tuesday and Thursday afternoon, and would bring out sandwiches with the tea, and bowls of pasta, even fish or steak. If it was a quiet night, she would sit with him while he ate. They buried themselves in conversation, heads bent low, oblivious to the sunset and the customers coming and going. It was as though he were her grandfather, or perhaps someone younger, and closer: a father, or an uncle. The girls hassled her – but she shrugged it off and continued to carry out his plate of food, grinning. Louise was bemused, and perplexed, because it wasn't pity, this. It was something less forced, less earnest, but unusual: a little unbalanced, a little obsessive.

No one objected seriously, until Tess pushed her luck, demanding that they start providing takeaway sandwiches for his lunch as well.

'Sweetheart, it's not a soup kitchen,' Margie said. 'You buy your friend food if you want, or give him cash to get his own, but I'm sorry, that's the end of the free meals from us.'

Tess refused to work for the next month, and Mr Deebing slipped quietly away into the night.

And now there is this girl. A phone call must have been made because she turned up unexpectedly yesterday at lunchtime, with a red backpack and three small cardboard boxes, while Tess was still at netball. In the middle of planting out the garden Louise stopped to make her ham sandwiches and didn't ask any questions. The girl seemed grateful for the silence, sitting at the table drinking down glass after glass of pineapple juice. Then she slept all afternoon. This morning she came out to the kitchen, just as Louise was about to leave, and seemed quite timid, and strange all over again, as though they hadn't met at all the day before.

'Help yourself to breakfast,' Louise said, pulling out a bowl, a plate, a mug. 'It's all in the pantry. Help yourself to anything you can find. And there's fruit on the table.'

'Thanks. I'll just have a banana.' She took one from the bowl.

'Are you going into town today?'

'I'm going up to varsity.'

'My son Jacob might be able to give you a lift. He has my car today. I think he's planning to leave around eleven.'

'I need to go quite soon, actually. That's okay.'

'So, are you doing all the same courses as Tess?'

'No. Only one. We did first year together, but I'm taking all the marine biology courses now.'

'Gosh, I imagine that would be fascinating. You know there's a laboratory just down the road here?'

'Yeah, I did some work there last year. I might go down this weekend. It's a good place.'

'And what's your particular interest?'

'Mammals, I suppose.'

'We get a huge number of dolphins coming through the Strait here.'

'Yeah.'

All morning Louise thought about the girl, wondering about her circumstances, wanting to know more. It was hard to tell whether she was sad, or cold, or simply reserved.

She asked Tess when she came down in the afternoon to eat a bacon sandwich. 'She's pregnant, Mum,' Tess explained, stuffing sprouts into her mouth. 'And her dad's way up north. She needs somewhere to stay for a while. That's all. God, it doesn't have to be *complicated*.'

Louise closes and locks the door to the restaurant. Walking quickly towards home she looks up at the sky, and it lifts and spreads over the water. She thinks how it is enough: the cold night, and the stars blurred and burning above the dark road. It is enough, it is plenty, to have all this. To have the café, with the occasional crises and problems, but the knowledge that they have done it, that it has been a success, and then the pleasure of Margie's good sense and humour. To have the silverbeet planted, and a book with a lighthouse. To have all this: a serious-eyed girl in the spare bed; a daughter who finds such people, notices them, and brings them home; a son who is learning to pay for what he uses; and Kevin, too, despite the awkwardness, now reconciled and safely inside the circle. And somewhere near the centre of it, her solitude, the hours of walking around the shoreline, heading south past the quarry

34

or north towards the airport, and coming back across the hills with the wind whipping up the flax on the banks, licking at salty lips and looking at the clear view out past the heads.

She has built it herself. Thinking of all this she feels a soft bubble of satisfaction rising to the surface. She sees it as a carefully balanced construction made from small planks of plain wood, and it pleases her, because she is responsible. It is the work of her own hands. She has spent nineteen years building a sturdy little bridge, and it works. A bridge gets you to the other side of difficult things, like the past, the cold bed, the times of wondering whether there was something else important that you were supposed to do, and the various absences that linger on the margins of the day. Of course, the trick with narrow bridges is not to look down. She has learnt now how to be disciplined, how to keep looking straight ahead.

They will eat at a restaurant tonight. This is what Tess is saying. It is a family occasion, and Ella imagines silver cutlery, organised in a specific, unintelligible order, starched white tablecloths and a menu of complicated, expensive items. Someone is likely to ask who she is, why she is there, and what connection she has. Then they will look at her in a concerned way. It is a horrible prospect and she does not want to go. Today she has had second thoughts about coming here at all.

This afternoon she came shivering through the door, late and frustrated. The bus route ends ten minutes' walk away at the desolate tail end of the beach, with a tiny dairy that sells only four kinds of biscuits, a dive shop, and a children's playground opening out on to the sand. Rusted fishing boats bob in the bay. To get to Tessa's place you walk further out along the coastline. Past the lighthouse – which is not a real lighthouse at all, but a small house in the shape of a lighthouse – you turn the corner and the wind is sudden and harsh against your face.

It has been a stupid day. She waited at the university bus stop for half an hour because she read the timetable incorrectly. It made her irritable, having to work out an entirely different set of arrangements just to get through the normal business of the day.

'Ella!'

Tess called out to her from the lounge, as soon as she opened the door.

'Ella, is that you?'

A flood of relief then, Tess being home, and calling out like that. A flood of relief because all day Nanna has loomed in her head, saying, I hope I'm not imposing, dear, it's very good of you, but I do hope I'm not imposing.

Here at this strange sea house she is surely imposing, and an imposter besides – not even family. None of this is hers, this strange family, living in this house with the crazing paving pathway and, inside, the jungle of green plants on the windowsill, and the tall palm tree in the corner. There are piles of papers and magazines everywhere, racks of washing hanging in the lounge, a tall bookcase with books squashed and stacked on every shelf, and then the wide view out over the ocean. The furniture is old, but comfortable, and everywhere on the walls there are posters and paintings, the colours clashing and rioting at random.

This is what she has been thinking about today, the little scene replaying itself time after time in her mind: she was five, or maybe six, helping Mum carry the heavy bar heater and extra blankets up the stairs to the spare room. Nanna had just arrived from Napier, sitting down with her cup of tea and calling out from the kitchen, I hope I'm not imposing – I don't want to put you out, love, and then Mum would look puzzled, and call back down the hallway, No, Claudia, of course you're not. It's a pleasure.

In Mum's family nobody talked about imposing – you just stayed and it was fine. Once, when she was five, she stayed at Auntie Jeanie's for six months, sharing a bed with her cousin Tilly, and she can't think now that there was any good reason for this, or even any discussion about it at all, although surely there must have been something said, some arrangements made.

After she turned seven, and Mum died, she moved to Napier and had to start at a new school down there in the city. She went back up to the coast for the summers, but hardly ever saw Auntie Del, Auntie Jeanie and the cousins after that. In Napier it was just her and Nanna. Dad came to visit sometimes on the weekends, the big ute pulling up late on a Friday night, and she would get out of bed when she heard the scatter of gravel in the drive, and run downstairs to be first to open the door. Dad usually brought Jaffas or Minties, and let her eat some straight away, shivering in her bare feet.

But most of the time Dad wasn't there – there was only Nanna working on the crossword in the kitchen, the fat cat tucked up on the spare armchair, and the low hum of the refrigerator. When Ella was eight, and nine, and ten, she would spend the afternoons alone in the front room, down on the carpet with the big faded roses, playing solitaire, or practising knucklebones. If it wasn't too cold Nanna let her go outside, and then she rode an old Raleigh bike around the block, or searched for insects in the layers of rotting leaves under the ngaio tree, until it was almost dark. The girls in her class invited her to come to their houses, but Ella never invited anyone back to Nanna's because it was a quiet place and Nanna didn't like too much noise or disturbance. Nanna's house smelt different from other houses and they didn't have a television, only a radio. After a while Ella didn't mind about the other girls not coming around, because there were plenty of things to do by yourself, once you got used to it.

Walking in the door, Tess had called out to her and then it hadn't seemed so bad. Although it was still difficult to tell, and she didn't completely trust the impression, it seemed that Tess was different. She didn't hover, or ask unnecessary questions. She had not once told her to sleep well, or eat well. Even the day they met, the day Ella cried, Tess had done something unusual: she hadn't asked why or tried to comfort her exactly and that was good, that made her feel normal.

That's the trouble with Andy, she thinks. In the end he is just like these others. Meaning like Dad at his worst, and many of the other people she has met in the city. Treating her as though she is small and delicate. She hates people treating her as though she is delicate, and trying to look after her. It would have become unbearable by now, Andy hovering with cups of

38

tea and insisting on rest, making her take folic acid supplements, buying her Ribena. But Tess talks sensibly and directly about other things. So Ella hopes that it might in fact work out well, staying here for a couple of weeks, until she can get herself set up. But then, how do you know if you are imposing?

Tess makes strong coffee. Ella brings out a packet of gingernuts that she bought from the dairy and they sit together on the carpet in front of the heater watching the sunset, and the waves all messy and lumpy in the wind. Gulls cross backwards and forwards against the line of the shore: innumerable flocking red-billed gulls. She remembers how the council has laid poison over on the small island. The airport wants to cull the gull population because apparently they crash into planes and cause accidents, or potentially might cause accidents, or maybe there was one accident, once – she's not sure. But the point about the poison is that there will be impacts, of course, on the ecosystem, and they probably haven't thought that through, probably haven't bothered to figure out what will happen when there's less shellfish consumption, or, worse, when there are hundreds of poisoned seagull carcasses interrupting the chain, changing the order around. It occurs to her that Tess probably knows about the poison, and the effects, and she wants to ask her. But Tess breaks the silence first.

'I think Mum's keen for us to eat at the restaurant tonight. It's good, actually: the food's good there.'

What restaurant, and how much will it cost? They haven't talked about board at all yet, but there are outstanding bills from the flat and it's tight, and that's only now – later on it will be worse. When she thinks about money her throat constricts and she feels uneasy in her stomach. Perhaps she needs to write home, just a short letter, not saying quite everything.

'Sorry, Ella, it's probably a bit ghastly for you, the big

hurrah family dinner and all that. It's Jacob's birthday, you see. Not terribly creative, but Mum just wants to do something and I guess the restaurant is the easy option. But, you know, if you're tired . . .'

The restaurant, she said. Not *a* restaurant. They go out so often that it's called *the* restaurant. And it's boring?

'No, it's great. Honestly. I'd love to, I mean, as long as it's fine with your mum and everything.'

'Hell, yeah. She loves it, she's totally into gatherings. There'll be a few extras – Chris, that's Jacob's mate – well, actually, our friend in general, and Margie, and my Uncle Kevin and – oh, god, does it all sound completely revolting?'

Tess sits up straight and pulls a face – a face to convey solidarity against whatever might be encountered at dinner.

'Look, if it's horrible, we'll leave, Ella, I promise. It's about one minute's walk so we've got a natural escape. We'll just leave – you kick me and we're gone: no drama, no questions. You just give me the look.'

Ella looks down into her empty cup. 'How much is it likely to be?'

'How much? Oh, shit, did you think you had to pay? No way, no cost, it all goes on the tab. I mean, what's the point in owning a café if you can't eat there once in a while? It won't cost us anything. It's pretty much like eating at home, actually, except easier. Same view even.'

Tess bursts into an awkward, loud laugh. Ella changes the topic.

'So how old is your brother?'

'Turning twenty-two.'

'Does that make him older or younger?'

'I'm flattered! I must come across as a competent, mature person. I'm younger – barely, though. Eighteen months. Have you met Jacob? Some people find him a bit of a moron. He gets practically catatonic at times.'

'I spoke to him just briefly last night. He asked me about

our bio courses. He seems okay. Do you get on with him?'

'Get on with him? I'd have to think about that. There are so many levels to getting on. I guess so, though. We used to spend more time together, when we were teenagers. But his mates are jerks, pretty much.'

'And they're coming to dinner too?'

'His mates? Oh, no, only Chris. He's different. Chris has been around for ever. I get on pretty well with Chris. He doesn't grunt, and ignore you. More charming. Unlike my brother. Who is about as charming as a dogfish.'

Arriving at the Breakwater Café it hits Ella like a new possibility, a reordering of the world, that Tessa's mother actually runs this place, just along the shoreline from the house. It strikes her as astonishing that people should do such things. That a person's *mother* should do this – should own and run a restaurant. She never even knew it existed. She and Andy had certainly never come here, and that's a shame because it looks fantastic, with the weatherboards unpainted, left to grey in the onslaught of salt and weather, and the green koru of the Aotearoa flag flapping wildly from the pole, angling out from the roof. Three or four picnic tables have been placed on the deck, also grey and worn smooth, and then there is a sliding aluminium door into this warm busy space, the sharp smells of garlic, cooked fish, coffee, and everybody wearing polarfleeces and woollen hats. Not a white tablecloth in sight. She takes it all in and realises it will be fine, completely fine. Then Louise is beside her, introducing her to a large smiling woman who comes over wiping her hands on her apron.

'This is Margie,' she says, 'and Margie, this is Ella, who is staying with us for a while. Ella's from up on the East Coast.'

Here it comes, she thinks. Here comes the question, and then the answer, and then the look: *concern*, or worse, *hiding the shock.* Professor Gregory had looked shocked when she told him she would have to sit the November exam early. People are shocked because she looks younger than she is – she looks younger than twenty – but still, it is rude. People, she thinks, are incredibly rude.

'Are you down for long?'

'Well, yeah, I'm not exactly . . .' A botched attempt at evasion that makes her look worse than if she had said it straight.

'Ella studies at varsity with Tess. She's particularly interested in dolphins. I've told her we don't do driftnet anything, so you'd better not offer her the tuna.'

Relief, and a sense of gratitude towards this Louise, who rescues her smoothly and sweetly, and then this other woman, too, who has moved along, is asking her whether she likes crayfish, and talking about the hoki done in a mild red curry sauce.

They sit at a long wooden table near the fire and it burns hot against her back. There is a coloured glass lampshade and the light picks at the red grapes, making them glow like port. She drank plenty of port in the flat with Andy. In fact, she'd quite like a port now, because she likes the little kick it makes at the back of the throat. There are ten or eleven lamps, all leadlight, all different. The lamps are dark and elegant, and don't seem to have any connection with the plastic pink flamingos planted in the flax bushes on the doorstep.

The friend, Chris, has yet to arrive, but there is another man here who must be the uncle. Louise turns from the conversation as he walks across the room, clumping his way between the tables in his large boots, saying 'scuse me, 'scuse me. He comes directly over to kiss Louise on the cheek and then stands hovering at the end of the table. Eventually Tess hauls out a chair and tells him to sit down. She starts pouring him a glass of wine.

'Actually, I'll go for a beer, Tess. You got a lager?'

'Sure. One beer for Kevin. Anyone for anything else while I'm up?'

'Steinie for me, Tess.'

Tess pulls a face at her brother's back.

'Anyone else?'

'Ah, Tess, do you have port?'

After all, she is offering.

There is a little flicker of surprise, but nothing more, from anyone. No dire warnings. No leaping in.

Focusing intently on drinking her port, she is taken by surprise at a sudden shuffling around the table. A young couple arrive, both wearing thick jackets. The girl is short and stylish, with cropped dark hair. She wears dark clothes and lots of makeup, and she is puffing and rubbing at her hands, silver rings glinting on each finger. Introductions are given all round, and she understands that this is Chris, and that he has unexpectedly brought his girlfriend Sally. She notices a quick look flashing between Louise and Jacob, and Jacob shrugging his shoulders, as if to say he knew nothing about it. But they accommodate, quickly and smoothly: a chair is pulled up, an extra wine glass and menu found.

When the meals arrive Margie emerges from the kitchen without her apron and carrying her own plate. She sits down beside Kevin. Conversation flows around the table and it strikes Ella then as easy, remarkably easy, to sit down at a restaurant with a strange family, at a stranger's twenty-second birthday, and not at all unusual to be doing so. Chris leans across the table and winks, and his blond hair slides down over his eyes.

'So Tess, where's Juan tonight?'

'Juan? Who? Oh, Juan, my fabulous lover, of course!'

Tess claps her hands together in delight.

'Juan is making some last-minute arrangements for an exotic night. Hiring the string quartet, that kind of thing. Actually,' she leans across the table and speaks in a loud whisper, 'I'm rather bored with these Latino men. I'm starting to think I prefer the Middle Eastern type. So much *stroppier.*'

Tess laughs loudly and winks at Sally, who smiles back shyly, uncertainly. Her hand slides off the edge of the table and down somewhere near her boyfriend's knee. It is strange to see Tess talking like this. The exchange appears to be awkward flirting, or almost flirting, or somewhere complicated in between, and difficult to read.

In any case, Tess is quite wrong about who is and isn't charming. Chris comes across well, and is pleasant enough to look at: tall, with a flop of blond hair and a broad, open face. But as soon as she mentioned marine biology he had nothing to say, until she mentioned kelp research, which launched him into a story about windsurfing, and he went on and on. He is basic, and completely lacks the essential thing. It is impossible to say exactly what is missing, but it's not there – the thing that turns you towards a guy, makes it suddenly urgent and important to talk to him.

Of course, everyone is probably blind to it in their own brother, but Jacob, at the end of the table, has it by the bucketful, nonchalantly eating his meal, drawing flickers of attention from every other woman in the room. At the table by the window, for example, three teenage girls take turns to sneak glances at him. Jacob has delicate, angular features, high cheekbones and a shy, intimate smile. That's his real trick, she thinks, the secret smile, as though he's telling you something important about yourself. He moves smoothly and gracefully, and he is slim, like Tess, but darker.

Dessert arrives, and coffees and hot chocolates. Jacob sits back and puts his arm around Louise's chair, and she looks young beside him like that. He speaks to her quietly about something. Sally is watching, and Margie is watching, and she herself is certainly watching. Tess is entirely oblivious. But, Ella thinks, Jacob isn't oblivious. He knows perfectly well what's happening.

Louise is tapping at her glass and a hush falls across the table. The couple sitting at the next table turn to watch.

'Well, Jacob. You managed to get away without speeches last year at your twenty-first because you were so drunk that I decided it wasn't worth it.'

Jacob has his head in his hands in an overplayed expression of embarrassment. Chris is rubbing at his mouth and smiling slyly.

'So I've decided to make up for it this year. I have a few things to say myself, but I wonder if anyone else would like to speak first . . . how about you, Chris?'

Chris looks slightly bewildered, but pleased.

'I don't know what to say.'

'*Go on. Do it. Give us the dirt on Jacob!*' Tess is reaching across, whispering, tugging at Chris's arm.

'All right. I –' Chris stands up, takes his napkin from his lap, clears his throat. 'I, well, Jacob and me, ah, we've been mates for a good long time.'

'Since standard three,' Louise interjects.

'Yeah, something like that. We met at school camp, when we were nine, remember, Jacob?'

'Yeah, absolutely,' Jacob says. 'You lost your paddle in the middle of the lake and the camp staff had to go out in the motorboat and rescue you.'

Sally starts laughing.

'Hey man, who's making the speech here?' Chris says.

'You reckoned you were trying to bash a shark with it, d'you remember that, Chris? A shark, in a freshwater lake.'

Sally is still laughing, but she's the only one.

'Anyway. So, yes, I've known Jacob for a long time. We started surfing together, and it's just sad to see that some of us have turned out a bit more committed than others.' He winks at Jacob.

'Well, I'm a bit worried about the sharks, Chris,' Jacob says.

'We've been through a lot, seen a bit of trouble –'

'Like the inside of a police cell!' Tess whispers loudly.

'Hey, we're not going there,' says Jacob. 'This is a family show.'

'More than a few escapades of one sort or another, but through it all, I can say that Jacob's been a true mate, and I'm proud to see him make twenty-two.'

There is a round of applause, and then Louise is on her feet.

'Well, thanks, Chris, and I also want to say how delightful it's been for me having you as another member of the family for all these years.'

'Thanks, Louise,' Chris says.

'Now. Jacob. You always were an engaging kid.'

A chuckle and nod from the uncle.

'And I think we'd all agree you've grown into an engaging adult. One of my favourite memories is of a three-year-old boy who would come up and tell me in all seriousness about the travel and career plans of his bear, Samson, do you remember? Samson was going to be a jet fighter pilot in Saudi Arabia. Not bad for three.'

Jacob is leaning right back in his chair now, relaxed, and smiling at his mother. All eyes are on him – all eyes around the table and all eyes at the surrounding tables too. One elderly woman is smiling across at him, knowingly, tenderly. It is extraordinary, the pull, the gravity he generates.

Louise keeps talking, telling tales about Jacob as a child, making everyone at the table giggle.

'And now the obligatory shaming ritual. I'd like everyone to take a look at just how pretty you were.'

Ella is directly on the left so the photo is handed to her first. She takes in the small naked boy in the bath. It is an outside bath, somewhere on a farm it seems, because there is grass, and perhaps sheep in the background. There is a boy with green eyes, the same shade as Tessa's, thickly lashed and shyly looking up at the camera. The image is of a particularly beautiful child, and she wants to keep looking at it, but everyone is watching her now, and she does not know how she ought to respond to the photo, so she smiles weakly and passes it on to Tess. Tess snorts and passes it on around the table.

'But, Jacob, beyond your imagination, and your energy, your zest for life, I think your best quality, which I would like to honour today, is your concern for other people, and in particular the way you've always worked hard and looked out for me and Tess over what have been some . . .'

Louise looks down and fiddles with the base of her wine glass.

'. . . some quite difficult years. In short, we're all very proud, and love you a great deal, and I have no doubt that it will go well for you in the years ahead.'

A round of clapping and people are on their feet, kissing and patting one another on the back. Ella stays seated and gulps down a glass of water, not comfortable with kissing and patting at all.

Chris hates talking about Marchant Ridge, but he thinks about it sometimes because it's an example. It happened four years ago now, but it still comes up occasionally. Jacob brought it up a few months back, when they went tramping with a bunch of girls overnight to Mount Holdsworth. Up in Powell Hut on the snowline, warm and full of risotto, six of them huddled around the candle with the night pushing in at the windows. The talk turned to other trips, faces around the table eagerly leaning forward saying, Yeah, Hector, gets wild up there, yeah, the Ruahines. Jacob told it in broad strokes, making light, skirting around the edges. Chris refused to meet his eye.

He had wanted to go and see Sally that night. He lay stretched out on the concrete driveway, hands behind his head, staring up at a grey racing sky. Jacob was on his skateboard, bored and restless on a Saturday afternoon at the end of summer, riding down to the kerb, spinning around and riding back, over and again. Finally he had flipped his board down and sat on it, peering down at him.

'So, Chris, what are we doing? What's up with the Maranui party tonight?'

He kept looking at the sky and batted the question away. 'Not on. So I hear.'

Sally had just returned from a year's student exchange in Spain. He hadn't written to her all year, and felt guilty, but she had called him when she first got home. Her voice was warm and familiar, and he urgently wanted to see her again, bring her chocolate and laugh at her stories about crazy host mothers and drunken trips to Barcelona. He had become friends with Sally in the third form when they sat together talking for hours at McDonald's. Back then he was the smallest guy in his class and on track to become the class clown. They stayed friends even after he grew a foot and a half in the fifth form and made it into the second fifteen. Strangely, the lines had stayed clear this whole time. They had never fumbled around on couches, had even avoided drunken passes at parties. He loved Sally in a straightforward way: she was funny and clever, and he wanted to see her again.

Jacob was restless. 'Well, if Maranui's off, we're going to find something to do. We need an expedition, Chris. I'm going to organise it. You're in, and let's get Andrew Barker. He's just got that Beetle, he can take us for a spin. Let's head out to Kaitoke, get some beers and go bush.'

'Well, actually, I thought I'd go see Sally tonight.'

Jacob regarded him for a moment and then kicked his shin gently. 'Come on, Chris. Don't pike on me, mate. This'll be good. I think it could be quite a time. Me, you and Barker, night out under the stars, a drop of rum to keep the chill off, what do you say?'

'Jacob. Look at the weather. It's cruddy. It'll be miserable and windy out tonight. I want to see Sally. Why don't you come see Sally with me?'

Inexplicably Chris had ended up at four in the afternoon in the back seat of the dun-brown Beetle with Andrew Barker at the wheel, speeding along the river road. Barker wouldn't stay but he'd agreed to drop them out there at the base of the Tararuas.

'So you'll pick us up tomorrow?' They tumbled out of the car, slinging packs on their back. 'We'll be out by two, I'd say.'

Jacob punched him in the arm. 'Chris, mate, we'll hitch back! I told you, it's a challenge, an expedition, up Marchant Ridge and back with no support crew. We'll be sweet. Don't worry, Barker, you go and have a good time with your chick. We're fine.'

———

49

Generally, Chris laughed at Jacob's plans and said no. Jacob pushed limits and Chris maintained the cool head. That was the deal. Like the day at Ngawi, a Saturday trip to the coast to catch the tail end of the cyclone. He pulled the car up to see waves smashing against the shelf, the wind offshore. The swell was there, but it was closing out, the whole length of the wave crashing down at once with nowhere to go, and the cross-current tricky, leading off to the reef. If you got caught on that you'd be smashed on the rocks or carried out around the point.

Jacob was ecstatic, insisting they go out – hadn't they woken at dawn and driven two hours to get here? He whooped and sprang out of the car, racing down to the shoreline as soon as they arrived. Listening to the wind banging at the boards on the roof, it was not difficult to laugh at Jacob and threaten to drive off to the tearooms and leave him there if he didn't get out of his wetsuit and back into the car.

But at Kaitoke he didn't protest. In retrospect, he thinks that day he was too mellow and apathetic after a long summer. And certainly, there was the desire to meet Jacob's recklessness measure for measure, to let it all unravel for once.

Two hours past the old whare Chris realised that since midday he had eaten only a punnet of hot chips and a slice of bread and honey. It was quarter to eight, the day was fading, and a gusty, rattling dark was springing up around them. It had been raining over the week and the track was wet underfoot, the sticky yellow clay sucking back at their boots. Up in front Jacob stopped and pulled out a chocolate bar from his backpack. Chris ran hard up against him, panting and grumbling.

'Jacob, I'm munted. How about we cook up the baked beans now?'

Jacob handed him half the chocolate bar. His stomach turned and he wanted to stop, urgently wanted to eat something solid, but Jacob said half an hour, just keep going for half an hour.

Further on they walked out of the scrub and into the beech forest. High trees swayed above them. It was dark under the branches, and watching his feet Chris found he could barely make out the layers of black bite-sized leaves that covered the ground. The soil was soft here, springing back against his feet, and the track had levelled out, but tree roots riddled the ground and had become difficult to see. He tripped and fell, swore, brushed at his knees and felt furious, weak and hungry; demanded then that they take a break. He undid his pack and pulled on a thin raincoat and woollen hat. Jacob hesitated, kept looking ahead down the track, and Chris's rage rose a notch further. Fuck it, he thought, he'd knock him over and make him stop. He stayed exactly where he was, flicked on his small headlamp and fiddled with the gas cooker. Fat moths whirred past and bashed up against his forehead. Finally Jacob swung his bag down and squatted beside the log.

They ate the beans and smoked, and they both became relaxed and pleased. Chris lay back against the log looking up through the black overlay of leaves and branches, and the odd shapes of grey sky. Then it seemed good to be out in the bush, at the end of summer, with Jacob.

Almost every evening that holiday had been taken up with discussion about study. Chris's father had leaned on the kitchen bench and said that marketing with the proposed law degree would make a highly sought-after combination. His mother favoured accounting, arguing that marketing was not a true discipline, with no real substance. Even his aunt and uncle had joined the fray over Christmas lunch.

'Get yourself some marketable skills in computers, Chris. Learn programming, takes you anywhere.' His uncle poured brandy sauce on his pudding. 'Plenty of cash in London with computers.'

He had debated the possibilities with them each in turn, and quietly worked out whether there would be room for a first-year philosophy paper among his compulsory credits.

In the bush, watching Jacob blowing rings up past his headlamp, he thought about the five years of secondary school. They had ended on a hot afternoon in November, with school magazines and water fights, and later, listening to Pearl Jam and getting sweetly stoned in Jacob's car, reminiscing about the first day of third form, when Mr Thomas had encountered them after school with fish and chips at the park, and given stern, terrifying warnings about eating in public in their uniforms. School had rolled over him day after simple day, and it occurred to him now that the same number of years lay ahead at varsity. It was odd to think about those years, and he wondered if they would pass gently over him in the same regular pattern, with no particular cause for excitement or alarm.

The moon came up and the shapes smattering the hollow in the ground brightened as the clouds skimmed off. They talked idly on, about skating gear, and climbing gear, and tramping gear, and he sat up to take a better look at Jacob's new pack, running his hand over the adjustable straps and sealed seams. Jacob tipped out the contents to show off his new knife. Two large books, a bag of bread rolls, a camera and a travel-size chess set tumbled out onto the ground. When would they play chess? he wondered. Did Jacob think they would be bored out here overnight?

Finding the knife, Jacob started carving the log. He worked in quick strokes, training the headlamp on the damp bark. The circle of light shifted from side to side as Jacob considered his work from different angles, his tongue moving around in his tightly held jaw.

'There!' he crowed, and snapped the knife shut. 'Right, let's go,' and started shovelling the books, buns, cooker and cups back into his pack.

'Hey! Where do you want to go?' Chris had taken a long sip from the hip flask and already pulled out a groundsheet and his sleeping bag, ready to bed down among the tree roots. 'A night under the stars, Jacob, an expedition, remember?'

Jacob was on his feet, pulling up his jacket hood and tightening the straps on his pack. 'Chris, what are you talking about? You said you'd do it. You said we'd go up to Alpha Hut. Fuck, you're an unreliable bastard sometimes. Can't trust you for anything.'

It was after nine. Chris was exhausted. Walking tonight his energy had depleted so quickly, and now here was Jacob, accusing, demanding. And lying besides. This was not what they had agreed. Jacob was never content to let it happen as they had agreed, and if he couldn't cajole you he'd turn to bullying.

'Screw you, Jacob, I'm staying here. If you go on, you're on your own.' He rolled over and punched a fist into his jacket, making an indent for his head.

Jacob muttered something, dropped his pack on the ground and wandered away without it. A short time later he returned. Chris lay still, watching the light swing as Jacob cleared twigs and stones from a patch of flat ground, finally setting his foam mat and sleeping bag out precisely in the centre.

Chris slept fitfully, starting at strange sounds. Around midnight he opened his eyes and it was black and cool against his face. He wriggled out of his sleeping bag to take a piss. There were drops on his face and within minutes it was a solid downpour. They both stood, torches on, staring out into the night. There was nowhere to go. The water fell freely, fat drops that gathered weight in the traverse down through the canopy. There was no low scrub to crawl under, no rocks, no tent fly. Chris swore loudly and shuffled back into his sleeping bag. He tightened the drawstring around the hood, pulled his legs up tight against his chest and turned his face to the earth.

When the rain eased, he sat up and drank the last of the rum. He checked his watch: one o'clock. Another five long hours until the dawn.

A possum flew overhead screeching out his name, and bats fluttered at his feet. He stood teetering on the edge of a precipice and saw Ms Maller, his drama teacher, fallen to the bottom, her red top torn in two, bare breasts pointing up to a sky of purple clouds. He put his head in his hands and was flooded with a sense of misery, and frustration, of trying to say something and finding himself unable to speak.

Waking at two a.m. he realised that the southerly had come up. It howled over the top of the ridge and the trees shuddered and creaked in long strains. His body began to shiver and he willed it to stop but it wouldn't. He felt the damp seeping through his jersey to the skin of his back, and the hot ache of tears pooling at the back of his head. Unconnected thoughts trickled slowly past his waiting mind. The stupidity of choosing a down sleeping bag rather than nylon, figuring that he would be unlikely ever to get really soaked. Sally, back in her own bed, lying in the room she had painted crimson. Her row of coloured glass pieces strung up at the window, glinting dark behind the curtains.

Several more times he sat up to press the button on his watch and stared at the green minutes ticking by. He turned over on the groundsheet and felt pools of icy water shift under his body. He sneezed, his nose pouring liquid, and wiped at it with numb fingers. Shuffling his body towards the dark shape of Jacob, he placed his head down near his chest. There was no warmth, but there was the sound of steady breathing, and he slept again.

Towards dawn it started to drizzle and the surrounding curtain of fine mist became slowly visible. As soon as Chris could make out the lines of the trees he hauled up and started stuffing gear into his bag, jiggling and shivering. The headlamp sat on the log, where he had carefully placed it in the night, beside Jacob's carving. The exposed red wood was bright against the black bark. Words, underscored twice: KING OF INFINITE SPACE. Whatever. Stupid bloody tosser. Fuckwit. He slung his pack on and walked out to the carpark, without pausing, without once looking back to check whether Jacob was behind him.

So yeah, nobody died. And in fact Jacob had loved it, going on and on up there at Powell Hut about how fucking cold they were, how saturated. How right he was, how they should have gone on, should have pushed through to Alpha, but hey, at the end of the day it was all quite funny and made for a good story. And Chris, getting so shitty in the morning and going off like that, going off like a stroppy girl. In fact he didn't say anything about the morning, but Chris knew what he would have said at other times, when he wasn't there. He knew what Jacob thought.

Chris doesn't like talking about Marchant Ridge at all. It was a long time back, and he knows a lot more about Jacob now. He knows it wasn't that straightforward – that he didn't cause it and neither necessarily did Jacob. He knows that Jacob gets like that at times and he's learnt to see that there is a pattern to it. He thinks of Marchant Ridge as an example.

Chris sits in his usual chair at the table and scans the columns of the newspaper. Social workers. Plenty of jobs for social workers. Policy analysts, ditto. And an entire page for programming geeks. But nothing for lawyers. Except here, at the bottom of the page, one small box, a firm in Christchurch.

Certainly, he doesn't want a job in Christchurch. His only clear memory of that city is walking with a parent (which parent he can't recall) through a stone archway into an open courtyard. There was a man standing there with long hair, playing the accordion and dressed in a blue fur coat, and they stopped to listen. He remembers standing in the courtyard, the sky grey and the ground wet, stamping in his gumboots, pulling at the hand, Let's go, let's go inside. When he thinks of Christchurch he thinks of grim stone towers, a city governed by grey men. But still, he checks it out – he follows up every possibility, even if it is unlikely, or awful, or would require him to leave Sally behind. His mother has been saying this to him now, saying, Chris, you can't afford to be fussy. It makes him wonder – does she think he's been turning jobs down? Or perhaps what she is really saying, trying to be subtle, trying to be positive, is that the time has come, that what it comes down to now is applying for McDonald's, finding a paper run, selling his body.

Every week she cuts out advertisements and pastes them on to yellow paper. When he turns up at home she kisses him on the cheek and hands him the yellow pieces of paper without a word. Around the edges of the ads she scribbles little comments: 'strong on litigation', 'small firm – might get broad exp. here?', 'OK if you don't want to practise'. His mother is not a lawyer, but a number of her friends are. He envisages anxious discussions over coffee about the Best Options For Chris.

Last spring he walked out of the room at the end of his Advanced Criminal exam and the weeks before Christmas were marked by an enormous sense of relief, and achievement. It was complete, an enormous task, and all the little tasks that made it up: the late nights at the library, the reading of a thousand perverse cases in tiny print, the scribbling and scrawling in exams to get down the right thoughts, in the right order, all finished, all satisfactory. After that, he slept in each day, lay in the sun and stayed up late into the night watching reruns of *Star Trek* and *Hogan's Heroes*. He had no guilt or concern, for he had earned this over five long years, and that's how he thought of it then – a holiday, the last holiday before he started work.

Of course, the best students in his class all had positions to go to. They had jobs sewn up a year before, law clerking for the big firms in town, and they spent that last summer on three-month bus tours around Europe, secure in the knowledge they were safely on the track, with an office – their own office – ready and waiting, and a newly purchased suit in the wardrobe. But these ones were still the exception, the elite of the class, and he wasn't worried back then. He wanted to say to his mother, and to his friends, and to Sally, and to everyone who asked, Look, I know it's coming, I know it's there, the right one, the one I'm supposed to get, the job that I've been primed for over the past eighteen years. And then, like a little blaze at the back of the mind, another question would surface: Did he actually want it, the right job, at all? Had he ever actually wanted it?

There was a flurry of applications and one interview in January, but nothing came of it. The holiday started to sour. The school year started and at home the conversation started to centre on his younger brother, Marcus, just starting seventh form, and with a full schedule of basketball, school and part-time work. An awkward gap grew where they used to talk about Chris and his study, his plans. He moved out of home, and then Easter came. Soon it will be mid-term break. He comes home for dinner once a fortnight, and now they are talking about what Marcus will do next year, but no one is talking about Chris at all, because there is nothing to say.

The bank continues to send him graduate brochures with pictures of shiny cars and computers. They will give him – well, lend him at least – up to five thousand dollars 'to assist in the transition into the workforce'. He has looked carefully into this, has considered the clean-shaven boy in the brochure, smiling in his black pinstripe suit, swinging a briefcase in his left hand. He has looked and considered, because perhaps he has a right to it, this money, and he is grateful that the bank has this unshakeable confidence in him, and in his degree, and he sometimes thinks he should honour this confidence, and take the loan, and buy a suit.

The Christchurch firm specialises in family law. He can't afford to be fussy, but even now he couldn't bear it, dealing with bashed-up women, and people squabbling over kids and houses. The two positions require previous experience.

'Do you want lunch? There's spaghetti on the stove.'

Sally kisses him on the head, gives his shoulders a quick rub.

'I had spaghetti for breakfast.'

'Okay, up to you. I'm just going to the gym, and then Fiona and I are going shopping for her trip. I'll be back about six. What are you doing?'

'Looking into some stuff. I might go biking later.'

He lies to Sally now. It is better than saying: Nothing, I am doing nothing.

'We might go into town later and catch Hobnail Boots. They're playing at Molly's. Do you want to come?'

'No money.'

'Chris, that's utterly hopeless. Look, I'll pay. You need to get out. You should come with us.'

'Ah, no. I'm not that into Hobnail Boots anyway. I've got stuff to do.'

'Well, what about Jacob, what's he doing tonight? Why don't you do something with him, something cheap?'

'Oh, yeah, maybe. Look, you go. I'm doing some stuff here.'

'Fine. Can you deal with the kitchen, then? I think we're developing compost in the fridge. It stinks.'

When he first moved in with Sally, in February, it was a respite and a variation, and he wondered why he had stayed living at home so long. It was glorious to spend every night with her naked body beside him, to reach over and have sex in the middle of the night, or first thing in the morning, just about every morning; glorious to get drunk with her and not have to go anywhere, to live surrounded by her odd style, her movie posters, band posters, and op shop dresses hung on the walls like paintings.

The flat itself was run down, small and damp, with the floral wallpaper flaking and peeling, and the first weeks after they moved in were filled up with domestic problem-solving: trapping mice, unblocking drains, replacing lightbulbs that popped one after another, as if set to expire within days of the old flatmates moving out. In a burst of enthusiasm they called the landlord and asked if they could paint the kitchen, slapping yellow paint indiscriminately over nail holes and uneven bumps. Sally found blue paint in the garage and did the cupboard doors, they bought a washing machine out of the newspaper, and Chris's grandparents gave him two old armchairs. In all this activity he was absorbed and happy, inordinately proud of the flat, and Sally. It makes him think he must have become prematurely old, or soft, or sentimental. It makes him wonder whether all he really wants is to become an old man, with a little wife and a little house; whether in fact he wants to skip straight to retirement, and forgo whatever it is – life – that's supposed to take place in the years between.

Sally doesn't want to skip that bit. Sally's landed exactly where she wants to be. She's just started at a small clothing design store out here in the Hutt Valley, and she tells everyone what a coincidence it was, taking the flat out here, and how it's close, and she can walk to work, it's so easy, and she can choose her days off because they're in at the shop over the weekends. He goes to pick her up late at night and she looks up at him, startled, with pins in her mouth, rolls of cloth piled on the table and coffee cups scattered everywhere. The student radio station plays loudly. One of the other women walks through, saying, Chris, you should see what Sally's come up with this time – it's fantastic, check it out. He's learnt the right words now, he can say, 'cut on the bias', or 'contrasting textures', but all he really understands is that it's hers, and she's good at it, and she gets off on it, totally – that it's what you might call a passion.

He makes cheese on toast for lunch, and decides to make a phone call. He will do this in order to generate a small sense of purpose, of action. It takes courage. Increasing amounts of courage are required for the ever-diminishing acts of his day.

'Hey, Jacob, Chris.'

'Hey, man.'

'What are you doing? Want to get pissed tonight?'

'Where?'

'What do you mean where? In town, I suppose. I don't actually care where we drink, Jacob, I just have a simple need to get plastered, abandon the conscious effort of the Life Project, get fucked, basically, and because you are my mate, and can generally be counted on, I am giving you the opportunity to do this with me. Are you interested or not?'

'I don't want to go into town.'

Just that, and silence. Jacob is in one of those moods, and that means it will be a difficult conversation, like paddling out through seaweed, in soupy water, and he really hasn't got the energy for this today.

'You don't want to go into town. Fine, then, can we drink at the Breakwater?'

'It's what, what day is it, Chris? Thursday? I don't think so. No.'

'I'm coming over. I'm coming into town and we'll figure it out. Anyone else we could call? What's Barker doing?

'No, no one else, don't call anyone else.'

He doesn't get it, really, but he's learnt that it happens, that there are these times when Jacob refuses to see anyone. It's as though his everyday self has been taken off and packed up into a box, and there is only a deflated balloon inside, a black rubber balloon, wrinkled and puckering, exhausted. Jacob doesn't want anyone then, and he won't go out, and sometimes he goes ballistic and tells you to fuck off when he's like that, so you have to tread carefully. But in fact Chris thinks that something within their friendship has developed because of these times, because if Jacob lets anyone in, it's him, and they sit together and drink, or don't drink, but either way Jacob is silent, and a sudden warmth will often rise up in his chest at these times and spread towards his friend, who despite everything is not always confident, or charming – who needs him, actually, when it counts, when it's like this.

There is a crackling and shifting down the line.

'Jacob, are you in bed?'

'Yeah, man. Keeping warm. Fucking freezing outside. Hailing.'

He pictures Jacob then, lying in his room in the dark, but today there is no warmth rising in his chest, there is only irritation, and he can't be bothered with it, any of it. He's got his own problems right now, and Jacob won't give a toss about that, because with Jacob you can be miserable on his account but never on your own. With Jacob it is always immense, always brilliant, expansive and wild or else there is this silence, the inability to speak, or move. But Chris is like the ant, scurrying below all this, and the feelings of ants are not an important matter. Well, Chris-the-ant is reaching the end of his patience.

'Jacob, forget it. I don't think I'll come in.'

Without pause, without a blink: 'Good idea. Stay home. Warmer.'

A matter of supreme indifference to Jacob then, his turning up, or not, even now, even in this mood. There is no particular place for Chris after all. It's probably time to let it die a natural death, he thinks. Time to get on with other people, Sally, and others – he can't think who right now – but others, people who are more normal, because after all he's the one who is unemployed and when you're unemployed friends like Jacob don't help.

'Any other kitchen things you need?' Louise asks.

'How about a spatula?'

Jacob is brandishing it by the handle, waving it in front of her face.

'Exactly when did you last use a spatula, Jacob? I'm surprised you know what it's called. You seriously want it?'

'For sure! How else are we going to make afghans? You need one for that, right?'

'Technically no, but take it. That's fine. What are you going to do about a vacuum cleaner?'

'I think Barker's dad has given him one.'

'And a fridge, is there a fridge there?'

'Fridge issue resolved. We got one for two hundred bucks. I told you that already.'

'I was talking to Kevin yesterday and he said he's got an old couch if you want it. We could pick it up this afternoon.'

'Nah, we've got two couches already.'

'And I've been thinking about a dehumidifier. It could be damp, and with your asthma, Jacob – I thought you could hire one, or I could. They're expensive to buy, but if it's damp . . .'

'There's a heater. We'll be fine. Mum, you're starting to flap. Let's just remain calm, eh?'

Cheeky boy. She bites her lip and turns to wrap plates in newspaper. They will need dinner plates, so she has pulled out all the old unmatching ones, chipped and cracked, that have sat unused for years at the back of the cupboard.

This one, with the gold and green lacing around the edge, finely frilled and stamped silver on the underside, is the last of the set she bought twenty-three years ago. She wraps it around twice and places it at the bottom of the pile where it is least likely to get smashed in transit. They were almost like a wedding present. She'd found them at the junk shop, and they were a present from herself to herself, in celebration of a beginning. The memory of the day tickles lightly down her spine but she packs the plate into a box with the others. It is simply a plate, ugly and of little use on its own. It will almost certainly get broken, she knows, because such things happen in flats. Kids don't take care: she knows that and it's all right, and what's more, it's best that Jacob doesn't see her like this, flustered about the plate, because he will tease her. Maybe it would worry him, and he doesn't need that right now. He needs to be left alone to get on with it.

'Sorry, Ma. I was being harsh.' He comes up behind her and starts massaging her shoulders with enthusiasm. 'And thanks, eh? I do appreciate all this stuff, you know.'

Kind, ridiculous son. Enough of the flapping. In any case, there will be a number of benefits to his leaving. Getting the study back, for one thing. In the two months since Ella moved in, book-keeping for both the house and the café has gone to the dogs because tackling that job without the study available would mean spreading papers across the lounge floor and being interrupted.

Now Ella will move into Jacob's room, the spare bed will go back out to the garage and the little back room will be reinstated as her own space. She might even put up some shelves, because the pile of books beside her bed is growing with nowhere to go. Perhaps she could frame the print she bought last year, the naked woman with cherry nipples reclining on the couch. Modigliani, she says under her breath, turning the sound in her mouth.

Certainly, it's not as though the house will be left empty. It has been almost too crowded, but she has become accustomed to Ella's presence and it no longer seems odd to have an extra kid in the house – a pregnant kid, with her little stomach starting to show. Ella is quiet and unintrusive, and rarely around. Some weeks after she moved in she began paying fifty dollars a week towards food and bills, quite on her own initiative, leaving the money in an envelope on Louise's bed every Monday without a word. She decided to accept the contribution gratefully and without making a fuss, because it helps a great deal.

They haven't talked about the long term, but secretly she has been thinking that Ella should stay up until the birth if she wants to. It's perfectly clear that she's enjoying it here, and that she doesn't want to go. There's family up in Gisborne apparently, and maybe that's where they'll go later on, but for now she wants to keep studying – a determined girl, in her quiet way – so really, she needs to be here. The best thing would be to broach the topic, to sit down together and ask her directly, but there hasn't been the opportunity, and Ella always seems slightly frightened, or busy.

'Ma, put that down! You'll sprain your back, you idiot – it's full of books.'

Despite herself, she likes it when her son takes this tone with her. She leaves the box at the top of the steps and returns with an armload of bedding.

Together they pack the car, fitting in a small bookcase, a chest of drawers, the old microwave and several boxes. Jacob drives over the hill into the city. The flat is near the centre of town, and Jacob's friend Andrew and his girlfriend pull up on the kerb at the same time, in a ute, with a double mattress flapping over the edge.

She wonders how Jacob will cope with the situation. She imagines it will be difficult being the third person in a flat with a couple. Jacob is the rent payer they require, and resent, and will attempt to accommodate. But then, perhaps someone will move in with him too; maybe that's what moving out is partly about – making space for a girl he's seeing. This is idle speculation because Jacob has not talked about any particular girl for years. When he started university he had a brief relationship with an older woman called Cindy who worked as a travel agent. He brought Cindy home one afternoon and she talked without pause for over an hour about her free trips to Fiji, New Caledonia and California. Cindy never came back and there has been no one since. Louise wonders occasionally if her son is gay, and when this thought occurs to her she wonders how she would respond, because there is no strong emotion attached to the thought, only a vague sense of surprise. Perhaps it would be different, she thinks, if Jacob actually came through the door with a young man, or an older man, on his arm. She might not be quite so tolerant, so blasé then.

But Jacob isn't with anyone, and he looks small and alone, standing beside the couple outside the new flat. He doesn't belong to anyone: he is twenty-two and leaving home but still, unequivocally, he is hers. She is not sure that he will manage. Perhaps it would be best not to shift Ella into his room just yet.

Jacob turns the key in the frosted glass door. Inside there are piles of rubbish in the corners of each room, and the windowsills are thick with mildew. Andrew's girlfriend brings in the vacuum cleaner, finds a rag and sets to, and it is easy for Louise to join in – appropriate to take the role of the mother who helps scrub down. Later she will go to the supermarket and buy vegetables, pasta, oil and herbs, a cheesecake and some fruit juice and then leave them to it: leave him, and go home.

All the lights are on at home. She makes tea and walks into the lounge. Ella is on the couch, writing furious notes on lined refill paper, papers and books spread all around.

'You're working hard. Got a test coming up?'

'Yeah, Monday. Sorry about all this mess. I'll go into the bedroom.'

Before Louise can say anything Ella is on her feet, gathering papers together. The politeness is annoying this time, because it occurs to her that it is not, in fact, completely polite, it is something else. It is almost a refusal to acknowledge the situation: that she is here, she is staying; that the family has chosen to make room for her. This silence, and absence, the trick of disappearing – it is as though Ella wishes to convince them all that she does not exist. She seems to want to avoid consuming anything, to avoid being in the way, she wants to remove any impression her body leaves on the furniture, to live among them so lightly that she does not mark or change the environment in any way.

In fact, Louise thinks, it's arrogant. She doesn't want to *live* with us. She thinks she's above it, or outside it, and it's starting to become really irritating.

There is mail on the hallway dresser. Something for Jacob. It might be worth letting him know about this. It may be important – perhaps something connected to his thesis – and he might need her to open it immediately. But of course he would see right through such a transparent excuse. She can't possibly ring him tonight.

She opens the bedroom door. It is empty now, the front room that catches the sun, bare except for a poster from the summer production of *Othello*, a bundle of old sports clothes and, in the corner of the empty wardrobe, a pile of abandoned books. Jacob's new books. She counts the spines. Eighteen, no, nineteen books, on Sri Lanka, and Mongolia and ancient Buddhist civilisations. Mainly hardback, with shiny covers, bought only a month ago.

She remembers Jacob rushing through the door that day with two large plastic bags and starting to unload them on the bench, his eyes wide and green, talking fast about the connections between Buddhism and romantic poetry, and something else about Sri Lankan kings, and caves. It hadn't made sense at the time and she had said, But Jacob, your research has nothing to do with this. I thought it was about Shelley and Keats.

He'd brushed her away, saying, It's relevant, it's all relevant, and then that night she came into the kitchen for a glass of water after midnight and he was still there, books open and page after page of spider writing spread across the table, in a language of indecipherable excitement. Now the books are here, in the wardrobe, irrelevant and discarded. He is a ridiculous, impulsive boy, she thinks, and he will have to learn to spend more sensibly or he will be out of money within a few weeks.

She takes the books out into the kitchen and piles them on the table so that she will remember to take them to him when she next drives into town. Tess comes in, her cheeks flushed from the cold and her pink knitted hat pulled down over her ears. It is not clear why Tess insists on wearing this pink hat, which looks so odd against her auburn hair, but Louise doesn't comment because to do so would be to invite furious words, or furious silence.

'You been on a spending spree?' Tess asks, picking up the top book from the pile and flicking quickly to the introduction. 'Buddhism, Mum? That's a bit radical.'

'They're Jacob's. He left them behind.'

'I didn't know he was into this. I mean, he's hardly the religious type, is he?'

'Well, I don't know that he is into it, not for himself in any case. I think it's for his thesis.'

'His very *wide-ranging thesis*, it sounds like. Anyway.' She drops the book onto the table and stretches her arms up above her head. Louise looks at her, surprised to notice how tall she is when she stands up straight like that. 'What's for tea?'

'That's up to you, really. I don't feel hungry myself. But there's plenty of pasta and vegetables, or frozen curry in the freezer. Is that okay?'

'Fine. So, what's Jacob's place like?'

Tess opens the freezer door and reaches past the open bread bag, pulling out a new one. She pushes aside pots and dishes on the bench and thumps the bread down. Ice crystals scatter onto the floor and melt into small pools.

'Nice. Quite sunny. You ought to go and visit him.'

'Yeah, I will, actually. I've got a three-hour gap in lectures on a Tuesday. I figured I'd head over there to watch the soaps and eat noodles.'

'Tess! How do you have time for soaps?'

Her daughter moves around the kitchen, pulling out a plate, a knife, the butter, honey. Her eyes and hands dart and collect. She plunges the toast down and then stands peering into the toaster, as though expecting it to pop immediately, stands there watching, hopping with impatience.

'Can I use the car tonight?'

'I thought you were working late.'

'Well, actually, the good news is, I've quit my job.'

'You've quit at the shop! Is that wise?'

'Very wise, because I've got another one.'

'A new job?'

Which is clearly a ridiculous question, and she braces herself for a sarcastic response.

'Yep, fifteen hours a week at Greenpeace, doing filing, letters, maybe organising events.'

Tess delivers this information in a calm and pleasant voice.

'Paid work? While you're a student? For Greenpeace?'

An entire stammering string of questions. She watches Tess slab thick layers of butter and honey on her toast – far too much butter – and gulp one slice down before she spreads the other.

'Of course it's paid. Pretty good, too – twelve dollars an hour.'

'Well, Tess, that's fantastic, it's exactly what you want, isn't it?'

'Yep. It looks good on my CV, too, and once I've got my degree I reckon I'll be able to get a full-time job with them. They're looking for scientists.'

'Tess, that's such good news!'

'I know. Anyway, the car, can I use it?'

'Sure. Back by ten o'clock though, all right?'

'I know, of course. Six more bloody months on my restricted. It's an eternity.'

For no particular reason Louise puts her arm around her daughter's shoulders and kisses her on the cheek. How long since she last did this? Guilt, immediately, because Tess has been here all along, trying her best, and she doesn't give her credit for it; she doesn't notice and she doesn't comment. She is often critical of Tess, and doesn't give her daughter nearly enough of this. But now there is only Tess at home, so she will notice, and it will be better. There will be more room, and more time for her now. She resolves to use it well.

That night Louise dreams of a helicopter. It is a cold day and she is in a garden, shivering, dressed inappropriately. The helicopter is swooping across and across, and there are men on it, and they are looking for her. She is in the garden and there is a baby in her arms. What she needs to do is to hide the baby. She has to put it down in a safe pocket, in the nook of a tree, in a bush, in the flax, but the helicopter is close and the sound is drowning her. It is difficult to think; the helicopter is black and shuddering, and crosses the garden, back and forth, and then the baby has grown strong and pins her down to the ground, and refuses to be fed or pacified. It is yelling in her face and she cannot move – she cannot breathe – and the man in the helicopter is searching her out.

Ella must have slept for a long time because when she wakes the light is fading. She hadn't meant to sleep this long, or even to sleep at all, and yet here she is, still wearing her long coat, because it was cold earlier in the afternoon and she didn't want to turn the heater on. Now the room is warm and she feels drugged, her limbs heavy and immobile. She rubs hard at her eyes and runs a finger over the pocked diamond pattern of the couch impressed into her cheek.

Every week now her body becomes heavier and she is starting to loll around – slobbing like a fat seal, she thinks. Increasingly she finds herself unfussed, unbothered when she should be bothered, and she should fuss. The tracksuit pants she wears day in, day out are dirty, marked with food spots, but she can't think what to do about this and it no longer seems important.

Right now it is time to get up, and to think. She needs to call Dad and let him know what time the bus will come in. If she doesn't call before nine o'clock tonight he will worry. She imagines him sitting with his gin, beside the radio, with the lamplight trained on his crossword. When he hears the pips and the nine o'clock news then he will know it is late, and if she hasn't called him by then, he won't be able to keep working at the crossword, because he will be distracted and worried, and perhaps he will even try to call her. He won't be able to find her number. He will have written it down somewhere but not remember where. If it gets to that he will be angry, and frustrated, and still worried.

The trip was planned two months ago and every time she has opened her diary since then, the weekend has glared back at her. It is the one with the dotted blue line around it and she has watched carefully as it has crept forward. A weekend is two little white rectangles, separated by a thin grey line of sleep. Empty white spaces. She does not know what will happen inside the rectangles, and she has been refusing to consider the possibilities. There is another blank day that is creeping forward, too – the day with a little red x on it – but that one is still two and half months away, so she isn't thinking about that either. And it's unlikely to be exactly that one anyway. It doesn't seem to her that Wednesday would be the best day. It is a middle day, a nothing, ordinary day. Sunday would be better.

At seven she will wake up and by nine she will be sitting in moderate comfort in the middle of the Newmans bus, with her bag and books on her lap, riding out of the city, up the gorge and on past the towns on the inlet. Winding up the belly of the fish, winding for ten hours, all the way home.

The trip is longer and hotter than she expected. There is a fussy baby, and at Bulls a group of girls board, ten- or twelve-year-olds. One sits beside her and another two across the aisle, and they chatter and giggle. The nearest girl has a flock of purple butterfly clips in her hair, and she doesn't like to be left out of the conversation so she leans over, saying loudly, Hey you guys, hey you guys, and points and gestures towards the boy in the row in front. He stares unblinkingly out the window and the tinny sound of Metallica sifts out from his earphones.

The coach stops at every small town along the state highway. The engine is left running as bags are loaded off and on, shuddering and making her stomach rise uncomfortably. For lunch they stop at the Putorino Sunshine Tearooms. Standing in the queue, Ella stares blankly through the plastic flap at ham sandwiches, egg sandwiches, ham, egg and cheese sandwiches, then further down at the meat pies, chips and sausage rolls. There is no soup. Which is the one thing she wants right now. Tomato soup. An old thin woman with an orange knitted hat nudges her in the arm and says, Aren't you just parched? Such a long time since morning tea, isn't it, love? In dismay, she nods and reaches for two ham and tomato sandwiches. The passengers sprinkle themselves across the tearooms, clustered into family groups. Those travelling alone fit in around the edges, apologising quietly. Her back aches and tingles, and she watches the fussy baby being fed a banana, taking it in his fat fist and smearing it into his clothes. Finally, they head off again. Past Wairoa it becomes dark, and for the last hour the bus falls quiet. Someone is snoring lightly at the back.

When she steps off her father isn't there. But they have arrived early and other people are waiting too, milling around the hatch to grab at bags, heaving them onto the footpath, stretching out their backs. They light up cigarettes and stamp to keep warm. There is no wind, unlike down in Wellington, but in September it is still too cold to wait outside for long. Ella moves inside the glass doors of the station and watches as one by one the other passengers are gathered up by friends and relations. They are swooped upon and kissed, their bags taken from them and they tumble into cars, slamming doors and driving off into the night. A backpacker with a Canadian flag on his pack makes phone calls under the blue glow of the Telecom sign, and the driver, whose name badge says Terry, loosens his tie and stacks packages onto a steel trolley.

Before he notices her she picks him, walking down the street under the white street lights. Tall and lean, with his familiar long stride, but then there is a brief moment of uncertainty because the man approaching the station seems to be wearing a red knitted jersey – bright red, with small white pocks, like snowflakes. It looks like a Santa Claus jersey, and is not something she ever saw her father wear. So she is puzzled, but then he is the first one to smile broadly and raise his hand in greeting.

'Gidday, girl!'

Reaching the station door he puts his arm around her, and there is the smell of smoke from the fire and cigarettes. There is the faint smell of dog on him, and something else mixed in – unfamiliar, and almost floral. He puts his hand behind her neck and pulls her in to kiss her cheek, makes a discovery about her body, and pulls back sharply.

'Ellie. Oh.'

'Dad, please, let's go home. I need to eat. Please, not here. Can we just go now?'

She knows she sounds desperate, and knows too that this strategy will not work, that there will have to be a conversation and not only with Dad either. The aunties will want to add their opinion, too. But while she can still create a respite she will. Because there is no doubt what Dad will want. He will want her home, right now, and if not now then certainly he will want them both home after the baby arrives. Dad will insist and demand, because he will want to look after her. And, at the end of it all, she will probably say yes, because there are no other options, and because his will is strong: stubborn and quiet, but strong. What Dad won't say is that he was right and she was wrong – about the city and all the big ideas, the studying, the science. He won't say this directly to her.

They drive out along the coast. It is completely dark now, a dark night with no moon, and silent between them. She is not afraid, and not uncomfortable. The space here, the long stretch of road and the distance, the absence of lights, these things astonish her. The land does this each time, as if for the first time, every time she returns. The radio plays love songs from the sixties and seventies; it plays 'Peaceful Easy Feeling', and she wants to let it lie between them, this song, and her father humming, and the night drive.

'Ellie, love –'

He clears his throat and she feels the impending rush of words coming from her right, feels the pushing, jostling torrent

74

of everything he wants to say, and braces herself.

'I guess you're not the only one with a few changes coming on.'

She looks sharply at him. He stares ahead, and as they swing around the wide corner the headlights catch a flicker of cattle, a stand of cows pushed up against the fenceline.

'I guess before we get home I should say, well, it's a bit different now.'

He says this in a shy and hesitant tone.

'Dad, what are you talking about?'

'Ellie, love, there's someone, we're, she, well, Ellie, Margaret's at home now, and she's putting on the tea for us. There'll be dinner on the table for us.'

'Margaret?'

'Well, come to think of it, more likely you know her as Mrs Loam.'

'Mrs Loam? Mrs Loam from the dairy? Mrs Loam is cooking me tea?'

Chocolate fish and toffee milks, and wrinkled hands with flashing rings carefully counting out twenty-cent mixtures. A floral nylon dress and purple curlers. Sometimes a smile, often a sharp comment. No kids allowed in the shop in school hours. Once, a slap on the hand for reaching out for the lollies before they were put in the paper bag.

'Yep, yes, she is, Ellie. There's chops and fresh new potatoes, lots of butter, bread, a big tea ready for you, love – you'll need that now.'

What is he saying? What exactly is he saying? That Mrs Loam is coming to cook tea because she is coming home? Never. Grumpy old cow. And besides, what about her husband, sitting in his old chair out the back of the shop, pottering in from time to time to rearrange the beans and the soap? Mrs Loam ought to be home cooking tea for him. But no, he died, Mr Loam; he dropped dead of a heart attack before she even left home. So clearly they are friends, Dad and Mrs Loam,

Dad and *Margaret*. She comes around, cooks tea. Without anyone else in the house. They are *more than friends?*

They both fall silent again then, and it remains for the rest of the drive. The car turns off the highway and starts up the back road away from the sea, and Ella turns the odd thought over and over in her mind. Dad is courting, then. Dad, up here, all through the winter, developing a whole aspect to his life that she could never imagine or anticipate. How on earth did it begin? Did Dad just go in there day after day, buying packets of Marlboro until the stockpile in the hot-water cupboard toppled over and swamped the hallway?

It strikes her as neither endearing nor disturbing that Dad should perhaps be in love. She is hardly thinking of him at all. Instead, she is considering how the picture that she has held in her mind has been wrong, and how perhaps this is like looking in a box for something you are sure you put there. You can see it in your mind, this thing that you need, this particular book, or a winter blanket, or a photo, and you are sure that you stored it right there, in that exact box, in that exact corner of the box, but then, when you look, it simply isn't there and you can't think where else to search. Now everything becomes tentative. As they make the final turn before the house she is anticipating that there will be a different way of approaching the first gate, or of closing it, or that the house will have moved to the other side of the fence, or perhaps that Billie and Toss will be dead, or have puppies, although they are too old for that now.

So she believes she is prepared for anything until Dad holds the door back for her and she walks in to see Mrs Loam, in slippers and an apron, carrying a plate of potatoes to the table. There is a vase of roses placed in the centre, which is a new vase, and can only belong to her, and then Ella sees that there are different plates on the shelves, there is a new fridge, and the curtains have been changed – they are dark blue, altering the whole aspect of the room. Mingled with the cooking smells is the foreign scent of lily-of-the-valley.

She feels heat on her face and ducks out of the path of Mrs Loam, who comes reaching, smiling broadly, towards her. She turns and walks back out the door, outside and around the house to the dogs. Acting like a child, like a small and silly child, and she knows it. Dad follows her around the corner, words first, tumbling out.

'Ellie, love, I'm sorry, love. I should have said. I know. I ought to have written it in a letter to you. I didn't know what to say, Ellie.'

She focuses on Billie, who is licking wildly at her fingers and whimpering softly. Dad leans against up the run, keeping a small distance away from her, but he is beseeching. His hand extends out towards her and he wants her to come and nuzzle in, soften and go to him. She realises that she has no interest in stubbornness or punishment, that it is late at night, that there is no point, so she does.

Muffled against the red jersey, she says, 'Dad, it's fine. Honestly. Sorry, I just got a shock. In fact, you did a lot better than me.'

He pulls back from her, keeping his arm around her shoulder, and lies a tentative hand on her stomach.

'So. A baby.'

'Well, it's not a kitten,' she hears herself mumble.

'He'll be a terror. A right royal terror. I can see it now.'

'Dad, it's not a he!'

'Is it a girl you're having, then?'

'Well, I don't know. I don't know what it is, but don't say "he", because we don't know yet, and that's not fair if it's not.'

Now he's the one crouching, rubbing the dog down with hard strokes, looking at Billie, looking away.

'So the daddy, what's happening with him?'

'We're not together. It's not his fault, though. It was my decision.'

'What do you mean your decision? You're bloody mad, Ella!'

'Hey, you don't know, okay, Dad, you don't know how it is! You can't judge me like that.'

'Oh, shite, he wasn't bad to you, was he, love? I mean, you're right to go if it was like that. I always say a feller can't expect anything from a woman he doesn't respect.'

'No, he wasn't bad, he didn't do anything wrong. It wasn't like that at all. I don't think I could explain it to you really. There were other considerations. Look, let's just leave it, eh? I don't really want to talk about it.'

She scrunches the dog's ear and they walk towards the house.

'What will you do, love? Will you come home? It might have been different, if I'd have known, perhaps we wouldn't – well, but Ellie, there's plenty of room, of course there is, and I'd like you to. Will you?'

'No, Dad, I won't come home. I wouldn't have anyway. I'm staying with some good people and I'm fine.'

And so she finds she has decided.

'What kind of people?'

'Oh, a family. Well, Louise, the mother, and my friend Tess. So two of them. McMahon. Tess and Louise McMahon.'

'And they're happy to have the both of you? They're happy to have a baby in the house?'

'Yep, it's arranged. Truly, it's fine. It's all organised.'

She lies, plainly and sweetly, and with peace. Whatever else, she won't be returning now.

'And will you bring him up to visit us?'

'Dad! Of course.'

'I don't know about the Kapuas, though. They're not going to like this at all. I'll be for it if you keep that baby down in the city. Will you talk to Jean?'

'Yeah, I'll talk to them, Dad. I will.'

———

Every part of her body aches. She lifts herself awkwardly into her old narrow bed, under the sultry eyes of Kylie Minogue and Ralph Macchio, the Karate Kid. She has left Dad and Mrs Loam sitting by the fire, because her legs were throbbing and because she would like to avoid watching them heading off to bed together. Mrs Loam has said very little beyond, Hello Ella, it's nice to see you, dear, and, Goodnight dear, sleep well, but all evening flashed a series of simpering smiles, and gave her extra pudding, and whisked her plate away before there was time to take it to the bench. And now, look, she has put flannelette sheets on the bed, and lying there on the pillow is a hot-water bottle ready to be filled, in a crocheted red and yellow cover. These are touches that Dad could not possibly achieve. These are the imprints of a new regime.

The old bed sags in a way she doesn't remember. She shifts and turns and when sleep comes it is uneven, broken by jolts and the struggle to roll to one side, then the other.

In the morning she wakes groggy, with a small tingling in her groin, with anticipation, wanting Andy, or not Andy; wanting to be touched, to be lifted away from her miserable body. She imagines him curled around her back, running disembodied hands across her waist, her breasts, her thigh. She never turns around and never touches him: his body is almost irrelevant. But this morning there is no escape because her body is too concrete: it is an immense construction and her mind will not let go. She shifts herself up to a sitting position and swings her legs to the floor. The sun beats hard at the back of new red curtains and the room is like the inside of an orange.

Tilly and Auntie Jeanie come with her in the afternoon to put the daffodils on the grave, and this makes it easier because she can stand there and say nothing while they sing, a long, low song that rises and falls and erases everything, until she is whittled back to tears. She doesn't know the words – she

79

doesn't know any of the words – and she never knows the right thing to do for Mum, but she puts the flowers in the vase and washes her hands as she leaves.

Then Tilly says, Why don't you come back to the house for a while? but she says, No, thanks, because it is easier to go back to the farm, where she can be alone. Mrs Loam – Margaret – is in town for the day, and Dad will be in the far paddock until dusk, checking on the lambing.

The bus home is almost empty. No one travels on a Monday. At lunch she buys new batteries for her Walkman so she can listen to her favourite, battered tape – *cry without weeping, talk without speaking, scream without raising your voice* – flipping sides over and over again, all the way down the island. She does not want silence, does not want to keep thinking about waving goodbye to Dad, arm in arm with Margaret, and she does not want to think either about the terrible, kind offer that Auntie Jeanie made. A decision has been made now, and it is best if it stays clear and straightforward. She does not want to wonder about any of this again. It will be good to get back. In the city, she thinks, you can keep the events of a day within a small white rectangle, and make them pass one by one, and get your work done, and not have to concern yourself with other people's days, the larger pattern.

All the way from Palmerston North to the city the baby punches and turns inside her and she feels a rising irritation. If she were alone she would tell it to be quiet, to sit still. Finally it ends. Stepping off at the city bus stop she searches for the red Corolla and it's there, waiting, with Louise and Tess waving, grinning and beeping. In the back seat she counts the familiar bridges as they wind around the city and out the long road home under the covering arch of orange lights.

'I think your grey jacket looks better.'

Sally steps back to the door and looks at Chris carefully, her head tilted to one side. It is her appraising look. This is the look that makes him feel as though he is in a steel cage, the smallest and runtiest in a litter of kittens. And the kitten knows, of course, that it had better start looking cute if it wants any chance at that girl and all her associated charms and benefits.

'I haven't got a grey jacket. What are you talking about? What's wrong with this one?'

'Oh, you have. I brought it from the shop, you used to wear it. Wait, I'll look. I think it's in the hall cupboard.'

'Leave it. Just leave it alone. I'm getting sick of this, Sally. As if it's important what fucking jacket I wear. Jesus.'

'I was just *suggesting*. You can do what you want, I don't care.'

'You go on and on at me – what I look like, what I wear. I'm sick of it.'

'Fine. That's just fine. Shut up, and let's go then, shall we?'

She slams the bedroom door behind her. This is always her way of ending an argument. Don't acknowledge anything, don't actually apologise, just move on: next thing, let's go. She is rummaging in the kitchen, looking for the car keys. Chris picks them up from the pile of magazines beside the bed and walks directly out to the driver's seat because she is clearly furious, not in a fit state to drive. She's likely to run them off the road in a mood like this.

He's not sure he wants to go out himself. Until right now he thought perhaps he'd pack it in, let her go alone and head for bed. There is a dull throb at the crown of his head that he can't shake off, despite the Berocca, the Panadol and the hourly glasses of water. It has been there, throbbing, for two days now. He wants to say how it hurts – all day he has been wanting her to come home so he can say, Sally, I've got a headache, and put his head down in her breasts for her to rub with her knuckles. But now she has come home and whinged at him about his clothes, trying to organise him, assessing him, treating him like a three-year-old. And then look at her, dressed in that odd, furred black skirt that makes her big hips bigger still, and she looks short in it, and squat, like a little dumpling lady, a muffin woman. For all her style, she is not always, he thinks, gorgeous. Not always.

But probably he wouldn't have mentioned the headache, because it was Sally who found him on Wednesday night, passed out on the kitchen floor after Jacob had gone home, and he doesn't want to bring that up again. She went on all night about what an irresponsible git Jacob was to leave Chris there like that. She's probably going to have words with him when they see him at the restaurant.

What she doesn't know is that it was only after Jacob left at eight that Chris had put on Pearl Jam and opened the vodka bottle, socking back shot after shot, letting the nostalgia warm him and the words blear into a different sense, their own private order. *Wheezing, rests his head in a shallow pool of morphine.* Listening, he sat down squarely on the lino, and then lay on the lino, and then it slowly became black, and cool, and the next thing Sally was pulling and pinching at him, leaning over him with her large blue eyes. You're a pisshead, Chris, she had said. You're really acting like a pisshead, and you've got to get it together.

Sometimes he thinks she is right. There are small moments, say on a day when he gets up early with her, and makes coffee, and watches the first light coming into the sky, when he thinks perhaps it is still there, within his hands. These moments are sweet with hope, and the physical rising of energy in his chest.

At times like this he thinks, Today I will go surfing, or out for a run, I will feel the water and air clean around me, I will clear out the cupboards, do the lawns, I will keep hold on the basic structure and it will carry me, and I will come through.

Last month he had a morning like this, and then another, and after three such mornings, three days of fulfilling small plans, it came, like a certain reward: a phone call from the Ministry of Transport. The woman sounded young, overly friendly, and interested in him. They had some work available – not full time, and not exactly *legal* work, but with potential for development. A part-time position taking care of the ministerial systems. Yes, he said, dazzled, yes, I would be very interested. He put the phone down and called his mother at work. Oh, she said, uh-huh, and suddenly he saw that it was no good and his stomach fell. He saw it for what it was. A part-time job as a government clerk, drafting letters to old men from Waipukurau, ensuring that the right forms are ordered and the filing up to date. Five years of study and this was what it came to. He called them back and cancelled the appointment, telling them another offer had come through. Now there are no more good mornings. Instead he listens to Sally moving about in the bathroom, and the kitchen, and waits for the front door to slam shut before he rolls back into sleep.

They drive into town in silence. He turns the radio up louder and swerves into the right lane, overtaking a ute, and then an old Holden packed with kids, arms flying out of the window as they go past. From the corner of his eye he sees that Sally is waving back at them. As she always does, in that ridiculous, friendly way of hers. Sally is the kind of girl who puts money in boxes for any and every charity, who unfailingly chats to acne-faced checkout operators at the supermarket, and advocates for unknown hitchhikers as they spin past on the state highway.

'So, do you know where the place is?' she asks.

'I've been there about a hundred times, Sally.'

'Sure. Just asking.'

But it is time to stop this now. It is time to make some kind of peace because soon they will arrive, and it will be embarrassingly obvious to everyone that they are quarrelling. The last thing he wants is Tess and Jacob noticing that this, too, is falling apart, that it has become this messy, this childish. And it's crazy anyway, because they are so good together, Sally and him: he is good to her, the relationship works. It is the one thing that needs to work. He believes in this. He is acting like a bastard. He is thinking like a bastard, and it is time to turn it around before the evening goes on and it gets worse.

'Tessa's got a new job. Did I tell you that?'

Sally doesn't reply. She is wary. Wary or stubborn.

'That's partly what it's for, tonight. A celebration.'

'But isn't she still at varsity?'

'Oh, yeah, it's part time, but it's a good job, some environmental advocacy kind of thing. It's her last year this year. Reckons they'll probably take her on full time when she's finished.'

'You talked to her about it already?'

'A bit, when she phoned, yeah, why?'

'Oh. Nothing.'

To which he doesn't respond, because he's not sure what she's saying here and he doesn't want to deal with it.

'Anyway, good for her, I reckon, because it's what she really wants. It is good when it works out like that for people.'

She is watching him. She is biting at her bottom lip. Perhaps she will cry. Which would be another matter altogether. Which would create a significant problem. He reaches for her knee.

'Hey, Sal, let's have a good night, eh? I'm being hopeless, I know. But I want it to be good for Tess, for you, for everyone. Can we just leave it behind? I know I'm acting like a jerk. It's just – I'm pretty down. I shouldn't take it out on you. I suppose it's Tessa's job, really, I mean it's great for her, but –'

She shoots him the look he was hoping for: the sympathetic look, her brow furrowed, pressing and releasing her lips. Concerned. He's won her back now. She loves it when he talks like this – slightly self-deprecating, generous. Her arm winds around the back of his neck and he can feel her fingers pulling gently at the curls there.

'– but, it's a bit like, salt in the eyes, or whatever they say. She's still studying; she doesn't even *need* a job.'

'You're doing fine, Chris. You're doing well. Something will come through. It will. I don't think any of us find it easy. Even Tess. I don't think it's supposed to be easy.'

'What does that mean? Unemployment as some kind of endurance test, like a sadistic rite of passage, making real men, real adults out of us?'

'I didn't mean that. Not just jobs, the whole thing. This whole bit, really. Leaving home, and, yeah, doing the great thing you're supposed to be doing, the job you said you'd do when you grew up. At school you always think it's going to be fabulous, and that it will simply happen, in this fantastic, ordered way. But it doesn't, does it? I think it's complicated for most people, most of the time. You don't expect that, though. It's like this horrible secret that no one tells you.'

'Uh-huh.'

He doesn't make the obvious point that none of it has been complicated for her. Except for him in her life, messing it up around the edges, it has all been a clear straight arrow into the future. She is one of the most single-minded people he knows. And now he is swept across with the sick feeling of difference, and despite his best efforts there is nothing further to say.

After the meal, at the nightclub, he finds he has drunk a great deal. He stands at the bar watching Sally dancing. She is circling her hips in wide circles and moving her arms in an odd way, flicking her fingers above her head as though she is shaking them dry. A shudder passes over him and he orders another handle of beer. He tries to watch her again, tries to see it differently, but this time it overwhelms him. He is embarrassed by her: the way she moves against the beat, her wide grin, her complete oblivion. She would like to believe she is a good dancer. Sally always wants to dance.

Up until now it has been a good night – a fantastic, glittering night in comparison with the past days and weeks. The mee goreng is still warm inside him, the burning taste in his mouth, and he is warm too with the sense that he has entertained them all, he has made them laugh, and he has talked seriously, and intelligently. He is as good as any of them – certainly as good as Jacob, who has his mind squeezed down into a small trap of dead English poets. Jacob is up tonight, way up, bounding with ideas and talk, dragging them off to go dancing before they had even finished the wine on the table. But even at his best Jacob can't make them laugh the way Chris can. And Tess has a real job, and there was a great deal to talk about over dinner, regarding the job. But now there is the sight of Sally, dancing. It brushes up against the surface of the pleasant night and he wants to swat at it, drive it out.

Tess had announced over dinner that she has, already, been put in charge of organising an anti-whaling demonstration. The way she announced it was quintessential Tess: proud, straightforward, demanding that they all participate. Jacob had been provocative, full of opinions about indigenous peoples' rights and any number of other things that, really, he knew nothing about. But Chris had conquered over Jacob, he feels sure of it now. The exact line of the argument has become hazy but he knows he was precise, and batted Jacob back with swift points. And he knows that Tess was leaning forward to listen to him. She was flushed with red wine and her eyes had gone dark in the dark room. And so they had tripped from one issue to another, on and on into the centre of things, until the bill arrived and he leaned back in his seat, satisfied, feeling that the world had grown larger, that he had expanded into it.

All night Sally had kept her hand on his knee but she was not talking about the whales, she was not listening to his line of argument, she was talking with the girl on the left, that pregnant friend of Tessa's, the girl with the name he can never remember. And every now and then he would hear Sally laughing loudly in his ear, and struggle to resist turning around and asking her to shut up.

The orange and red lights wind down, the glitter ball splashes slow dots across his chest, and an arm, tattooed with roses and a dagger, reaches across the bar for a jug of beer. There is an armpit in his face, and the sharp stench of salt. Sally looks across, moving slowly now, and waves to him, and in that moment he sees that there is something ugly, something ill-formed in the way he feels about her. This causes him to feel desperate. He thinks that he would like to turn around and punch the face of the man with the roses and dagger on his arm, the one who shoves his armpit into people's faces. He imagines kicking over the chair, smashing the glass down on the bar and walking out of there, pushing past the transvestites and the pretty boys in their spangled lycra singlets. He wonders who would follow him out, who among his friends – Jacob, Tess or Sally – would come out first. Who would put their arms around him if he sat down at the bottom of the steps and made it perfectly clear that it was not all right?

He watches Jacob leaving the dance floor, ducking and slipping between the girls in glittering low-backed tops, manoeuvring his way out, placing a careful hand on a waist, a shoulder, an elbow. He pops out by the high stools, searches the crowd for Chris and walks over to the bar.

'Damn, it's hot in here. Just water for me, mate, thanks.'

There is a girl over there, where Jacob just passed, who looks familiar.

'Hey, Jacob, who's that chick in the red dress? Do you remember her?'

'Where?'

'Over there, by the door with the two guys in suits. You know her, eh?'

'Oh, god, yeah, what's her name? She was Tom's girlfriend, years ago. Very hot. For a fifteen-year-old. Remember he took us all out for a drink straight after he first got with her, told us all if we touched her he'd kick our heads in.'

'Yeah, vaguely.'

'Then one day old Barker starts chatting to her at the bloody supermarket – remember she worked there – and that was enough for Tom. He was watching. Sitting there, watching her at the supermarket all the time, waiting for her to finish up. Think he slashed the tyres on Barker's Escort for that. What the hell was her name?'

'Can't remember. God, he was a mad, possessive bastard, wasn't he?'

'I don't know. Mad, yeah, but, I mean, it was all on back then, wasn't it, scoring each other's girlfriends. It was a different world, Chris. We were kids. It was all pretty stupid. And look at her, she is a damned attractive woman.'

'Not that we ever thought *they* had anything to do with it.'

'What do you mean?'

'It was like, you know, we thought *we* made all the choices. About who we scored, who *owned* which chick. And then the girls had this entirely different view on the whole thing. I mean, ask her what she thinks about Tom now. Knight in shining armour? I doubt it.'

'How the hell would you know? What makes you think you understand what the girls thought about us?'

'Well, I talked to them, for one thing. More than you did.'

'Nah, don't kid yourself, Chris. You were just trying to get in their pants. The slimy way.'

'That's where you always got me wrong.'

'Could never be sure that I trusted you, Chris. None of us could.'

Chris sucks in a sharp breath, feels it whistle between his teeth. His heart is a tin drum in his chest, insisting on a little tune, ga-donk, ga-donk, ga-donk. He walks away quickly, down the narrow steps of the club and out into the cold night, where there is the smell of vomit, and a group of girls rolling and falling down the street, tripping in and out of the gutter.

'Don't touch me! Don't fucking touch me – get away, get off me, you pricks!'

It is her voice, her own voice rising to that high shriek, and there is panic in it, and fury, and it rings in her ears. The words, the sound of that voice, hit up against the faces of her friends and they are alarmed by her – they are taken aback and do not know what to do. Even Louise steps back, looking across at the nurse with concern. But it is all blurred and groggy. There is the voice racketing around the ceiling, and then perhaps someone else speaking, moving towards her and speaking, but she cannot understand the words and lets her eyes close. In the darkness she drops further down, and it is everything and embraces her: it becomes so black and terrible that it is almost beautiful.

And then, at the deepest point, for a brief moment it breaks and she comes clean to the surface. There is respite and it is bearable once again. Relaxation swarms across the surface of her mind and once again she can take it in. In this one brief moment swelling up with relief she takes in the surprised faces of Tess and Andy, the angry cream walls staring back at her, admonishing her for bad behaviour, the stench of disinfectant and the clop of heeled soles down the passage outside. There is sweat on her face. The midwife is leaning across, not touching her. There are no hands anywhere on her body now, although there have been hands everywhere today: she has been rubbed right across the surface of her skin and nothing has been left alone.

The midwife is saying, Ella, that's good, you can say what you want, it's all right. You say how you want it. It's up to you; we're listening. It's all up to you. The thin lips shape and purse as they form the words and she watches for the quick flashes of crooked teeth. The midwife, whose name is Wendy, is a small woman with a fine-boned face, and in among her thick black hair there is a shock of silver, running from the centre of her head down to her temple. Every time Wendy has visited, Ella has had to stop herself from staring at this silver chunk of hair. But now she does not even try, she stares boldly as the midwife speaks, knowing that this silver hair will burn into the memory of all this as one little piece that she will recall later, a small image to hang on the necklace of the day.

She will remember this in the same way she will remember waking, sweating and disoriented in the early morning, knowing that it was beginning, far too early – four weeks early – but beginning nevertheless.

She will remember Louise with her in the bedroom, kneeling down beside her as the early pains crunched her abdomen, rocking and swaying, hearing herself cry out for the first time, and noticing that one small breast had slipped free from beneath Louise's blue pjyamas, watching the soft brown nipple bobbing back and forth in time with the hand stroking her back. Being wrapped around in a checked blanket and walking outside to the car, clutching at herself with the jolt of each step down to the road, the air damp and still, the first streaks of light coming across the sky, and the seagulls going berserk on the telephone poles.

She has this one small moment of reprieve and it is important to get the words out now: she has to say it because soon it will start again and then there will be no speaking.

'I don't think I can do it. I can't keep going. I want to try the gas now. Can I have the gas?'

Once again there is that exchange of looks over her head, Louise and the midwife conferring silently, because they are the two competent people in the room, they are the people here who understand what is going on. Louise has stayed, although they never discussed it. She has been taking photos – not asking her, or, thank god, telling her to look, or smile, just snapping them, now and again. Louise is here, which seems to be the most important thing.

Tess has learnt that towels need heating and has figured out how to do this, is performing the task over and over again with dogged faithfulness. Every three or four contractions Ella notices her coming back in at the door with the steaming plastic bag and handing it to Louise. But no one is talking to Andy. He is sitting against the wall and looking at the bed, then out the window, then back at his hands. Why is no one talking to Andy? No one will ask him to leave, so it would be better if someone spoke to him, directed him, put something in his hands that he could usefully do, because he will not of his own accord come over, and he will not touch her.

Ella was surprised to see him walk into the room an hour ago, just as a new, lower burning started to grip at the bands across her back. How does he know? she thought. Who told him to come? Andy wasn't supposed to be a part of this. She hadn't asked him – that was never the plan. She was even more surprised to find that she wanted him to stay, wanted him here after all, despite everything.

She urgently wants Andy to come across now. She wants him to do something, say something, not stare like that out the window and at his hands. Andy, Andy, come here, she hears herself saying, and it is as though there is no line between the thought in her head and the words falling from her mouth. It is a shock to see that she can no longer control the boundaries of her body, for the body is functioning alone now, and according to its own logic.

In the last instant before she dives back down into the next wave of pain, she notices that his face is startled, that he is on his feet and moving across to the bed. His face is startled but composing itself into confidence. He is a stupid, kind man, she thinks. And this is all his fault. And I hope the baby doesn't look like him.

They give her a little gas, she vomits and the room sprinkles out into fine dots, and laughter. They should be laughing, all of them, can they not see it, how stupid and pretty it is? The muscles pull and flex but they belong to another world now, another body. Her mind is separate from this action of her abdomen, and observes it coolly. Then, after a time, the dots gather back into the shape of the room, and once again it is agony: simple, terrible pain. She is hungry, and thirsty, and they let her take a sip of blackcurrant juice.

The specialist comes in and pushes her T-shirt up to her breasts. She lies there on her back, bush and belly up. The man sticks a hand into her – she can feels him inside – and it occurs to her that everyone is watching this happen. This does not seem unusual or a matter for embarrassment. Her head flops to the left. There is a sharp pain where he is poking. Seven centimetres, the specialist says. You're doing well, very well.

The end comes with a rush. Her mind narrows to a pinpoint of light and she focuses the light down, and inwards, and she is entirely there, pushing in great, relieved gasps. But perhaps it is over now, because it suddenly feels as though she has let go and lost control of everything. There is a foul smell and she finds that she has. But there are five full pushes more – long, difficult pushes.

Words are falling out of her. *Mum*, she hears herself saying, *Mum*, but it is Louise grabbing at her hands, making a fist with her, holding it there until it comes, swimming, slithering down between her legs. They lie it down on top of her and she has to sit up to take a proper look at its mawing, screaming face, like scrunched paper, and a single arm flailing, and the little bloody stump between the legs.

In and out. In and out. In and out. It is a small, fine movement, his chest lifting, barely visible beneath the tight wrapped blanket and the lid of the plastic cot. But it is there, below it all, and it is steady. The nurse says it's unlikely to happen again, and Ella mustn't panic or be upset because it's common, this sort of hiccup, a small disruption in breathing in the earliest hours of life. But the nurse panicked when it happened – she didn't look calm at all, walking efficiently into the room to find Ella sitting up in bed, thumb pressed hard on the red button on the wall, lap cradling the still, blue body. They are monitoring him now, and she is monitoring too. She watches carefully for ten minutes at a time. Then she breaks away, noticing her own slow breathing, and pads down the hallway to the neon-lit kitchen, where she makes a cup of tea in an Arcoroc mug, picking between the clumps of sugar in the crusty jar. She drinks it fast, standing up in the kitchen, because they won't let you take hot drinks in near the babies.

Because he was early, and because of the breathing, they have decided to keep him in the neo-natal ward for a few days. And so she is staying on at the hospital, sleeping long hours in the afternoon and waking at dusk to walk down the three levels of stairs to visit and feed him. Neither of them is doing well at that, but this too, they say, is normal, no matter for concern. The nurse spent half an hour today showing her how best to hold him, how to get him to open wide and latch on, and later, helping her express milk for the overnight feeds.

In the evening sleep comes easily again, heavy and unbroken. Lying in bed she feels swaddled by the slow tightening of skin, the close fall of the blanket over her empty body. Sometimes the mewing or screeching of other babies comes to her in the dark, and then she is aware of his absence, but she is calm, because it is enough to know that he is here in the building, under the same roof, and in the meantime she can rest and rest and rest, drinking great quantities of it, the pour of warm golden water through her limbs and mind.

Walking back to the cot, she sees Andy coming into the ward with two packets of gingernuts.

'Hi. Bought you these.' He kisses her cheek. 'How's he doing?'

'Not bad. They keep telling me not to worry, not to panic. It's starting to get to me actually. It's starting to *make* me worry.'

'Well, they're probably used to flapping, crying mothers. Which you're not, Ella.'

She ignores this, wary of criticism, and changes the topic, talking fast.

'Hey, he's really quite spunky, this boy. Look, he's got this Tintin tuft going on with his hair today. And see his ears – check out the little elf bits at the top. Is that your family? Have you guys got ears like that?'

'Are you kidding? Look, perfect rounds.' Andy pulls off his cap and tucks his hair back. 'Must be a throwback. But you're right, odd. They're cute, though.'

'Oh, *definitely* cute. But I think he's quite a ratbag. He's giving me these really cheeky looks when he first wakes up, like he's saying, I bet you don't know what I'm thinking.'

'Breasts. What the hell else do they think of?'

'Yeah, all of them.'

'Who's cheeky now, Ella?'

And he grabs at her, whipping his arm around her neck and pulling her into his chest. She catches her breath against his shirt and takes in his smell. The older, thin nurse is walking past and smiling fondly over at them. She can see what the nurse is thinking, and Andy is probably thinking it too. But it isn't right, he has misunderstood, and she doesn't like this pretending, this acting as though it's all suddenly different. She pulls away awkwardly and sits down.

'So, Ella, what happens now?'

'What happens now? Dinner, I think. Boiled cabbage and fried meat. I have no idea how a sick body is supposed to heal itself on this food. Not that mine is. Sick, that is.'

'I'm asking a serious question.'

'I know.'

'So what happens?'

'What do you mean exactly? What happens with you and me, or what happens with the babe and us?'

'Both. Either. Isn't it the same?'

'No, Andy. They're separate questions.'

She sits down next to the cot.

'Look, Andy, you're Dad. No one's arguing about that, me least of all. It's good, and you'll be good at it, and you can see him and have him whenever you want. I think we can work it out together, and be reasonable. But you have to understand, it is a separate question.'

'To us.'

'To us. Who aren't. We're not an *us*, Andy.'

'Fuck, Ella, do you have to be so harsh *all* the time? What I don't get is how come you get to make the choice, you get to make all the choices, and then I just have to live with it. Do you have any idea, Ella, what that's like? It's not right. You know that. It's not right for him either.'

She stares down at the packets of biscuits, not angry but sad, sad for his open, grumpy face, his clear need.

'Okay, fine, I need some space here. I'll come back later.'

He walks out of the ward at pace, swiping at his eyes. The nurse wheels a trolley of equipment past and raises an eyebrow.

As she picks the baby up, because his eyes are batting open, he seems solid, a small weight to hold down her scattering thoughts. Hello, she says, hello, boy. Further towards the window a woman is reaching into an incubator. She is stroking the baby's head and Ella hears her speaking to it in a language that she cannot understand, and cannot name. *Meeshka*, it sounds like. *Meeshka tina*.

Sitting up in bed she flicks backwards and forwards through the pages of a *Cleo*. It is strange – these magazines, producing these stupid articles each month and yet still making you want to read them. More than that, making you urgently *need* to read them, convincing you that they have information you need – warnings, facts, insights into yourself and others. Information that will make everything clear. *Career Killers at the Corporate Christmas Do. Ten Simple Steps to Better Summer Sex. Have You Turned into Your Mother Yet?* The headlines seduced her in the kitchen and she picked up the magazine, bringing it back to bed. She hasn't started revising at all, and she promised that today she'd make a start. But all afternoon there has been a constant high-pitched cry from the room next door, and the shuffle of visitors coming and going, and it's hard to find the energy to take the book out of the bag, let alone start concentrating and taking notes.

'Hey, Elle. That boring, huh?'

Tessa's face appears around the corner of the door, grinning widely. It is her third visit today.

'It's pretty bad. Come in. God, Tess, I'm seriously in need of a distraction.'

She lowers her voice and tilts her head to the left.

'The woman next door had a caesarean this morning and it didn't go well. I think there's something funny with the baby because the doctors have been in and out all day. It howls and howls. It's just stopped now after an hour. It's ghastly here, Tess.'

'Can't be worse than that woman screaming next door while you were in labour. It sounded like someone was slowly inserting needles in her eyeballs.'

'What woman screaming?'

'You're joking. Are you serious? Do you know, the nurse told me she'd been in labour for thirty-six hours. That's pretty cruel.'

'Honestly, I don't remember hearing anything. I must have been somewhere else altogether.'

'Wow. Bizarre.'

Tess sits down heavily on the end of the bed and looks at her meaningfully.

'So. Does it completely freak you out, Ella?'

'What?'

'Being a parent. A *mother*. Having a kid.'

'Yeah, I've gone to pieces.'

'I can see that.'

'It's good. I think. It's good not being pregnant, anyway. I just want to go home and wear jeans. And eat lots of avocados. I'm craving them, and no chance of getting them here. Or much that's edible at all.'

'I'll bring you some tomorrow. And when you finally get to leave, I'm taking you out for kebabs. I found this great place in town. Really cheap.'

'You'll have to take us both. Do they let babes in?'

'Of course, you geek. He can have an iskender. Lots of hummus – it's great for them.'

'He'll get what I get. Recycled.'

'Oh, lucky guy. Hey, I know what I have to tell you. I saw your Professor Gregory at varsity today. Can you believe it, he asked how you were. All paternal and concerned. Very touching. Very delighted, too, and wanting to know what your plans are. Seems you're quite the teacher's pet, Elle.'

'Where did you see him?'

'He took our lecture today. An hour on orange roughy.'

'Yeah, he's pretty obsessed about that.'

'Reckons they'll be wiped out in a decade.'

'I had a whole term of it. He gets pretty upset, eh.'

'Hell yeah. Not a big fan of the fishing industry, is he? I'd hate to see him go head to head with my uncle Kevin. Anyway, Gregory clearly wants you back up there slogging away in the lab.'

'I might call him. He said I could sit my exams early. Of course that was when I thought the babe would arrive smack bang in the middle of them. But I might do them early anyway – get it over and done with.'

'I didn't know you were doing exams. That's a bit mad isn't it?'

'Tess, of course I'm doing them – I'm not wasting a whole year! All I'm missing is the last three weeks of class. And he'll be fine. He can just sit in the corner for a couple of hours and I'll feed him if I have to. There's a special room, you know, so it's no big deal.'

'Yeah, I guess.' Tess hops off the bed and yawns, stretching her body up to its full height.

'Are you staying for a coffee? Supper comes in ten minutes. I'll give you my biscuit.'

'No, I have to go. I have get the car back before ten, and Mum wants a whole huge list of stuff from the super-market.'

'All right. Might see you tomorrow, then?'

'Yeah, definitely. In the afternoon. Sleep well.'

Tess bends across the bed and kisses her on the cheek. She is almost out of the room when Ella starts speaking, quickly, getting the words out before she changes her mind.

'Oh, Tess.'

Tess turns around.

'You know, I meant to say thanks. I mean, before. I meant to say it before. For staying for the birth. And everything. You were great.'

Tess shuffles, screws up her face.

'It was pretty amazing, you know. I've been on this weird high ever since. So has Mum. She's hanging out for you guys to come home. I can see her turning into this complete clucking grandmother.'

'Yeah, she was here this morning. I'm, you know, I'm grateful. To both of you. For letting me stay. And everything. I'd be – I don't know what I'd be – well, just, thanks.'

'It's *fine*, Ella. As if we'd have it any other way. As if Mum doesn't think this is the best thing that's happened since she bought the café. Look, it's extremely cool to have you. Both.'

After she leaves, Ella reaches up to turn out the lamp and settles down to sleep. The day rewinds slowly past her, starting with Dad on the phone this morning, stunned, and quietly delighted. 'Well done, girl,' he said. 'Well done. Mum would be happy, love.' Dad sounded like he might start crying then. Later on there was Andy's stroppy scene, and then the relief of talking about other things with Tess. She thinks briefly about study, flicking through the names of various categories of algae; and then just as she is about to topple over the brim of consciousness he is there. Her son, breathing in and out, a tiny body that changes nothing, and everything.

He seems improbable. He is making only a shallow indent in the universe. His place here is not yet secure. His fingernails are intricate, as vulnerable as the pale discs on a new frond of maidenhair fern, and they remind Louise of matters she thought she had forgotten. Of cancerous children, their round bald heads like globes of light, eyes big with second infancy. And others, damaged by cars or falls, needing nappies changed at five, and six, and seven years old. Young skin, thin and translucent as tracing paper, and then the fine blue thread of a vein in an elbow, the syringe almost half the size of a child's forearm. Night crying, and coming towards it, rubbing a small knobbed back, and knowing that none of the kind words will suffice, or carry meaning. Ten years of paediatric nursing come thudding back at the stretch and curl of his yawn.

She finds it unbearable – his delicacy, the slight weight of him in the crook of her arm, like the wheat-bag she puts against her neck at night, like a package of desiccated coconut, like the little blue penguin she found injured in the gutter last week and carried back across the road. Unbearable, almost, to have him here now, in her house. His home. Because if they leave tomorrow (they won't, they can't, there will be no going away now) it will still be home, the first place he came to. She realises that she is in danger of being swept away by all of this: the material fact of his presence here all through last night, the upward purse of his thin lips, the whorl and lobe of his ear, the sour milk smell of him, and she has a strong desire to let herself go, out to sea, to swim in the ocean of all this, to let it overwhelm her. But she contains herself because he is not hers, this one: not her child nor her grandchild. There are boundaries.

Yet it seems to her that something happened within the

sterile cream walls of the maternity ward, and then the three weary days in and out of neo-natal, which changed the order of the relationships, which shifted the steady categories of blood and not-blood out of the way entirely. She doesn't know what, if anything, this translates into. And she doesn't know what Ella thinks either.

So she checks herself and watches nervously as Ella lifts him from the wicker bassinet, negotiating her wrist into the cavity at the back of his neck, jostling him awkwardly into the bones of her shoulder. It is the first day, for all of them. They are all trying to breathe steadily in a new element.

'What time is the midwife coming, Ella?'

'At eleven. I thought maybe I'd try and sleep before then. For an hour. Just an hour of sleep. But I don't think he's going to go back down now. I'm not sure if it means he's hungry or what. I only fed him about an hour ago.'

'Why don't you try him again and then let me have him while you sleep?'

'Do you think that would be all right? I mean, you could wake me if he fussed.'

'Ella, it's fine.'

She brings her a cup of sugared tea and briefly takes in the two of them in the armchair, fussing and fiddling over the nipple. Hey, pup, says Ella, hey, bubs, come on now, come on. He is one week old and unnamed. Perhaps he is Caleb, perhaps he is Hemi, perhaps he is Connor. He wears his uncertain identity well. For the present he is alternately bubs, pup and fella. Louise has resisted the urge to make suggestions, or to hurry the decision along. Tess, on the other hand, has been forthright on the matter. Max, she says. Please, Ella, call him Max. I would have really wanted to be Max if I was a boy. It's a fantastic name.

Louise doesn't tell her daughter the name that she almost certainly would have been given, had the doctor announced a small penis instead of the fine curling line between Tessa's baby legs. It would have been Tessa's father's name – because Louise would never have got away with it twice, registering a son with a name of her own choosing – and therefore the wrong name. But when the second child turned out to be a girl the rules were immediately different and it was left entirely up to her, the matter of a name, and then all subsequent matters as well.

Ella kisses his forehead and leaves for the bedroom and then he is deliciously in her arms, blinking like a bat, his jaw performing its signature shudder. Left alone Louise wanders around the house jostling and singing. Out in the hallway she catches a quick image of herself in the mirror: a tall, tired-looking woman in a faded yellow sweatshirt, clasping at the checked bundle. She is irritated by her hair: the cut outgrown and a half-centimetre of grey showing through at the roots. She is irritated by it all – the limp hair, the sweatshirt and the tired face, and most of all by the unwelcome idea that she is turning into the kind of woman that she has never liked. A middle-aged woman, cooing over the babies that her retiring body can no longer produce. The eternal hovering great aunt: advising, admonishing, essentially lonely, *left out*. Conniving greedily for snatched minutes. Feeding an unhealthy need. She shudders. This baby is not hers. It is a different matter entirely now to what it was twenty years ago, and her knowledge might not count. She has to be prepared for that. She has to let it pass by, the temporary presence of this baby in her house, and attach herself only lightly: take a mild interest, support but not take over. Keep a critical distance.

After all, she tells herself, there is her own life to get on with and the road does not go backwards. And she hasn't, in fact, forgotten the washing, the squalling, the vomit on clothes, the red-faced screeching *will* of them, and the occasional fleeting desire to smack their little heads against the windowsill. She brushes her lips lightly against the pulse in the skull. Yes, she has done her time already, and under difficult – extremely difficult – circumstances. Really, the last thing she needs is to be in charge for another round.

After a week he is still below birth weight but gaining steadily, his fine folds and wrinkles filling out daily. Louise sees that Ella is terrified but in fact handles his body well, supporting the neck, watching out for the fontanelle, and she is not afraid to hoist and roll him, to push and pull a little. Feeding is still difficult but she is persevering. She is a tough girl, sitting there in the evening holding her breath and tensing her shoulders as he sucks at her cracked, raw nipple. There are no routines – the pair of them eat and sleep at random hours – but that will settle in time. Ella has even managed to get out one night, into town for an early evening meal with Tess, and they took the baby along too, despite her offer to babysit.

Ella is an exhausted mother, but not an unhappy one. Louise keeps her eyes peeled for any sign of depression. It would hardly be surprising, under the circumstances. But she is waking easily, and chatting, talking almost more than before, and most important, constantly searching out his filmy grey eyes, and speaking to him, and running her hands up and down his darkening skin.

It strikes her as equally remarkable that Tess should turn out to be so competent. It astonishes her that this daughter, who as far as she is aware has never been saddled with an infant in the flesh for longer than three hours of evening babysitting, should calmly take the screaming newborn body out of Ella's hands and jiggle like an expert, swaying him back and forth until the wailing drops into gasps and then the gasps subside and he plummets like a stone into sleep. Where can she have learnt this? She is endearing, this Tess – all angles and attitude with her mother and brother, but displaying an intuitive touch with infants.

Not for the first time Louise is reminded how little she really knows about her children, how she only ever witnesses a small part of their lives. How, despite her best guesses, she can't really predict what either of them might do, say, in an emergency, or in a situation requiring an unusual degree of personal integrity. When they were still at primary school she would sit them down at the dinner table, outlining step by step the plan for a fire and the plan for an earthquake. (Don't try to get home. Stay where you are.) But always it was the hidden life of her children that concerned her. What would they actually do?

A similar thought strikes her on Saturday morning when she goes into Tessa's room to wake her for lunch at twelve o'clock and finds the bed made and empty. *How little I know about my daughter's life.* Tess has not come home, or possibly went out early, very early, before Louise woke at seven. She is neither alarmed nor surprised, for of course it is reasonable that at twenty Tess should do this – spend the night wherever she wants – but usually she would say where she was going. That's all. Usually Tess would let her know.

'Hey, Ella, do you want a sandwich for lunch? I bought some avocado and brie this morning.'

'Yeah, great, thanks.'

'Uh, Ella . . . did Tess say where she was going last night?'

'No. I don't think so. I don't think I even saw her. Isn't she here?'

'She's probably at work. She didn't mention it, that's all. Or maybe she did tell me, perhaps I forgot.'

'No, she's definitely not working today. They gave her the weekend off after Thursday's demonstration, remember?'

'Oh. Right.'

'I guess Tess went out while we were down at the café yesterday.'

'Yes, but I thought she was here when we came back. I thought I heard you talking with her.'

'No, I definitely didn't see her last night.'

And then there is her guarded look. It has become less frequent, this cool mask of suspicion, of caution. Lately there have been occasional wide smiles, and a certain eagerness at times to participate, to chat or confide. But right now, on the basis of this small confusion, Ella is shutting down, retreating back into the safe bubble of herself.

'Hey, it's okay, Ella, I'm not blaming . . .'

Then Tess walks down the hallway, directly into her room with the straightened bed, and shuts the door behind her. Outside the window Chris Ferguson is driving away in his little green car, pulling away from the kerb and staring straight ahead, both hands on the wheel.

Waiting and letting Tess unfold the story in her own sweet, stormy time is the sensible thing to do, but she doesn't feel like allowing her this luxury because there are other people to worry about now. Tess cannot always be at the centre, creating scenes, dragging them out. So she knocks on the bedroom door with determination and walks in, finding Tess flung face down on the bed, sobbing loudly. The little store of anger and worry dissipates into the air. Hey, love, she says, her hand stroking Tessa's curls, hey, what's wrong?

It is new to be doing this, and there is a letting down of love, a small rush of it through the body. The sensation makes her think of milk stains on Ella's T-shirt, and it is pleasant. She suddenly wants to coddle her adult daughter, wrap her up and soothe her. But it is all new and it is slightly awkward, the situation, this way of handling, and she hesitates, unsure of herself, because Tess doesn't cry in front of her mother, ever, and there is no practised response. Tess will stamp and slam and yell, but if there are tears they are shed alone, and as she is generally the cause of the problem she has never been welcome as a comforter. But today it is different because Tess has come home in this state, bringing it in from the outside world. Chris was pulling away from the kerb. So perhaps she stayed over with her brother, and if so it seems likely that

Jacob has said or done something to put his sister in her place. Something horrible and inane – something she will have taken utterly, utterly to heart.

'What's happening, love, what's wrong?'

There is a muffled response. A muffled response is a big advance on the silence she had anticipated.

'Tess, I can't hear you, sweetheart. Roll over, come here, come on.'

Propped up against the headboard, her skin is pale, freckles standing out in dark contrast, and eyelids already puffing into fat cushions. Outside the door the baby is starting to cry, slowly winding up.

'Is it something about Jacob? Has he done something?'

'Jacob?'

'Oh, well, it's just . . . I saw that you came home with Chris. Were you at Jacob's last night?'

'At *Jacob's*?'

'Well, yes, Jacob's. That's a reasonable thing to think, Tess.'

Snappy, and bad. She is handling this badly. The trick is not to let it get to you, this tone, the incredulous look. Try not to feel put down, dumb, out of the frame of reference within which this particular drama is unfolding.

'God, no, I wasn't at Jacob's. Forget it, Mum, just leave me alone.'

Tess flops back onto her stomach. Outside the baby's crying reaches a new pitch, the breathing shorter and faster between screams, and the sound of it drums along her nerves, picking her up, her pulse rising in response. Is Ella with him? Has she lifted him up yet? No, Ella knows what she's doing, she thinks. They will be fine. The trick is to focus on the matter at hand. She takes a deep breath and lets it slowly out, holds still, waits.

'Tess, I think you need to realise –'

Still lying on her back she interrupts, words coming in a muddled rush.

'All right, Mum, all right. It's about . . . I . . . Chris and me, we, well . . . something happened last night, and it's all wrong, because he doesn't . . . he said . . .'

It's like trying to read a short story in French and suddenly seeing the full sense of the first sentence. Like finally getting the pun after a year of walking past Jacob's black sticker on the fridge, the words bouncing backwards and forwards with the new, obvious meaning: 'Radio Active'. It is a small realignment of the ordering of the world, a shuffling and melting of set boundaries. *Tess and Chris*. Chris Ferguson. Tess in love with Chris. And Chris mucking it up, mucking her around. The bastard. The sweet, dear, selfish jerk.

'And, it's worse, because, you know Sally?' Tess says.

Oh, she had forgotten that. The short dark girl with the high red cheeks he had brought to Jacob's birthday, without warning, without asking. Sally, the girlfriend, the live-in partner, which makes Tess . . . what exactly? The fling? Of all the strangers in the universe that he might want to behave like that with, why in god's name would he choose Tess, his best friend's sister?

But then, perhaps there is another perspective. It could, after all, be real: something important, something long buried, smouldering away through years of after-school teasing, of surfing and cricket, and mashing up milkshakes, giggling, three of them, always giggling. She speculates wildly and then realises she has skipped ahead – too far ahead. Tess needs to talk, she needs to explain it, all of it. But the thought is still thumping against her, odd, and not entirely unattractive. Tess, with Chris. Chris loving Tess. Like man and woman. Not kids. But not messy, and ghastly, not mucking her daughter up, not like this.

'Anyway, it's over, it's nothing, it's stupid, and he's a fuckwit, and I'll be fine.'

Tess looks ill. She looks decidedly awful. And outside the wailing hasn't stopped. It sounds as though the baby is undergoing death by fire, by slow torture. Her ear tunes back in and she can physically feel it in her arms and chest, the urgent need to go out there, to take him and soothe him. A separate energy turns her torso towards the door and she has to will herself to stay still, to stay and finish this, to focus.

'He's mucking you around, Tess?'

'He says . . . He told me he'd broken up with Sally, and she'd moved out, and then this morning –' Her voice catches, but there are no new tears now. Her chin is fierce.

'This morning he said that he'd lied. It's not over at all – she's just away, in Masterton, for Christ's sake, at some kind of design conference. For a week. Less than a week. She's back on Tuesday.'

'Oh, Tess. Oh, love.'

The baby's distress is working up to a new, undiscovered level and she can hear Ella speaking to him as if to a grown child. All right, that's enough. I said, that's enough. Stop it. Stop it, you little fuck. Did she say that? Did she really say that to him? Ella's voice is firm and low, tight with contained anger. What is going on out there, and how to intervene, gracefully? She looks across at Tess on the bed, wild, and distracted.

'Look, Tess, you need some time to yourself. Let it settle, and then come out for lunch and we'll talk about it calmly.'

And she leaves the room quickly, so as to avoid taking in any look of puzzlement or betrayal from her daughter. She takes the baby from Ella without speaking and Ella sits on the couch, burying her face in her arms. The baby continues to wail and Louise rocks harder and faster, holding him firm between her arm and chest, clucking and ticking at him. Eventually it slows down, drops a notch in volume and pace. And so the world steadies, and her nerves slowly disentangle.

Then the baby sleeps, and Ella sleeps, and Tess perhaps sleeps too, and Louise lies down on her own bed in the sun, holding her novel, staring at the words, which spin and jitter across the page, refusing to settle. She feels unaccountably tearful and furious, and she realises that this is because she is carrying it all.

While each one of them sleeps and sloughs off the frustrations of the morning she is left alone, wound up, unable to read or think. She is reminded of the silverbeet growing up in the garden, in urgent need of treatment for white butterflies, and of the McCahon exhibition she hasn't seen yet, and of this slim novel, about Clarissa Dalloway and her plans to hold a party. All persistently unfinished. She wonders how it has come to this so quickly: being swept up entirely in the eye of young storms, with nothing of her own, no space to breathe. How has it happened that she is here once again? Taken over, and separate from her sense of self, which she sees as a shadow, quickly becoming thin and transparent, and walking now in a different direction.

At three o'clock on Saturday afternoon Chris puts the jug on, flicks a spoonful of coffee into the plunger and leans against the pantry door to think. A fat square of white sunshine lies along the floor, lighting up the blue of the cupboard doors and forcing his mind into focus. It is the middle of October and the sun creeps further around the side of the house each day. But the weather, the month, the coming of summer: these are distractions, these are not important matters. What is important now is to think, carefully and logically. He has three days. He needs to get this right, because he believes it could come out well, even now: it could all be for the best. He notices that he is breathing fast, and that his mind is clear, is working at an unfamiliar edge: meticulous, braced to achieve what is necessary. He has not felt quite this good, this alert, in a very long time.

On the other hand, if he gets this wrong – if he steps or speaks where he shouldn't, or fails to speak where he should, or puts the right words in the wrong order, or allows himself to dither, or become confused again, even for a moment – it is over. It is all, he thinks, utterly over. He will lose them both. And I shall go and jump off the Avalon bridge, he thinks. Or find pills. Or whatever is necessary.

He recites the facts. We had sex. In our bed (yes, Sally, *your* bed). He thinks how dark, how newly green, the duvet looked this morning, with her pale arm over it, the lines of fine freckles trickling down to her wrist. And then, how he had peeled back the cover, hoping she would stay asleep, to look where there were no freckles, only white, unmarked skin, and the tendons and bones visible, the architecture of her strong body. And pale nipples tugging upwards in the cool air, living pebbles to turn his tongue over and over. Waking her. Slipping her out of sleep.

He sips at his coffee and slowly, consciously, runs over each detail of this image. Then he puts it to one side, carefully laying it down, placing it in a box labelled Tess. He is allowing himself this one day to sort and label each fact and each memory and to put them all safely away, then close the lid. He will start at the beginning. He will itemise.

The first image: walking through town. She slips one cool hand quick and clean between his rib and his arm, wraps it around. *Takes* his arm. Proud, walking down the street with her holding on to him like that. Proud, walking with this tall, familiar woman, but ducking a little, keeping an eye out, going through the back ways because anyone might see them – anyone at all, and Jacob in particular.

The second image: lying on the rug, here in the lounge, her hair spinning down over her wide shoulders, her small breasts lolling sideways as she props herself up on one arm. The two of them awkwardly giggling. Cupping his hand under her breast and remembering her years ago, on the couch at home, in a white blouse and a blue jersey.

The third image: Chris I haven't done this before. No. Not right. What she actually said was: Chris, do you know that I haven't . . . She didn't finish the sentence. He wasn't certain, then. It stopped him, and he would have let it go, taken her home, despite the ache of it, the red wine, everything. But she was quite certain, and direct. She said, Chris, what about the bed, because the floor was too hard and her skin was itching against the woollen rug.

He is sitting down now, on the lino, head and back braced against the wall. He is a little bit exhausted, a little bit excited. But the essential point is not to get confused. The way to move forward is to look at it all, honestly, and adore it, and let it go, because now he is sure of one fact, one solid fact at the centre of his life, like a table bolted to the floor, around which all else must be organised, accommodated. He loves Sally. He pictures her face fleetingly in his hands. She is fine, a fine woman, and she is at the centre. She is his blood and his bone, she is his day and his night, and he cannot, simply cannot, lose her. It is like waking up with a clear head for the first time in a long time. And he believes that he could not have come to the fullness of this knowledge any other way, terrible though that seems – and inexplicable.

And Tess, sweet, gangly Tess, who has always been there, perched near the edge of his consciousness for years, his best friend's sister. *Practically my sister*, he thinks, shifting on his haunches under the weight of the thought. Practically family. Then there is an image of Louise, standing before him, frowning, furious. It is terrible when Louise is angry at him. This has hardly ever happened but the two or three times that she has looked at him like that he has felt himself wither, felt his insides turn into something like the carved-out, rotting guts of a fish, because Louise is always kind, kinder than his own mother, and if she doesn't approve of him, then, he thinks, it must mean he's failed in some essential way.

Like the time he and Jacob took Margie's son out surfing. The kid was twelve at the time and they took him out to the break off the island. He was too small and he got bashed around, nearly flung into the rocks, and then he was too terrified to swim back so they had to tow him across the channel lying on his board, with the tide buffeting hard against them. He was blue and exhausted by the time they got to the shore, and Margie told them that he slept for two days straight, and woke up screaming in the night for a month afterwards. Louise looked at him just like that then, and said in a shaky voice: You are irresponsible, you are foolish.

But Louise shouldn't be angry about this, he thinks. She mustn't be angry because Tess is delightful to him. She has not diminished; she is more now, not less. Tess has white skin and breasts he has cupped in his hand and he knows her completely, and it is both different and the same. And he does love her, because she is lovely. She is his lover. He is astonished by the rushing in his chest, by his delight in both of them, Sally and Tess, these two women, and all their various ways. They overtake him, both of them: his heart, his mind, his body are entirely taken up with them and he is becoming quite giddy.

Don't fool yourself, Chris. He stands, hearing the warning echo in his head. He starts to walk, paces the lounge in tight circles. Don't get complacent. This is not a stable situation. You could lose it all. Do you understand that? Do you understand what is at stake? He needs to be firm with himself, he can see. He needs to ensure that he stays focused, stays clear. Everything is in the balance. He stands before the bathroom mirror, looking directly at his unshaven face. This is a serious junction in my life, he says aloud. The phone rings violently in his ears.

Watching the weather come in over the water, Louise remembers why she lives on the coast, and will never leave. The weather is the best asset of the house, situated with its back to the city, braced into the wall of rock, face turned out toward the wide strait. It has become a quiet delight to Louise, being the first to know, the first to see the storms arrive, before anyone in the high glass towers, before the suburbs of settler cottages. She spends slow minutes observing the changes in the water, the light, and the patterns of the tide against the wind, minutes that no one knows about, but which make a difference, she believes, to everything.

She sips coffee in her dressing gown at the living-room window, watching the Sunday morning sky darken over the headland, and is pleased, as always, by the sheer fall of land down to the sea. Clouds pour in over the hills, fat with cold rain from the south-west, and the gulls are wheeling inland, so the ocean will be whipped into chunky, difficult waves by the afternoon. There will be no walking around the bays today, and down at the café the windows will steam up, and the customers will order second coffees and hot chocolates, grumbling about the unseasonable onslaught in October, when in all justice it should be warm and green.

Jacob kicks his shoes off at the door and pads behind her in his socks, coming into the kitchen still panting, his cheeks red from the wind.

'You should have called me. I would have come and picked you up.' She automatically starts to make more coffee.

'I wanted to walk.'

'It's a long way, Jacob.'

'An hour and a half. I feel good, though. I feel better now.'

'What kind of better? Were you feeling sick?'

'Tense. Just tense. Barker's pissing me off. I'm pissing Barker off, whatever. I needed to get out for a while.'

Among all the developments of the past few months, this part has seemed so smooth: Jacob leaving, setting himself up. It's four months now since he left home, and aside from occasional requests for cash he has been on his own, and doing fine.

She drove up to the house one Saturday afternoon with his mail and a couple of extra things for the flat – a chocolate cake, some salsa and corn chips, a large bottle of orange juice – arriving to find all three flatmates at home, watching a video together, companionably sprawled across the worn furniture. And although chaotic, with every surface covered in dishes, magazines and Andrew's sports gear, it wasn't a *dirty* flat, and there was a pleasant buzz about it, she thought, with posters on the wall, and someone (probably Trisha, the girlfriend) even had a cactus collection carefully arrayed along the windowsill. Hey, Ma! Jacob had shouted back at her when she opened the front door, calling out tentatively. Come in, he said, come on in! He cleared her a space at the table, offered her beer, played host. So she had been satisfied, pleased that this one thing had been well accomplished: her son established in his own life, independent.

But now he is back here, standing in the kitchen with flushed cheeks, having walked furiously all the way down to the coast because there are difficulties. Both of them are embroiled in difficulties, then, struggling to stay friends with the various friends around them. Tess had some kind of ghastly phone call with Chris in the afternoon yesterday, and when Louise went to bed at midnight she was still up, blank and brooding in the lounge. It is past midday now and she has yet to surface.

'So, did I tell you that Ella has named the baby?' she says, handing him a mug of black coffee.

'Oh, yeah?'

'Yes, finally. Connor. Connor Tamaiti.'

'What does that mean, Tamaiti?'

'Good question. I don't know, actually. I didn't ask her that.'

'Well, I'll ask her.'

'She's not here right now. She's gone up to varsity. She's sitting an exam in a couple of weeks.'

Telling him this she feels a small tug of guilt because really, she ought to have offered to keep the baby here for the morning, ought to have let Ella go and get some proper work done for a couple of hours, without all the bother and distraction of nappies and feeding. But she didn't offer. Ella stepped out the front door looking as though she were pregnant once again, with the baby a blue padded lump in the frontpack, and her thick coat wrapped around them both. All Louise felt was relief, for the silence, for this few hours of absence.

'Exams, eh? That's keen.'

His voice is flat, and he holds the blue mug in his large hands, lifting it to his face. The gesture is one of a child – the same child who would pull his morning Milo into his thin chest, guarding its warmth. It is a familiar sign, with a specific meaning. Jacob is feeling wounded.

'So, out with it, Jacob. What's going on?'

'Um, you know. Just stuff.'

'Normal flat stuff?'

'I guess so. I wouldn't know. I've never been flatting before, have I?'

'Well, I wouldn't know either, particularly, but I imagine you're always going to face some tension.'

'Oh, sure, yeah, sure.'

'Don't be sarcastic. I'm not saying it's necessarily *easy*, Jacob. Just that you should stick at it. Don't you think?'

Stick at it. She is suddenly aware how often she has said this to Jacob over the past twenty years, at various times, and with varying degrees of bluntness. Regarding flute lessons and soccer teams, school plays and School Certificate French.

Sometimes he does, and then the results tend to be stunning, as with his degree, the line of pretty As running down the transcript page. But so often the enthusiasm passes, and without will or discipline the latest brilliant plan is left to subside, usually with another set of expensive, unused equipment stashed in a corner of the garden shed. Stick at it: her constant refrain, and perhaps, she thinks, not always the right advice.

'I don't know, Mum. It's really not working for me there.'

'Is it because Andrew and Trisha are a couple, do you think? I do wonder if it would be easier with a fourth person in the house.'

'Nah, I don't care about that. That's fine. God, nobody extra – that would be worse.'

'So what exactly is it, then?'

'Well, I need my space, for one thing. You know, I reckon if a person wants to be up and working overnight, they shouldn't be hassled.'

'Well, yes, sure, why should that be a problem? But, Jacob, why *are* you working overnight? You've got another whole year to get your Masters done.'

'Oh, it's not the thesis. I'm doing some other writing. My own stuff. And I find it comes best late at night, or really early in the morning, three or four o'clock. So I get up and I get on with it. And Andrew gets pissed off, because he reckons I wake him up, walking around the house, and putting the stereo on, just really quietly.'

'Well, that does sound fairly inconsiderate.'

'No way! No, I reckon Andrew just wants to control me. I don't think I wake him up at all. He's like that – he's a controlling bastard. He's really petty and pathetic and he gets in these furious moods if you do something wrong. He's so hard to live with.'

'But if he doesn't wake up, how would he know what you're doing in the middle of the night?'

He talks past her then, ignoring or not recognising the fundamental logic in the question.

'In any case, it's fucking awful there – it's not good for me. I want to get on with stuff. I've got work to do, heaps of work. I'm talking to people. There's a couple of projects I'm looking into.'

'What kind of projects?'

He leans in close, and he isn't pouting any more; he's gleaming at her, and moving his hands, moving his fingers around quickly in the air.

'Well, publishing, actually. The fact is . . . I'm going to set up a business. I'm going to start publishing my own stuff. And then expand.'

'Oh, Jacob.'

'What does *that* mean?'

'Look, there's a hell of a lot of work involved in setting up a business, and you have to be steady, you know, really steady. I know what I'm talking about here, and I just don't believe you're ready for something like that . . . Where did you get this idea from? And what about your research?'

'I can do both! And it's not just an *idea*, Mum, it's happening. It's already under way. I've been talking to some banks.'

'Don't be an idiot! You are *not* going to borrow money.'

'*Sure* I am! There's no problem. It's going to go brilliantly, they all think so. I've found this niche in the market, and no one else has got to it yet. It's guaranteed success. They're backing me –'

He breaks off suddenly, peering into the fruit bowl.

'What the fuck is this doing here?' he asks, plucking out an egg.

'I just put it there.'

'You put an *egg* in the fruit bowl?'

'Yes . . . just leave it. I'm about to make a cake. Look, Jacob, you already have a huge student loan.'

'Well, a few grand,' he says, passing the egg from hand to

hand. 'Okay, twelve grand. But everyone's got a loan; it's not as if that should count against you. Mum, hell, you know, I really thought you'd be into this. It worked for you, didn't it?'

'You're going to drop that.'

'No, I'm not.' He starts to toss the egg a little higher, back and forth, tracking it with his eyes.

'Sure, the café worked out for us, but we were careful. There were two of us, and we had other investors as well, and besides, we already had a reasonable percentage of the capital we needed up front. And we did our sums, we thought it through very carefully, step by step. Who's in this with you, anyway? Who's asking the difficult questions?'

'It's just me at the moment. I'm going to get it started and then perhaps bring some others on board. But anyway, look, the *reason* I'm telling you all this is that I need to move out of that flat. I can't work there. It's too constraining.'

'So what do you propose to do?'

'Well, I did have one idea.'

'What?'

'I thought I could move in with Kevin.'

Her head is spinning with it all. He can't borrow money. He mustn't, he simply mustn't. This is the only matter clear in her mind now, this one bright urgency, pricking at her, causing her head to pound. Whatever else, Jacob can't get further into debt, not for something so flighty, so risky. Just what kind of publishing is he talking about?

'What do you think?'

'About Kevin?'

'Yeah. I'm sure he could do with the company when he's at home, and then when he's away at sea I'd look after the place, and have complete freedom to do what I want. Perfect. Shit.'

The egg drops, and cracks open on the bench.

'Sorry, Ma.'

'Wipe it up. And get another one out of the fridge for me. It needs to be at room temperature.'

'Where are they?' he says, gazing in the fridge door.

'At the back. In the box. Look, Kevin's place is miles away from the city, and I don't know that he would want you staying. It's just a small cottage, Jacob.'

'I'm *fine* with that. All I need is my bed, and a desk.' He places the new egg down, precisely, between two kiwifruit.

'Okay. Stop. Perhaps I'm wrong. Perhaps it's a good idea. Look, this is a bit much all at once. Let me think about it for a while, all right? Just let me think.'

Her first clear thought on the matter is that it wouldn't be fair to inflict Jacob on Kevin. Nor, for that matter, Kevin on Jacob. Two odd men, she thinks – two similar men, driven as they are by some strange inner life, something individual. She tries to imagine them drying dishes together at Kevin's battered bach and nearly laughs aloud.

But then, after all, it was Jacob who sought Kevin out in the first place, without her knowledge, without asking or telling her. Jacob, at fifteen, who tracked down the phone number using the electoral roll and called Kevin out of the blue one day, introducing himself as a nephew.

They never have talked about this, but she wonders what on earth Kevin thought. A phone call on an ordinary Tuesday or Wednesday and suddenly the sister you haven't seen for over a decade has this assertive, smart-talking son. When Jacob was a baby, and Kevin only eleven or twelve himself, she would visit Nelson and leave them together for hours in the front room, Kevin building towers out of the red and yellow wooden bricks, Jacob squealing and knocking them down. Well, then, perhaps it could work, this unusual idea. Perhaps they ought to ask him.

'I'll think about it, Jacob. Let me think about it. Kevin's away now in any case.'

Kevin is on a long trip this time, with a new company, the big ship circling down towards Antarctica. In recent weeks her pulse has skipped each time she's heard the opening music for the six o'clock news, terrified that there will be news of an iceberg collision, images of grey bodies in a cracking sea.

'All right. Fine, you think about it. But I can't see any problems myself. I'd have to buy a car.'

'Exactly. There's the first problem, I'd say.'

'Pessimist! Enough, I'm sick of this. We'll talk about it later. So, anyway, where's Tess today?'

'Still in bed.'

'You're joking! What a slob.'

'Well . . . she's . . . unhappy, Jacob. In fact, you might like to go and talk to her.'

Surprisingly, Jacob takes up this suggestion, walks out of the kitchen and knocks on Tessa's bedroom door. It closes shut behind him, and Louise is left alone in the kitchen with her cold cup of coffee, perturbed, and irritated, and wanting to get out of the house, to leave them all to it and get on with various tasks that need doing down at the café. She's annoyed that it is past two in the afternoon and nothing has been achieved. My son, she thinks: he is odd. At the least he is impulsive, and wildly frustrating. And then there is the old familiar nag, the boring song of her brain circuiting around the worn track: is this my fault, could it have been different, did I do the right thing after all? *For Christ's sake, I'm not going over that again.* She walks out of the kitchen, says the words aloud: I am not going over that again.

At dinner no one is talking about Chris, or about publishing, or about flats. Everyone is talking in calm, even sentences about Connor, his fine features, his future as a piano player, or perhaps a Buddhist monk, or a tiger trainer, while he sleeps quietly on Louise's lap. This is a celebratory meal, a meal out at the restaurant, because Louise has decided that she, for one, needs to celebrate something. Misery, an almost palpable presence, descended on the house this Sunday afternoon, and it has quite exhausted her. There has been no formal event to celebrate Connor's birth, and as he now has a name, and with no christening ceremony in sight, it is a good excuse.

Louise is hoping that all of this – the good food, the wine, the focus resting for a while on someone else (someone small, new and triumphant) – will help Tess and Jacob get their troubles into perspective. Drama queens, the pair of them, and particularly Jacob, posturing around the house this afternoon saying, I'll fucking kill him, Tess, he's using you, the lying bastard, and Tess shouting back at him from behind the bedroom door, Shut up, Jacob, this is my business and I don't want you involved. Like three-year-olds, she thinks. Storms in a teacup, and look at them both here, her scatty children, pale and grumpy creatures at the table. Then there is Ella, with her dark hair pulled tightly back, moving smoothly with this satisfactory child, a full six hours of study at the library, her serenity and her silent purpose. And Ella, she reflects, is younger than both of mine.

The storm has come in and perches overhead, slashing and banging at the windows as the grey light fades. After dinner they squash into the car and drive the four hundred metres home. Louise runs up to unlock the door so that Ella can get the baby inside quickly.

In the middle of the night the phone rings, loud and persistent, and Louise struggles to wake up. This is about Kevin, she thinks, the idea suddenly fixed and cold as she picks up the receiver. *Something has happened to Kevin.*

The thin male voice down the end of the phone belongs to a man called Glenn, and he says he is from the hospital, and it is about Tess. Oh, she says, confused, but my daughter is here. Yes, in fact, I'm sure she's here. But no, that's not true either, she's not quite sure, and she can't be sure, just now, with the red digits flashing 2:35, exactly where Tess is – whether she went out, whether she said anything about leaving or staying. Sorry, madam, the voice, Glenn, replies. I'm very sorry. Your daughter has been in a car accident. She has sustained severe head injuries and has been taken into surgery. You should come to the hospital immediately. But, no, what do you mean? How do you know? Louise hears herself ask. Are you sure it's Tess? The driver gave us your details, madam, he says. The driver? she asks, bewildered. Someone else was driving? And she is thinking, *Jacob*, is Jacob here? I'm sorry, he says, I don't know all the details, but I can tell you that the car was a red Toyota Corolla, and the accident occurred along the Hutt Road. It would be best if you came to the hospital straight away.

When nursing, Louise had, on occasion, been given the task of supporting the parents immediately after they had been told that their Jonathan or their Sarah or their small Hamish had been diagnosed with cancer. She was always struck at those times by the way in which people would become confused by the facts at first, would posit other, logical solutions to what they had heard. Shock, pure shock, held off – waiting, she supposed, until they got home and were left unguarded, performing some small, everyday task, to sink its claws into the back. Oh, the parents would say, but we thought it was anaemia, we thought it was a rare form of diabetes. Can the doctors be absolutely sure, they would ask, are they certain?

When the phone rang she was certain that it was about Kevin, and she had seen then, quite clearly, an image of the boat tipped over and sinking into the ocean, the men scattered and clasping at bits of board, nets, one another.

It is this image that stays with her. This is all she can see. It takes up the entire frame of vision. She dresses in trackpants and, strangely, a suit jacket. She wakes Jacob. They go outside. But there is no car to take them to the hospital. No car. No red car at all.

TWO

I didn't know they would do that. But you ought to have known, Louise says to herself, because you know that's necessary when they operate. They have to do that to get at the scalp. They have opened up a flap of bone and released the intracranial pressure. You know that. You have seen this before, she tells herself sternly – little heads, dark like that, little shorn heads. You have trundled children with heads like that down from recovery yourself. You ought to have been ready for this. *But she looks twelve. She looks ten, she is too small, she is blue, she is small and blue and vanishing.*

It rushes in like a strong, focused wind, funnelled straight at her, this small head, tufty, with the dark stubs of hair shrinking in around her swollen purple face. The unfamiliar line of a cheek, puffing out, expanding unnaturally into the white space of the room. A bandage is wrapped from ear to ear and the rest is submerged by tubes, in nose and mouth, and arms, delivering liquid, oxygen, blood. The doctor reaches over, checking, fastening. There is a bare torso, breasts like small globes of dough, everywhere bruised and cut. Louise realises that she has cupped her hand around a foot that is sticking awkwardly out from the covers. And look, this is Tessa's foot, it certainly is, because look, see how the last toe turns slightly inward and the nail is pitted and rough because of the accident with the bike when she was two.

But I don't know this little vanishing head. She wonders then what they do with all the hair, and whether they have thrown it away, whether it is lying tangled somewhere in a sterile bin, somewhere in a plastic bag. She wants to go and check the bins right now, to go and turn every bin in the place upside down and rummage through, scattering aside needles,

127

swabs, used gloves, coffee cups, and hold it up, the long red curls of it: hold it up in the air, hold it up against the light, and start putting it back.

Chris knows that his arm is wrong, although no one has examined it yet, not properly. Spikes of pain shoot down to his fingers and splice across his shoulder blades. His neck is wrong too. He hasn't tried turning it to the left yet. In the ambulance he lay flat on his back because he felt giddy and thought he might faint if he stayed sitting up, so he lay down and looked up at the white roof. After a time he noticed that the rush had settled down. The small precise words that had been shooting back and forth between the paramedics had stopped, and the rustle had stopped too, and then he wanted to look: he wanted to find out if they were still moving across Tessa's body with quick certain movements. He hoisted himself up at the waist and turned his entire torso in one piece because, definitely, there was something wrong with his neck, and he didn't want to try turning it then, and still doesn't.

Now he is sitting here in the Emergency Department, in a green plastic chair, cradling his left arm in his right, and not turning his neck at all. There are fifteen – no, sixteen – people in the room now, and in some cases it's impossible to say who is the injured person and who is the person here to do the looking after. Of course, that's not true for the man opposite, holding a swab over his eye. The swab is turning slowly crimson, and his mate is saying, Are you right, Jim, are you right? No, says the man. Jesus, I'm not. The mate puts his arm around him, lets his hand rest there on his shoulder, but it's awkward, and the mate's not all right with this, not really, so he coughs and shifts and takes it away again. The man with the swab on his eye doesn't seem to notice much, either way.

Then there is an older woman right next to him, bent double, with her arms wrapped around her stomach, her nose almost on her knees, swaying, and the skin at the back of her neck turning slightly yellow. She's wearing a dressing gown and her husband is here with her. He is rubbing her back constantly, up and down, and these two aren't talking at all.

There are some drunk kids, and a man with a baby in a pushchair. It's hard to say what's wrong with the baby because it's asleep. Perhaps it's not the baby at all – perhaps it's the guy, with something broken, something smashed up somewhere inside: nothing visible, nothing obvious. It could be that he was home alone with the baby and so he had to bring it in. Another woman has two children with her – a boy who stares up at the infomercials on TV, and a smaller girl who likes the plastic house in the corner, pulling the blue door shut behind her and then screaming out to her mother to open it back up. Again, it's difficult to say which one of them is having the emergency, the woman – or the boy. But probably not the girl, he reckons: she looks fine, boisterous and giggling like that.

It's good to think about all the possibilities, and to count and recount the number of people in the room, and to keep a lookout for the first nurse he talked to, to keep watching the door, wondering if she will come back and send him in to be checked over. It's good to have all this to look at and to think about because it keeps his mind ticking and moving and he doesn't want to let his mind stop. He thinks that they might have said fifty-fifty. That could be wrong, but he thinks that's what the taller paramedic said to the three nurses who came rushing up to the ambulance doors and slid the trolley and the tubes and drips down onto the tarmac. It's fifty-fifty, Tom. Those were the words he heard, the exact words. Well, that could be some kind of system number, a code, the amount of blood she needs or anything – it could mean anything at all.

It is too difficult to think about, those numbers, and her hair clotted with blood, and her face too. He couldn't see any of her face under all that blood. Most of all it is difficult to think about the song the radio was playing, and how he had noticed these things: her hand moving towards the tuner knob, the silver car up ahead, the sticky pine smell in the strange car, the smeary blaze of the traffic lights – orange and red. It is difficult to start thinking about the way he had noticed everything apart from the important problem approaching from the left.

She is borderline. This is what he is saying. We can't offer you a great deal of reassurance. Then the doctor keeps talking, keeps holding on to her arm, but Louise isn't listening any more. She hears herself saying, Yes, thank you, I understand, but she has to breathe, she has to get outside immediately. She goes down in the lift alone, through the rush of warm wind just by the Red Cross shop, past the buckets of drooping lilies and daffodils. She walks along the gleaming lino, faster and faster all the way out, following the yellow tape on the floor. Out onto the street.

The earth cracks open beneath her, and the soil here is not clay brown, like in the garden, it is not soft and mixed with pebbles, it is black, it is peat. There is a pit all the way down to the edge of vision, down to lapping water, a pool of salt. The body bobs on the tide, in the black ocean under the cracking earth. The cold glove slides across the body and takes it down, takes it inside so she can't see it any more, can't see the slashes and the bruises all down the torso, can't see the shorn head. There is only black water, and the soil crumbling in, and the body slipping away. There is a hand floating on the surface of the water, but the light is dimming; the light will go soon, and then she will not be able to see at all.

Terror begins in the stomach and peels out across the skin of her back, her breasts, her arms. She stands outside the main entrance of the hospital, with the rain spitting in her eyes. She retches onto the concrete below the red sign that says Emergency, and between spasms she whispers, Live, god, please live. The words are a little mantra, a little raft, and she is clinging, and scrambling, and holding on. Live, god, please live.

When he sees his mother come in through the waiting-room doors Chris feels the pressure of hot tears, and he wants to crumple then, to let down all his defences and cry.

'Mum,' he calls out, 'Mum, I'm over here.'

She comes across, anxious and brisk, and puts a hand to his cheek, pulling in to kiss him.

'Chris. Are you all right?'

'I'm okay, Mum.'

'Oh, darling, look at your cheek. That's a serious cut. But they've stitched it. When did they stitch it?'

'When I first got here.'

'Did they look you over thoroughly? Have they checked for fractures? Which doctor can I speak to?' She is looking around the room, charged, ready to assert herself, to ensure that he is taken care of.

'Mum, I'm still waiting to have my arm checked. They did what they could, but they were focused on Tess. She's pretty badly hurt, Mum.'

'Tess McMahon, you mean? Jacob's sister? She was in the car too? Who else?'

'Just Tess. Mum, it's bad. It's really bad.'

'Oh, god! Is her mother here? Have they called her?'

'I guess so. I don't know where they took her. I gave them the phone number. They must have found Louise or they would have come back to me.'

Then he is swallowing hard because he really mustn't cry now, he mustn't let his mother see him like this. He winces against the scald of salt tears stinging the tight sore on his cheek.

'Oh, Chris. It's frightening, I know, it's all right.' His mother puts her arm around him.

133

'Mum, I don't know where they took her,' he says, hiccupping and swallowing. 'I'm really not sure that she's going to be okay.'

'We'll find out as soon as we can. But there's nothing you can do for Tess right now, and we need to get you looked at.'

'But do you know what I'm saying, Mum? I'm saying it's really bad. I don't know if she will – I don't know.' He looks at his hands, and he wants to throw up.

'Chris, I understand what you're saying. It's all right. You can't think about this now. We will find out about Tess as soon as we can. You can't do anything now. They will be doing everything they can. They will look after her. We need to make sure you're okay. What hurts? Does your head hurt at all?'

'No, my head's fine. My arm feels really bad, and I can't move my neck much.'

'Probably whiplash. Did you have a seatbelt on?'

'Yes, of course. My arm hit the steering wheel.'

'Oh. You were driving, Chris?'

'Yes, I was driving! That's the point, Mum, that's what I'm fucking trying to say!'

He stands up and paces the few steps out the door of the waiting room, stops, breathes, and turns around. His mother is watching him anxiously. He walks back, sits down again in the green chair.

'Look, it was her mother's car, right? Tess is on a restricted licence. She wanted to stay, but I said I'd drive her home.'

She keeps looking at him, and she's concerned, but she won't interrupt him.

'It happened at the traffic lights, at the Melling Bridge, I think. Or maybe further back. Maybe Avalon. I can't remember. I need to think. I'm not sure.'

'Hey, that's enough. Really, it's okay Chris. You don't need to do this now. There will be time later. Shush now, shush.'

'Fuck, Mum! I'm telling you this. I'm telling you what happened. Just listen.'

'This isn't good for you. You're agitated. You're getting too worked up.'

'And the other car crossed the lights early – they can't have seen me at all – and maybe I crossed late. A little bit late. I think that's what happened. I think so. The car hit the passenger door, directly. And then, I don't know, some spinning, and I don't know where we ended up, just the hit, I know they hit on her side.'

The nurse calls out Chris Ferguson and his mother jumps up, relieved, and says, Yes, we're here, over here.

They are letting him leave now. He has a sling around his arm and a brace around his neck. Sleep, the nurse says, but not for too long, and any signs of unusual drowsiness, bring him straight back. She looks at his mother. We'll check up in a few days.

'Excuse me,' Chris asks, 'where is my friend, where's Tess?'

'Your friend?' The nurse asks.

'Yes, she was in the accident too,' he says. 'She was injured. Quite badly injured, I think.'

'Sure, I'll try and find out where she is.' The nurse looks concerned. 'What's the last name?' She pulls out a slip of paper and a pen from her pocket. He is comforted by this, because it is clear that the nurse is on his side, prepared to take action, prepared to intervene on his behalf.

'McMahon,' he says. 'Her name is Tessa McMahon.'

The nurse writes it down, turns and walks back to the office.

Back in the waiting room he sits beside his mother and they don't speak. All the people who were here earlier have left now, except for the man with the baby. The baby has fallen asleep on the man's shoulder and he is standing staring at the television, and occasionally walking around the small room. His mother unzips her handbag on her knee and starts fishing around, searching for a tissue, or her lipstick, or a key.

Chris picks at bits of fluff on his black pants and wonders suddenly why he is wearing these, his only good pair of trousers, bought for his graduation and rarely worn since. He can't think why he chose to put them on this morning. It seems like an extremely long time ago. It is a bad joke: being here at the hospital, waiting to find out about Tess, in the middle of the night, in his best trousers.

'Now, Chris, I'm going to phone Dad. He'll want to know what's happening.'

'Dad? Where is he?'

'In Sydney, darling, I *told* you that. I called him before I left home. Hours ago. He'll be worried. I'll let you speak first.'

She finds the mobile phone and starts dialling, but then he notices the nurse coming back through the doors and jumps up and runs towards her. The nurse isn't smiling, but she doesn't exactly look upset either.

'I've managed to get some information.'

He is blank. He cannot think what she will say next. He cracks his knuckles, bending his fingers to one side and then the other, and notices that his hands are quite cold.

'Tessa is in theatre. In surgery.'

'Yes,' he says, his forehead beading with relief, but greedy for more, and impatient. 'So what does that mean?'

'It's likely to be some time before anyone will be able to see her. I think, really, Chris, it might be best to head home, and call the hospital when you get there. I'll give you a number that you can call anytime, and the Intensive Care Unit will explain exactly what the situation is.'

'No,' he says. 'I want to stay, I want to wait here.'

His mother is behind him now. He can hear her talking to his father about the brace, and the stitches. Sure, she says, yes, tomorrow morning. Yes, I'll tell him. Bye, then.

'Well, it's up to you,' the nurse is saying. 'I could direct you to the recovery area. You could wait up there until she's able to be seen. But it may be quite some time yet.'

'Tessa's being operated on?' his mother interrupts. The nurse nods.

'Well, Chris, love, we should go home in that case. We're certainly not going to be able to do anything for Tess tonight.' Her hand is on his shoulder. He shrugs her off. It might not be rational, but he believes that if he doesn't get to see her, now, tonight, it's going to make a difference: it's going to change the outcome.

'I think your mother is probably right,' the nurse says. 'It's important that you get some rest quite soon.'

Sides have been drawn and no one is moving, no one is saying anything. His mother gives up, walks over to the waiting area and sits down. Chris stays standing with the nurse and can't think what to say next but he's not going to move. He's confused and exhausted but he's determined to stay there, silent and waiting, until he gets what he needs.

'Chris!' Someone is yelling behind him. 'It is you! What the fuck?'

Jacob is paused on the landing of the small flight of stairs, just outside the waiting room. Chris leaves the nurse, turns and races up to him in four or five leaps.

'*Christ.* Jacob, I'm glad to see you. What's happening? Where is she? How is she?'

Jacob stays quite still. He is staring at the sling, and the brace around Chris's neck.

'Hey, look,' Chris says, 'I'm fine   this is nothing. Tess, what's happening? Can you take me up to her? Come on, man, let's go. She's in theatre, they said. What have they told you?'

'You were there? You were with her?' Jacob says.

'Yes, I was there. I came in the ambulance with her. Look, Jacob, I already know it's serious. I just need to know how bad.'

He wants to put his hand on Jacob's back and start leading him gently back up the stairs. He wants to put him in motion, to start the mechanism moving that will lead him towards Tess, whatever state she is in. He wants to know the worst of it. It is important to see, with his own eyes.

'Chris?' His mother calls out from the foot of the stairs. 'Oh, Jacob, hello.' She comes up to the landing too now. 'Is your mother here?'

Jacob is staring at Chris and doesn't seem to hear the questions.

'Who was driving?' Jacob asks in a small voice. '*Who was fucking driving, Chris?*'

There is silence. His mother breaks it.

'Jacob, this isn't relevant right now. We're not going to talk about this at the moment.' Her firm voice bounces back off the smooth walls. The woman at the counter is watching.

'Cunt.'

Jacob pushes past them both, down the stairs and out the main door. Chris stands there, looking down at the receptionist. Move, his brain whirrs urgently – follow him, talk to him, explain, explain. But when he gets outside the door the street is empty, the traffic lights are fixed on green and Jacob is a small bent figure walking fast towards the city, already well past the bus stop.

There is a nerved energy tingling down her legs. Louise has drunk five cups of coffee in the past five hours. There is a blaze of astonished exhaustion at the pit of her neck. But she is still here, still functioning, capable somehow even of noticing that Mr Kelly, Tessa's neurosurgeon, is also very tired. Sitting opposite her at the table in the visitors' room he rests his temple on his hand and presses his fingers into his scalp in tight circles. Jacob sits beside her and puts his head down on his arms, falling directly into a jolting half-sleep.

Despite herself, Louise is starting to be concerned about Mr Kelly now: concerned about the red lines of his eyelids, and his hanging, unshaven jowl. This seems ridiculous, and it makes her furious, this instinct for worry. Why should she be concerned about this tired stranger – why now, when all she ought to have room for is Tess? I guess that's how it is, though, she thinks. We're in this together, and Mr Kelly as well, all of us working with whatever instruments we have to hand to keep her here.

There isn't much to see: only the outer husk. The essence of her is away for a time, wandering somewhere unknown. But just being beside her, holding a hand, lightly running fingers down her arm requires everything, requires a concentrated presence and attention. Tess is an immobile, silent body demanding the last atom of energy and strength available.

At seven this morning the duty doctor came in to check the monitors, the vital signs marking out the progress of her invisible life. He stood at the head of the bed flicking back through the graphs, and firing acronyms at Louise like pithy insults. 'It has been thirty hours since the accident now,' he said. 'If she makes it through the first forty-eight hours her chances are very much improved.' Of full recovery? Louise had asked. 'Of survival,' he answered.

Louise picks at the Chinese takeaway that Jacob has brought in. After two mouthfuls she lays it to one side, feeling queasy. Mr Kelly has come to brief them.

'It's been a good day, Mrs McMahon.'

A good day. A day during which Tess did not breathe, eat, move or open her eyes.

Louise arrived at six this morning. She had woken at five, after three hours of uneasy dozing. The night before, she left the hospital some time after one o'clock in the morning when the neurosurgeon finally said that Tess was stable almost a full twenty-four hours after the accident. Tessa's night-nurse urged her to go home and try to get some rest, assuring her that they would ring at the slightest change. Jacob had been home to sleep earlier in the day, and so he stayed on, armed with volumes of poetry. Go, Mum, he said, you look terrible. Eventually, she let herself be convinced and returned to the house, tried to rest.

Waking to the dark this morning she was sure that this was a mistake, certain that she should never have left. She sat at the kitchen table, blank, unthinking, letting her cup of tea grow cold for twenty minutes until she couldn't stay still any longer. She arrived at the hospital to the sun breaking through at the north window, and the view out over the buildings, over the suburb and on into the centre of town, with the summer light picking at the red roof of the Tip Top factory. The weather changed mid-morning, turning to rain. She noticed this when she went downstairs to stand outside for a brief minute, eating a toasted sandwich from the cafeteria.

All day workers have been working, everywhere here in the hospital, and in the city beyond: innumerable important tasks completed, stocks traded, every kind of item bought and sold, papers signed, stories published, houses cleaned, children taught and fed, lawns mowed, negotiations completed, planes brought safely to earth, and now at last the long day has ended. The clock on the wall has ticked its slow red second hand around, and the minutes have lurched past, each following the one before, until evening came. A day during which Tess kept quite still, and didn't die. A good day.

'I want to be cautious here.' The neurosurgeon props his elbows on the table, and makes a precise triangle with his fingers. 'But I do think we can afford to be slightly more optimistic at this stage.'

Well, Mr Kelly, Louise thinks, I'm sorry to tell you, but I'm already taking it rather further than that. We think she's going to live. In fact, we think Tess is going to live first of all, and then she's going to get completely better. We really do believe this, Mr Kelly, because we feel, Jacob and I, that there is no alternative. These other scenarios, Mr Kelly, I am refusing to contemplate. And Kevin hasn't even heard yet. She can't get a message through to him. Kevin is not coming home to a dead niece, she thinks grimly.

'How long do you think she will be in the coma?' she asks.

'Look, I'm sorry, we're unable to make predictions like that. At this stage it's about survival, and beyond that we really can't say what the outcome will be. Certainly we are talking about a number of weeks at the least.'

'But her signs are good?'

'Well, we need to be careful, but yes, I do think that Tess is showing positive indications. We are seeing some reaction of the pupils today, which brings her rating on the GCS up.'

'So what happens next?'

'If she continues to improve we will work towards weaning her off the respirator. The monitor records show that she is breathing spontaneously about thirty per cent of the time. But it will be a gradual process. We certainly wouldn't take her off until we're reasonably confident that she can breathe adequately on her own.'

'We've been worried about the tube, actually: she's gagging a lot. Can anything be done about that?'

'I suggest you mention it to the nurse. They'll ensure that the secretions are suctioned regularly.'

'Doctor, I need to know – in your opinion – do you anticipate that there will be permanent damage? I am a nurse myself.'

Tell me the worst, she thinks. Say it, tell what you think, and then I can make up my own mind. Then we know what we're facing here.

'Well, Mrs McMahon, I want to be frank with you. Your daughter has sustained significant subdural haemorrhaging, and her recovery is likely to be slow, and possibly limited. We will do a further CAT scan tomorrow to see whether the left-side swelling has reduced, and we may be able to offer you a more detailed prognosis by then. Look, we do understand how difficult this is for the family . . .'

No, Mr Kelly, she thinks, something suddenly growing hard and solid within her. I beg to differ. I don't believe you really do understand, because I thought I knew too – I thought I had an empathy as wide as a small ocean for all those broken, fringe-dwelling parents, the fathers who forgot to eat or sleep, and the mothers who wandered around the ward like zombies, and only ever looked normal and present when seated beside their sick child, chattering about toys and small domestic matters. I really did believe that I knew what that was about at the time, Mr Kelly. But you have no bloody idea. I had no idea, because what I realise now is that this is something else again, an indecipherable country with no north and no south. It's not what you expect at all.

Oh, but look at you, Mr Kelly, she thinks. You look exhausted.

———

142

The light is grey, and thin, and she wakes with her cheek in a damp pool of dribble. The baby is crying in the room next door. It is evening. No, she thinks, that's wrong. It's morning. It must be morning. I should be there. I need to go, I need to get back to the hospital. She reaches across for her watch and it says nine o'clock. It must be evening. It is nearly dark.

She came home to rest for the afternoon. They suggested she take a break for a few hours because it has been three days since the accident, and she hasn't slept for more than a few hours at a time. Visit your GP, the nurse said, get a sleeping pill, but she doesn't want pills because they act like a sledge-hammer. You forget time with a sleeping pill, you forget every-thing, and even though every hour the cool facts hit her like the dull thud of a fist in the back, it seems important to keep hold of it, this strange black time with its different chronology. I will need an intact record of this, she thinks.

In the kitchen she pours a glass of water and remembers her dream. She has been dreaming of water, of being rolled in the surf, skin scraping hard along the shingle surface. Coughing and tossing and not knowing where to put her feet down, not knowing where the surface was. It was difficult to breathe, and the water was filled with thousands of lurid fish, tiny pink and yellow fish, churning in the crest of the green wave. Keep your mouth shut, that's what she had to remember in the dream – keep your mouth shut – because the fish are poisonous and dangerous and you mustn't swallow any. Keep your mouth shut.

She drinks the glass of water and the colours of the kitchen seep away. When Jacob comes into the room he starts to tell her something, he starts talking, but then he stops and seems to think better of it. He comes across and wraps his arms around her, stroking her hair, rubbing her back, and she gives in to this. She allows herself to stay there for a short while, held against her son's thin chest.

'Hey, Ma, hey there. Are you okay?'

She pulls back, wipes her eyes and laughs.

'Oh, yes. Okay. I'm okay.'

'I think she's doing great, you know, Mum. Really. When I saw her this morning I thought she looked different. Pinker skin. A little bit better, didn't you think?'

'Maybe, yes. Jacob, thanks. That helps.'

'Mum, honestly. If someone does his best to kill your little sister, you get furious, and then you get in there and do what you can. This is a crisis for us, and I'm going to deal with it. What did you expect?'

'Christ, Jacob! What are you talking about?'

She takes a step back and looks at him, alarmed, her head groggy, trying to make sense of this sudden shift in the conversation.

'He hasn't even apologised to us yet. Mum, he hasn't said anything.'

'Chris? Are you talking about *Chris*? It was an *accident*, Jacob. I imagine Chris is suffering terribly. I'm going to call him in a few days. Once it's clearer. What are you saying?'

'I've got my own opinions, Mum.'

It is outrageous that Jacob could think like this, talk like this. But when she had to explain to Margie about the accident, and about Chris driving, it was there, a moment of irrational, unbidden rage, at the injustice of it, at the fact that Chris walked away unscathed and Tess didn't.

The truth is, she doesn't want to think about Chris's sweet familiar face too much, because it might be quite difficult to see him in the same way now. Let Jacob handle the situation with Chris in his own particular way. She has no energy to argue with him about this. She has no spare energy at all.

Sometimes, when she sits watching, she tries to imagine that Tess is sleeping. She blocks her ears against the soft continual beep of the green screen marking out the rhythm of her heartbeat, and turns her head so that she can't see the other plotted lines measuring oxygen saturations. She blurs her eyes, blotting out as many of the tubes and bandages as she can. Then she looks at Tessa's face, and nothing else, and she tries to see it as a resting face, tries to believe then that she is only asleep, that nothing is out of place, that she is whole, simply healing and dreaming her normal dreams, and with this trick Louise can lull herself into a different state of mind: one that is a little away from the edge, a state of mind in which she can be bright, and speak in a normal tone, can say, Well, Tess, what's the news today, kiddo? What have I got to tell you?

Another trick is to look at only one part of Tessa's body at a time. Her right hand, for example, which rests, white and perfectly formed, on the bed cover. If you don't look at the wrist, the plastic band with her name on it and the line into the vein, you wouldn't know that anything was wrong. Not even her nails are broken.

After five days Tess is taken off the life-support systems and they move her out from intensive care and up to the ward. A little routine establishes itself and in this way the days fill out, and start to unfold in a measured and expected way. Louise spends every day at the hospital from first thing in the morning until two, then goes home for lunch, and perhaps a short rest, returning again at four. Jacob comes in at lunchtime, and Ella spends an hour with her later in the afternoon.

Margie usually visits around eleven, once the morning shift at the café is under way. Margie has been a saint, a saviour. She's spent the past two afternoons cutting between offices and making long phone calls, organising the ACC papers and negotiating with the insurance company. Just give me all the papers, she said to Louise, I'll get that part sorted out. That's something I can do. She's been in contact with Chris, too, and taken down the necessary details of the accident for the claim. Louise has signed a form saying that Chris had permission to drive the car. It's stretching the truth, but there's no point making the process more complicated than it has to be. Margie says that the police have been involved too, asking Chris questions. It's good that Margie's dealing with all this, because it would be difficult to have such discussions. She hasn't spoken to Chris at all yet.

When Margie arrives at the hospital in the morning Louise takes a short break. She is making it a habit to have a quick cup of coffee over the road at the new café, the one with the large bowl of yellow tulips in the window. She orders the same latte bowl every day, and reads the paper for ten minutes. The best thing about this café is the exhibition of paintings by a young, local artist. There are ten of them on display, all around the walls, with objects such as stones and shells and pieces of wood stuck into the paint. Her favourite one hangs above the table used for water jugs and cutlery. It is a long narrow painting, a series of four images. Two are painted, and then there is a leaf, dipped in some kind of gold, and a feather. If she can get the table by the window the view is perfect. When she sits back in her chair and looks at this painting the balance of anxiety shifts, replaced by a brief sense of proportion, and release.

The hospital social worker has called in twice now and each time she has said, Don't overdo it, Louise. Coping with head injury is a long-term change. You will need your energy over a number of months, or longer. You can't afford to burn out, she says. Think of it like the aeroplane. What do they say, in the safety instructions, when the oxygen masks appear? Attend to yourself first. That's the rule. And that's exactly how it is, Louise. You can't help her if you don't help yourself first.

But she doesn't feel exhausted, spending these hours at the hospital. It seems right, because if she isn't here she will fret and pace and won't be able to keep her mind on anything, and that's when she gets tired. The routine works, it carries her through the day, until the long evenings which simply need to be survived, to be diverted. Driving home in Margie's borrowed car, she drops in at Video Ezy and grabs two or three trashy American comedies. She watches these one after another until it's past midnight and her eyes are drooping. She's becoming very familiar with the mannerisms of Steve Martin. With careful planning she can fall directly asleep, and not think about anything at all.

Three days after they move Tess on to the ward Margie doesn't turn up. Louise is hungry, and knows she should go and eat anyway, but she doesn't want to leave Tess here alone. She doesn't want to miss anything. Just past midday Ella arrives with the baby strapped to her stomach.

'Hi, Louise.'

'Oh, hi. I'm glad you're here, Ella. Do you think you could sit with her for twenty minutes while I get a quick bite to eat? I'm starving. I mean – you don't have to. She will be fine, of course. But if you want to?'

'I was heading up to varsity, actually. But, yeah, sure, I can wait here for a bit. Can you hold Connor for a minute first, while I go to the loo?'

Ella fumbles quickly at the plastic clasps of the frontpack and lays the baby down on his back, on the black vinyl stool at the foot of the bed. He stays asleep. One fist stretches out. His eyes open, and then drift slowly shut once again.

'Here,' she says, placing him in Louise's arms. 'Ta.'

He is heavier, she notices. Hello, she says, touching her finger to his nose. Hi, little feller. She wonders then how they are getting on, because she hasn't had a chance to ask – she's barely thought about them. She hasn't picked him up since before the accident. It's going to be difficult for them now, she thinks, because I haven't got it in me, really I haven't. Sorry, Connor, she says aloud, sorry, little boy, thinking how Ella will be struggling and battling, with no one to help quiet him down now, no one getting meals, and god knows what left in the cupboards. I'd better get some groceries on the way home, she thinks. I'll get us a pre-cooked chicken, and I'll get her some yoghurt too, because she needs dairy products, and she needs iron. And gingernuts, that's what she'll want. He's less than a month old and Ella is still learning. This isn't going to be easy.

She is thinking about all this, holding Connor, watching his eyelids jitter with dreams; she is laying a multitude of little plans, but then quite suddenly it is as though a plug is pulled and the small accumulation of energy and concern drains out of her, like a delusion. I can't do it, she thinks. I simply can't look after them. Perhaps Ella needs to go home – perhaps she needs to find somewhere else to stay for a while.

When Ella comes back Louise shoots her a bright smile. Right, she says, here he is. I'll see you very soon. She swings her handbag over her shoulder and walks out through the main doors where she repeatedly presses the lift button.

'Louise! Louise!'

Ella comes running through the ward doors, chasing after her. What, Louise thinks, with a tight irritation now, her head prickling with the need for coffee and food. Can't it wait?

'She's opened her eyes, Tessa's opened her eyes, come and see!'

Louise phones Jacob, burbling with excitement, and he comes straight down to the hospital with Margie. The nurse pages the duty doctor, who comes into the room, pulling at his chin and nodding his head. Several of the other nurses on the ward come too, and Seamus and Jill, the young couple with a sister in the cubicle next door, and so they are all there, crowded around the bed, everyone smiling and talking at once, and Tessa's blank green eyes stare back vacantly at them all. Look, Jacob says with triumph, they are beautiful! Look at those eyes, Mum!

148

Photographs arrive in the mail, carefully pressed between squares of cardboard, with no letter. They have to be Andy's photos: black and white close-ups of the baby's hands, his feet, his closed eyes. He must have taken them while Ella was sleeping. Andy always liked taking black and white photos with backgrounds of rock, sand and grass. He always said that black and white film worked best with contrasting textures.

Ella stands in the hallway and flips carefully through them. She chooses the best one, a shot of his hands, so close that you can clearly see the tiny moons at the base of his fingernails. She puts it in the silver frame on her bedroom windowsill, replacing a faded picture of her, aged about fifteen, with the dogs at the farm.

Damn, she thinks. Now I'm going to have to call him. She is standing there, looking at the image of the hands, pleased by the way the shadows fall and accentuate the lines of the skin, pleased and irritated at the same time, when the phone rings. She pads back down the hallway to answer it.

'Hi, Ella,' Andy says.

'But I was just about to call you!' she says, taken aback.

'Really?'

'Yeah. I got your photos.'

'What do you think?'

'I like them. They're great. Thanks.'

After this initial rush of conversation there is silence. She can't think what to say next.

'Well, how's things?' he asks.

'Terrible, actually. Something terrible has happened.'

'Oh, god! What?'

'Not to the baby. You know Tess?'

'Tess who was at the birth, you mean?'

149

'She was in a car accident. She's in a coma.'

'You're joking.'

'No. She has head injuries.'

It's strange hearing herself tell Andy this, hearing herself explain about the accident. It makes her feel responsible, and important, the same way she felt at the hospital, when Tessa's eyelids blinked, and lifted, and she was the first one to notice. It was as though she had been let in on a secret. She had to call Louise back then – she was the one to let everyone know.

'But she was there, at the birth . . .'

Andy sounds bewildered, as though there is some incongruity in the facts.

'. . . when?'

'Just over a week ago. Nine days today. Not long after I came home from hospital.'

It has been nine days now since she woke up early in the morning to an empty house. That seemed odd at the time, but she washed, dressed and got on with the ordinary tasks of the day, until the afternoon, when Jacob came home with thick, red eyes and told her that Tess was in hospital, that she had brain damage, that she might not live. Then she realised that all day, while she had been eating, drinking, doing the washing, feeding the baby, changing nappies and listening to the radio, the entire time something horrific, something important was happening to her friend, and no one had called to tell her, no one thought that she needed to know. She felt furious then, and desperate, because she wanted to see Tess; she wanted to go there immediately. Not now, Jacob said. It's not worth it. I'll take you down in the morning.

Later she saw Louise and felt stupid, because she realised that none of that was important: the only important thing was Tess.

'Jesus, that's awful.' Andy sounds quite upset, quite emotional, and this surprises her because he doesn't know Tess well.

150

'Yes. It is.'

'Ella, is it all right for you to stay there? Do you need somewhere else to go?'

'No, thanks, Andy, it's fine,' she says firmly. 'There's no problem about that.'

'Christ. Well. Other than that, then, how are you? And how's my son?'

'Well. We're good. I think I've decided on a name.'

'Oh?'

'The one you liked. Connor.'

'*Connor*. That's great. Connor. It was my grandfather's name.'

'Yeah, you said that.'

'And what about a middle name?'

'I thought Tamaiti.'

'Hmm. Is that one of your family names?'

'No. I just like it.'

'Oh, right. Fair enough. Connor Tamaiti.' He pronounces it slowly, sounding out each syllable. 'Yeah, I like it – I think we have a decision. What do we need to do for the birth certificate?'

Just as well you like it, she thinks: I've been calling him that for two weeks now.

'It's fine. I'll take care of it. Look, Andy, I can hear him crying. I've got to go.'

'Oh, really?'

'Yeah.'

'Okay, sure. Well, I'll . . . speak to you soon. And I hope Tess gets well.'

'Yeah. We all do. See you later.'

She hangs up, and walks back to the lounge, and turns the stereo up, because the house is empty again this morning. There's nobody here except Connor, lying on the rug, kicking his bare legs in the air.

———

In the afternoon she straps him into the frontpack, hoists up a bag full of all the stuff he needs – a ridiculous amount of stuff – and walks out of the house, along the shore with the wind blowing cold on her face, and around the corner to the bus stop. When she walks through the main door of the hospital she whispers to Connor, Look, see, this is where you were born. She follows the yellow line, keeping hard to the left so as to let the shuffling people in pyjamas pass, and the occasional stretcher being rolled towards the lifts.

The first time she saw her she didn't believe it was Tess. She didn't know what to do, but Louise was there, watching her, so she went and touched the hand hanging out from the covers, and said hello. She looked around, at the circle of machines, dismayed, and Louise put a hand on her back and said, Don't be frightened.

After the first time it was easier, but still, she looks at her friend lying in the hospital bed, crooked up like a handicapped calf, a thin body with a shaved head and a tube in her nose, and the pieces do not fit, the connection is difficult to make. It doesn't really seem to be Tess at all, and so she finds it difficult to talk to her, or touch her, although she does try.

Today Jacob, Margie and Louise are all here at the hospital already. It's crowded in the room, and hot, and there's no spare place to sit down. Tess seems to be sleeping: her eyes are shut and she's not moving. Ella walks around the far side of the bed, says, Hi, Tess, and touches her arm for a few seconds. Then she hovers, listening to Louise and Margie discussing some kind of scan Tess had this morning. She stands by the bed, listening, and trying to follow, but her back quickly gets sore. Jacob is in the big armchair right up close by Tessa's head and she wants to ask him to move. She wants to unstrap Connor from her stomach and give him to Louise to hold for a few minutes. But Jacob is stroking Tessa's face with the back of one finger, he's talking to her in a low, intimate voice, and he's completely absorbed. Louise is at the foot of the bed, on the stool beside Margie, talking in an agitated way. She looks distracted and has barely said hello, simply nodded and smiled when she came in.

Ella wanders over to the window and looks out at the city, covered over by a low mist. She sways the baby back and forth, pivoting around on her hips in a small rhythmic movement. When she turns back to face the bed everyone is in exactly the same position, and she notices that the scene is balanced: each of them has one other person to attend to. I might head off, she thinks, and then she says it, aloud: Well, I might head off. Oh, really? Louise says, surprised. Yeah, Ella says, I'm actually on my way to meet someone in town. She bends down and kisses Tess quickly on the forehead, and her skin feels cool and sweaty under her lips. I'll see you a bit later on.

You are gorgeous, Chris thinks. He watches Sally undressing in the low bedroom light. God, you're beautiful. She climbs into bed and her skin is warm against him and he says this to her. Sally, he says slowly and deliberately, you're gorgeous, do you know that? Why thanks, she says and starts kissing his face and neck, running her palm smoothly down his side.

'Ow,' he says, wincing at her lips near the cut on his face.

'Sorry,' she says, pulling back. 'It's still really sore?'

'Yeah. It's getting there. It's okay.'

'Hey, Chris.'

'Mmm?'

He is wishing he hadn't interrupted, because she's stopped touching him now; she's taken her hands right away. He reaches down and starts tracing circles on her hip.

'Is there any more news about Tess?'

He stops moving his hand over her skin then. Irritated, because she has spoken the question out loud, the one that nags and constantly scratches at him. Each morning he has been waking up thinking, What is happening to her? What is happening? Is she still here? But he knows she must be more or less the same because otherwise he would hear about it. Jacob would still ring him first of all, if things got worse, or suddenly much better. He's sure of that.

'I don't know. I haven't heard.'

'Will you ring them?'

'I keep thinking about it. I want to. I want to know how she is. But then, I don't think they would want to speak to me, not yet. I told you, it's been really ugly.'

'Her mum will talk to you. Louise likes you, Chris.'

'Well, she used to.'

'You can't go on like this without knowing what's

happening with her. I mean, Chris, what if she dies?'

'Don't be fucking stupid!'

He yells it at her, and then he gets out of the bed and pulls on his bathrobe roughly.

'Chris, that is pathetic. You are being so reactive.'

'I'm going to take a piss. *You* are being dramatic,' he yells, stabbing his finger at her, 'and you haven't got a clue.'

'*Listen*, Chris. I know it sounds harsh, but it's a reality. From what you've told me, it could happen, and I just think you need to be in touch with the family. Shit, I can't believe I'm the one that has to tell you this!'

No, he thinks, you're right, that's unfair. You have no idea how unfair this is.

'I mean, this woman, your friend, turns up on the doorstep all upset, you end up *kissing* her to make it better, on the way home you crash the car, and then I'm the one who has to tell you it's good manners to find out if she's still bloody alive! How do you figure that out?'

'Shut up. Just shut up!'

He slams the door behind him and leans against it, breathing fast. He wants to stop his ears up with clumps of cotton wool, with clumps of earth, with anything to shut out her voice, and these questions.

Sally had come home from Masterton the day after the accident and he was ready. It was raining hard outside, blank sheets of water sluicing down the windows, and he was alone, waiting at the flat, ready with a box of Mövenpick maple walnut ice-cream.

He was preparing himself to tell her the five facts: that the neck brace and the stitches were the result of a car accident; that he was driving at the time of the accident; that Tess McMahon was in intensive care because of the same accident; that he was driving Tess home because she had come around to visit him; and that she had come to visit him because they had slept together the previous night.

These were the five relevant facts. These were the five things he was ready to tell her.

She had swung through the kitchen door, her red jacket dripping, old green suitcase in hand. She saw the brace, and the sling, and dropped the suitcase, shocked.

'I've been in a car accident,' he said. 'I was driving.' And that was two facts, straight away, just like that.

'*Oh, Chris*,' she said, rushing over to him. 'Are you all right? God, what happened?' She was biting at her lip, looking at his cut, running her hands through his hair.

'I'm okay,' he said, 'I'm all right,' kissing her cheek. 'But Sal, it wasn't just me in the car.'

'*Jacob!*' she said. 'Is Jacob hurt?'

'No,' he said, 'not Jacob. It was Tess.'

'Tess, his sister?' she asked, confused. 'Tess and Jacob?'

'Yes,' he said. 'I mean no. I mean, *yes*, Tess, in the car. Not Jacob. Look, Sally, she's in intensive care. She might not live.'

He knew this was true, because he had called Jacob four times in a row on Monday afternoon. He heard the exhaustion in the voice saying, 'Hi, Jacob here,' but then when he started to speak the line went dead, leaving the little pips humming in the air. On the third call Jacob didn't introduce himself at all, he just shouted straight down the phone, 'Brain damage, Chris. You got that? *Fucking serious brain damage*, and she could still die. It's on your fucking shoulders, you prick.' Then he hung up again. The fourth time, Jacob didn't answer the phone. After that Chris decided he wouldn't go back to the hospital; he would do the right thing and stay out of the way, and wait.

It wasn't difficult telling Sally the first three facts. She was frightened, and worried, and they sat at the table silently for some time. Then he started talking, telling her about lying in the ambulance, and not knowing what was going on, about the moment when the smash came, and the way that the car had slid, forwards and to the right, and then the spinning, and the darkness, the sounds of other cars skidding, sounds of running and shouting, and not knowing what had happened, not being able to understand where the other car had come from. He told her about the policeman who stopped him before he got into the ambulance, put a hand on his shoulder and said, Sorry, mate, but I need you to blow into this. But I wasn't drinking, Sally, he said. I hadn't drunk anything.

Then he didn't want to talk about it any more, so she told him about her conference, about the new designers coming out of crazy hick towns like Carterton and Te Kuiti, and she started brimming with it all, enthused, describing an outfit she had seen made of silver latex – some kind of dress, and pants, a dress and pants set involving lots of zips – but it was hard to listen to her, hard to follow.

Later in the evening they ate the Mövenpick and Sally asked, 'Chris, how come Tess was in the car with you?'

'Because she came round to visit,' he said. That was four facts. Four out of five facts.

'Listen, Sally,' he said, 'Tess was upset, and sad. She's facing some issues at home – there's been a lot of tension. We talked about the situation, and it became confusing. We ended up kissing, Sally, but I stopped, and I realised she had to go home. She wanted to stay, and she was refusing to drive back, because of her licence, and the weather, and the time. We kissed, and then she wanted to stay, but it was all wrong, and so I insisted on driving her back to town.'

This was all true. It was all true, and then he had told her four and a half facts, and perhaps he would have told her the rest, but Sally didn't answer, she just left the kitchen and he heard the front door slam shut, and the wind chime, swinging in the draught, sounding a circle of notes back down the hallway.

He sat there at the kitchen table, watching the ice-cream melt into an even pool in the plastic container. He sat there, quite still, for half an hour, and one little thought ran around in his mind, lonely and circling: the simple thought that there was nothing he could do. He realised there wasn't a single action he could take to improve this situation, or any of these situations. *I am paralysed*, he decided, sitting and watching the ice-cream melt for half an hour.

Sally came back, with puffy eyes, and a three-litre bottle of Keri orange juice. She slammed the juice down on the bench and said, 'Okay, Chris. I'm willing to talk about it. I'm willing to hear what you have to say.'

'I'm sorry,' he said, looking at her standing by the bench, her red coat dripping, the bottle of juice a bright orange square to the side of her arm. 'I am sorry about what happened with Tess.'

Fuck, I am so sorry about everything that happened with Tess. He put his head in his hands, and then her wet arms were around him, and everything seemed to be more or less all right with Sally after that.

Tess has been in a coma for twelve days. No. Louise mentally rephrases: today is the twelfth day of Tessa's coma. This is a better way of saying it – stronger, because although the twelfth day implies a thirteenth day, and probably a fifteenth, maybe even a twentieth or, at the very worst a thirtieth, it still implies something finite, a given amount of time to be marked off, a time to endure and then to be done with. *Something you get past.* When she says it this way it sounds like something purposeful and that's how she is coming to think of it now, this coma, as a dark friend, a dark hollow for Tess to bed into, to let the stillness work and work and work, a billion neurons slowly reattaching, picking up the line, reconnecting.

Last winter a young cabbage tree was knocked down in the garden. The secondary branches snapped off and the broken roots waved in the grey air, ugly and damaged, out of their element. She replanted the tree and it shrivelled down, the bundles dying off one after another, and she thought that would be the last of it. But in the end it was fine, because it was happening all along, the secret knitting of the soil. Today is the twelfth day, which means that Tess has served two hundred and eighty-eight hours of time, and all of that counts, it has to count.

This morning the doctor came around and said, What we think you should do now is talk to her. Keep talking to her constantly. We believe this can make a difference.

So even though they have talked and read to her often, today they have not stopped. This afternoon the nurse propped her up in the bed, and sitting that way she almost looked as though she wanted to chat. She is breathing for herself now, and the wad of bandages has been removed from around her head. There is only a square pad left covering the surgery wound, and already, everywhere, the fuzz of hair is thickening on her head. The bruises on her face are in the final shades of yellow and green.

Tess sat there today, propped up, with her left arm flopping unnaturally. They took turns in the comfortable brown armchair, and talked for a full seven hours. Louise, then Jacob, then Louise again, then Margie and her husband, then Ella for half an hour this afternoon, some old school friends, and then Louise again, speaking solidly to her blank face until five o'clock this evening, sitting beside the bed in the brown armchair and pouring out a torrent of words, a hundred jumbled stories, explaining the low-pressure system over the South Island, talking about the baby throwing up constantly and starting to smile, about an earthquake in El Salvador and twenty people found buried alive in a biscuit factory after seven days, about a man at the café with a pugdog and a green beret, and his girlfriend with spangled bracelets up to her elbow. The day wore on and Jacob began reciting half-remembered poems, and then in the humidity of the afternoon Louise resorted to Three Blind Mice and the Lord's Prayer, pouring out over her daughter whatever inane words came into mind, holding her here with memories and gossip and trivia, stroking her hand constantly over an arm or a foot, rubbing in circles around her ankle, or on her thigh.

And she did respond, or seem to, her eyes staying open for much of the day, and once or twice small guttural sounds gurgled in her throat. There would be a slight squeeze when holding her hand, the semblance of an expression on her face. Each tiny movement thrills in the chest, and Louise has found herself running out to call Jacob, or Margie, yelling down the phone, Guess what she did! Each spasm, each movement is immense, a gesture of infinite hope. Progress.

Driving home, the moon is high and brilliant. Light catches at the waves and at the top of the steps it floods across the front lawn. Louise notices that the grass has been mown today, and the path to the house freshly swept.

There is a box of Roses chocolates on the doorstep, but no note, and so she assumes it is from one of Tessa's many friends. These friends ring twice a day, and show up at the hospital with grapes and magazines – all sorts of things that Tess can't use but her mother can. Then she plays back the messages stacked up on the phone and there is Kevin's hesitant voice: I'm home now, Louise, I got your messages on the phone. I came around. I don't know what to say. Call me, he says, as soon as you can.

This makes a difference. He's home, and he knows. He knows, and he's ready to help. *Thank you*, she says silently, unwrapping the box right there by the phone and picking out the hard caramel with the pink and black wrapper. You're dependable, Kevin, she thinks. Thank god you've turned out to be so dependable. She wonders whether she should call him right now, whether he would come around straight away, even though it is close to eleven at night.

It's difficult to say exactly why it seems so important to talk to Kevin in particular. She knows that she has been reticent since it happened, with Margie for example, and even with the social worker, holding back a number of thoughts and questions, as though waiting for Kevin to return, and she doesn't know why this is. It is perhaps the sense that Tessa's accident is Kevin's particular concern, in almost the same way that it is hers, and Jacob's: the sense that he carries an equal stake and is inside the circle with her, suffering and doubting, not beyond, like all these other friends who are kind, concerned, upset, helpful, but essentially unaffected and unchanged.

She imagines talking to him about all this: about grief, and the black unknown future. She decides to make a chamomile tea first and take the phone to the couch, so that she can discuss matters in comfort if he can't drive over right now.

———

In the kitchen, dirty dishes are scattered across all the surfaces. The butter and milk have been left out, and all the cupboard doors are open. As she walks to the sink her left foot slides in a puddle of liquid between the microwave and the table. The kitchen is so disordered that for one moment she panics, thinking of intruders, and experiencing an urgent need to check her back, and turn on all the lights in the house. Seeing herself reflected in the dark kitchen window she observes the fright and confusion in her face, and relaxes. Get a grip, Lou, she says aloud. Over by the sink the large electric frypan has been left out and she checks inside, poking at the thick rim of fat and scraps of bacon, potato and sauce.

The sensible thing to do now would be to walk away and ignore it all, but it is disgusting, worse than a student flat, and she feels a quick, tight wave of fury; she feels unaccountably hurt, and tearful, and wants to go and yell at Jacob and Ella, get them out of bed, and force them to clean up immediately.

She is planning to do this, but by the time she has put the carton of milk back in the fridge alongside the chutney jar she finds she has lost momentum. She doesn't have the energy to rally, and hustle, and boss them into action. She doesn't even have the energy to sink down onto the kitchen floor and dissolve into sobs. Instead, she sets to stacking and rinsing the plates, moving at a slow, deliberate pace.

She peels back the yellow rubber gloves and folds one hand into the other. Her watch says twenty past twelve, and it is now far too late to ring Kevin. She finds a pen on the windowsill and makes a note on her hand while she remembers, *ring K*, because it is vital to contact him first thing, before he heads out for the day. Then she wipes down the benches, cleans up the mess on the floor, ties the rubbish bag, takes the pile of books on the table back into the lounge, and lifts the cat off the couch. He wriggles in protest but she doesn't back down, and carries him directly to the front door.

Passing the phone she impulsively picks it up and dials Kevin's number. He answers immediately. I'm sorry, she says, it's late, I've woken you.

No, he says, I wasn't sleeping, and she can hear the noise of the television, the nasal woman excited about the benefits of Blueblocker sunglasses. She has watched this advertisement a number of times in recent weeks. There is a long silence, and in the background the woman, talking rapidly.

Are you right, Louise? he says eventually, and she feels slightly disappointed then, and almost laughs aloud, because it's a ridiculous question. The answer is *No, of course I'm not all right*, and yet she can't say this, not straight off the cuff.

'I'm not bad. For this time of night. Look, Kevin –' she knows she is sounding efficient now, and brisk, '– I know it's late and I'm sorry to call at this time, but I wanted to ask if you would come to the hospital tomorrow. I think it would help Tess tremendously to see you.'

'Well, yeah, of course, of course. I'll be there. Just, ah . . . just tell me where I should go.' His voice fades in and out. He must be stretching the cord, looking for a pen. This is going badly, this is not the way this conversation is meant to unfold.

'Ward 32. The main hospital. You know where that is? Just go straight to the ward and ask any of the nurses. They all know her.'

'Ward 32. Got it. What time do you reckon's best?'

'Anytime, Kevin. Perhaps after lunch. She's generally more alert after lunch.'

'All right. After lunch. What, say, one? Two?'

'Two is fine.'

'Can I bring you something?'

'No, nothing. Just come and see Tess. That's all.'

'Sure. Right.'

'Okay, well – I'm really glad you're safely home anyway. The trip went well?'

'Bit rough. We had a few dodgy spells. But the fishing's

163

magic down that way. Gotta give it to these guys, they know what they're doing, all right. Hitting the jackpot every second day.'

'Full nets?'

'Hell, yeah. You wouldn't credit the tracking gear these boats have got now. Fish haven't got a chance. We're hauling in forty, fifty tonne a day. Only wish it was shares. No chance of that on these outfits, though. Bastards are too smart for that.'

'So when do you next go away?'

'Six weeks. Same ship. Same deal.'

'Six weeks?'

'Yeah, it's decent. But I guess there's a fair bit going on here anyway.'

'Why, what do you have on?'

'Well, I, ah, just meant Tess, really. Getting her back on her feet.'

'Oh. Well, it's not just physical, Kevin. You might get a shock. She's not . . . Tess can't do much of anything at this stage.'

'I can imagine.'

'You see, there could be long-term effects. The doctors can't predict how much of a recovery she will make.' She is spelling the situation out because the last thing she wants to have to deal with is Kevin going to pieces at the hospital, in front of Tess.

'You know, a guy I crewed with once had something similar. Fell backwards off the top of the pilothouse in high seas and smacked his head on the deck from ten foot up. His head must've cracked on it like a fucking egg.'

Thanks, she thinks. This is cheerful, this is what I need to hear.

'The guy was bleeding like a stuck pig. Out cold for weeks, he reckoned, Louise, and he says he didn't walk or even talk for close to a year, but he was back fishing by the time I met him, and a bloody good sailor at that. I was thinking about that guy today. I reckon Tess is a pretty tough kid.'

Well yes, she thinks. Exactly.

'She is. You're right. And I think it will be good for her to see you. We think she's starting to recognise people now.'

'I dunno that her old uncle's worth getting too worked up about, really. I've grown a beard. Probably frighten the living daylights out of her.'

'Could do her the world of good.'

'Might do, might do. Well, I'll see you tomorrow, Louise. It's a relief to hear from you. I was waiting.'

Later, lying in the dark, and turning from one side of the bed to the other, she realises she didn't thank him for the chocolates, or for taking care of the garden. Her memory is failing her every day, in these small, irritating ways. It's difficult to tell if it's simply the stress of the situation, or, more disturbingly, the creeping effects of age. She turns the light back on and makes a second small note on her hand, because tomorrow morning she has an appointment with the woman from the Neurological Foundation, and she can't afford to miss it. The staff nurse referred her, and also gave her some photocopied information from a clinic in the States which has had success in the field of coma arousal.

The young male nurse who comes in on the weekends told her that she could get information from an Internet site and she looked it up at Margie's yesterday. It is specifically dedicated to head injuries and has stories from various survivors. Lucinda for example, twelve years old, from Ohio, thrown last year from her horse at high speed and landing without a helmet on a concrete path. There are photos of Lucinda, a daily journal kept by her mother, comments from friends and supporters.

All this makes clear is that it's going to be bloody hard work, and that nothing is certain. She may not talk, the nurses tell her, she may not walk. Louise, Mr Kelly says in serious tones, Tess is likely to be left with some kind of disability. *Cabbage, cabbage girl*, a little voice sings in her head. Louise wants to look them fiercely in the eye and tell them they are wrong. She wants Kevin to go to the doctors, and the friends, and everybody else involved, and tell them his story about the fisherman who recovered.

Above all, she wants to dive right in, and work and work and work, and not have to sleep, not think. She doesn't want to be left alone with these terrible dreams, and the tendrils of fear that unfurl in her stomach every morning when she wakes.

Ella is changing the third nappy of the morning when she remembers. She lifts his legs to clean the yellow slime between the cheeks. His lips pucker and prepare to howl in protest at having his bottom bare in the cool draught.

One month! She says it out loud and kisses his nose. One month today. God, you're doing well, she thinks. Don't know about me, but you are doing extremely well, my boy. She slides the clean nappy under him, flips back the plastic strip and tapes him tightly in, lifts him to a sitting position and tugs a clean woollen singlet over his head. Stinky nappy in the bin, dirty clothes in the overflowing basket. The small movements that have become habit already, fluid and automatic.

She pulls up her top and lets him latch on to her breast. This too is easy now, and sometimes it even feels delicious; sometimes it tingles down through her body in a familiar way. She hadn't known it would feel like that.

While he feeds, she pulls the new photo album closer, going back over the pages. It's a proper one, expensive, with dusty black pages and thin plastic sheets between. It opens with the sequence of photos that Louise took at the hospital. First, there is one of her on the bed, arched like a snail, her face buried down in pain. The photos go right through to the end, with a close-up on his purple face.

You'll want them, Louise had said, clicking the camera at her before they left the house, you'll want these later on, and she was right, although the one that shows his head coming out is a bit much, and she's kept that one aside, put it away in an envelope. At the back of the album are Andy's photos, one to a page, placed carefully in the centre, clean and beautiful.

He called again yesterday and they chatted politely for some time, about the baby, his sleeping, and his weight. It's civil between them – they can discuss such matters – but certainly it's not resolved. Right now it seems a little too much, in fact; right now she can't deal with it. Although he's getting bigger, she thinks, feeling a tight pinch of something uncomfortable, he's going to look different already. But then, Andy only has to ask. He could come around whenever he wanted.

She hasn't had a photo album since she was ten. It's been strange to see these photos of herself, the first she has seen in years. Look at all my hair, she thinks. It's getting longer, and really scruffy. There she is sitting with Louise on the couch, smiling, the day he came home. Bleary and tired, but smiling. And fat, she thinks: I didn't realise my face had got so fat. She traces the line of her cheek on the photo, and then runs her finger along her face. She traces the same line on Connor's cheek, pushing in for the hard press of bone.

Of course she hasn't shown Louise the photo album, although she'd quite like to. She hasn't shown anyone. It isn't the time for that kind of thing. The house has grown foreign in the two weeks since the accident. It still seems unreal, and every now and then she catches herself waiting expectantly, an ear cocked to the small noises of the house, sitting feeding on her bed perhaps, or getting breakfast in the morning. She finds herself waiting for Tess to come through the door, kick off her shoes and start moaning about the heat, or talking about the latest scandal at the Greenpeace office.

She keeps visiting down at the hospital, but as Connor grows this seems increasingly difficult. Some days it takes her more than an hour to get ready and travel to the hospital. It takes at least ten minutes to walk around to the bus stop, and there isn't always a bus at the right time. Jacob goes down in the morning in Margie's car, but Connor's still sleeping then and she can't go with him. She doesn't go when it's cold, or spitting, because he's still a little underweight.

Certainly, it's fine once she gets there, enjoyable almost,

sitting and talking to Tess, putting on some good music, and moisturising her legs, or tickling her wrists with a feather. It was fantastic last week, for example, watching the physiotherapist sit Tess up in the bed. That day Tess held her own neck up for almost half a minute. Connor's just learnt to do the same thing, and she wanted to point that out to Louise, but she was worried that it might sound like a joke, and even if it was kind of funny Louise might not laugh. Louise is always there, hovering, and sometimes you get the feeling she'd rather you left them alone.

Louise is away at the hospital all day, every day. When she comes home at night she is agitated, snapping at Jacob to do the dishes and tidy up. Then she lies on the couch most of the night and sips red wine. She watches videos and sometimes starts to giggle in a falling, uncontrolled way, so that you worry that she might end up crying. But she never does.

Last night Ella watched Louise pouring out her third glass and thought: I ought to talk to her. I ought to ask her how she is. You're supposed to talk about your problems when you're under stress. If I could just get her talking it might help. That's what you're meant to do in a situation like this. But the thought of such a difficult conversation is terrifying, and she can't imagine what words she would begin with.

Instead she keeps vacuuming the house each day, and brings in the mail. She makes sure the plants are watered and she writes down messages from the phone calls that come in each morning, unfamiliar voices that ask whether there is any progress. Last week she mowed the lawns, swept the path and weeded the vegetable garden, because the thick summer grass had grown up past her ankles and the fennel was starting to take over. Once or twice she's made an apple crumble as a treat for everyone, and left it in the fridge, only to come back the next day and find it completely gone. She tries to do these things, even though she is tired, constantly tired, always craving a little more sleep, and so it's difficult sometimes to find the energy to do extra jobs. She acts in these invisible ways, and hopes that it's helpful, that Louise will have an easier time because of it, and that through some strange transfer of energy this will translate into Tess: into Tess getting better quickly.

The baby lies on the sheepskin and bats vaguely at the hanging shapes above his head. A red teddy bear, a blue starfish, a green butterfly. Blowing raspberries on each cheek, she notices how his eyes are tending to blue today – a surprising, pale blue, not like her eyes or Andy's. But they are still changing. It's hard to tell where they will end up. She wants to ask Louise about it, or, even better, Tess. If Tess were here she would say something like, Wow, chameleon eyes. She would say, what if they end up one brown, one blue? She would say, they're not exactly attractive, are they, babies' eyes?

Jacob paces in and out of the lounge, talking on the phone and fiddling with the alarm clock he has taken from Tessa's room. She could ask him. What colour do you think Connor's eyes are, Jacob? But this is stupid, because Jacob won't be interested. Jacob, like Louise, has enough on his mind right now.

'Ella!'

She startles, as if he heard her thinking. It's as if he were listening and is angry at her.

'Yep, in here!'

'Hi,' he says, appearing back at the door. 'Sorry. I didn't notice you in here before.'

Right, she thinks. I know, I'm easily overlooked.

'How's it going?'

'Good. Yeah, good.' *What, Jacob?*

'Look, I was wondering . . . have you seen Tessa's *Zooropa* CD?'

'No, I haven't.'

'I think it might be missing. I can't find it anywhere. It was pretty important to her, you know. She went up to Auckland to the concert.'

170

'I haven't seen it for weeks.'

'It would be good to play it to her. The thing is, I'm pulling together a collection of stuff to take down to the hospital – her own things, you know, to work on stimulating her memory. I've got some of her books which we can read to her, and posters, and music. What else?'

He's about to walk back out of the room, preoccupied, and it's not clear whether he's actually expecting a response or not.

'You could take some photos.'

A new wall of photos has appeared in Tessa's bedroom, pinned up above the headboard. Photos of Jacob and Tess as kids, playing in a sandpit; of Tess riding a horse, thirteen or fourteen perhaps; Tess, Jacob and Louise with thin smiles, all dressed in smart clothes, standing very straight and tall beside a black car; tramping shots, girls with strong brown legs up on the tundra, boiling tea. In the middle, a close-up of Tess with a mouthful of fingers, pulling at her cheeks.

This is a tribute, she thought when she first saw them – no, a memorial. It had made her want to cry, that close-up shot, the screwed-up nose and crossed eyes. Jacob must have put the photos up because he is sleeping in Tessa's room now, and perhaps this means he's left his flat altogether. Perhaps he's living here permanently.

'Yeah, photos could be good.'

'I've got one of Connor if you want.'

She is hesitant, saying this, because maybe he will think this is a dumb idea; maybe he will think that Connor is irrelevant, and that a photo of him won't help Tess get better at all.

'Oh, sure, chuck that in.'

He is fingering something small, flipping it in his hand. It is a ring, or a necklace, or some kind of stone.

'What's that there?'

'It's Tessa's ring. The one Mum gave her for her birthday

171

last year. The paua shell one. I found it on her dresser.'

'Oh, I like that ring! That's a good idea, she should wear it. I think she might notice it.'

'Well, actually, I think I'll just keep it for now. I think it would get in the way, with all the stuff the doctors are still doing. I'll keep hold of it.'

Sure, she thinks, I know what you're going to do. You're going to walk around with that ring in your pocket and think about your sad sick sister every time you put your hand on it. Very helpful.

But if Jacob is obsessive and dramatic it's only because he can't bear to be simple and happy when Tess is like this. But I forget sometimes, she thinks. Like yesterday, shopping in town. She completely forgot about Tess for the entire afternoon, until she got on the bus to come home. It was as though it didn't matter, as though it weren't important. Jacob wouldn't forget about it, not for a second. And I am supposed to be her friend, she thinks. I'm probably one of Tessa's best friends. But still, that's not the same as family. Not when it's like this.

The clock on the wall ticks loudly and the little sound bounces off the plastic yellow walls. She is alone in the small examination room. Outside she can hear people talking and laughing, and then a car driving past, and then perhaps a dog barking. But actually, the dog might be further away. Outside, people are relaxing, sitting in the sun and unwinding, but she is in here, inside the yellow room, and the minutes are flipping past, and now her mind must become like a clear pool: a silent, steady pool, with the facts lying beneath the water like perfect shells.

She turns the pages of the exam paper, scanning carefully, and then sinks in deep, naming cetaceans, identifying tail flukes, commenting on experiments. *Cephalorhynchus hectori*, Hector's dolphin – there it is, the one with the odd, lump-shaped fin. There is a question about a phenomenon called sulphur bottom. She remembers the photos from Andy's book – the silver, and yellow, and greenish gleam of the whale at Kaikoura – and scribbles quick sentences about diatoms, microscopic algae with siliceous cell walls that attach to the underside of the blue whale in Antarctic waters.

It's all coming easily, and it's like riding a bicycle, fast, down a hill. It's like running, striding along the beach in the middle of winter, with the sky a slash of blue and the wind hard and cold in her face, the gulls lifting and rising around her. It makes her want to laugh out loud. She is running and swooping and scribbling down the words as fast as she can, and this strikes her as astonishing, because she hasn't been able to concentrate at all up to now: she's struggled along with a head full of sludge and a low exhausted ringing constantly in her ears. But not today.

When she hears Connor whimpering she looks up, dazed. For the final twenty minutes she plugs him onto her breast and turns back to the beginning of the paper, checking each line and each box, making small alterations, guessing at the two or three gaps she has left. The supervisor comes back into the room, looks at her student card and takes the paper from her. That's lovely, she says, smiling. She strokes the baby's head as Ella burps him over her shoulder. Gosh, he's very good, isn't he? she says. Aren't you so good! The woman suddenly steps back and starts flicking her hand in the air. Uggh, she says, oh dear, as a thin curdle of vomit runs off her arm.

That afternoon the phone rings and Jacob calls out, 'Ella, it's for you!' It might be Dad, she thinks. It would be good to talk to Dad. It would be good to tell him about the exam today, and the new things Connor is doing. And about Tess, she thinks. You haven't told him that yet. But perhaps she wouldn't tell him about the accident anyway, because he wouldn't really understand how important it was, it wouldn't really mean anything to him. She is thinking about this – how strange it is that Dad doesn't know Tess at all – as she walks into the kitchen to get the phone. Then she is surprised, because it's not Dad.

'Oh, Andy, how are you?'

'Good, thanks.'

There is a long pause. This is difficult, already. Well, she thinks, you rang me. What do you want to say?

'How's Connor going? How are you going?'

'Good. Great. I took him down to Plunket last week, and he's put on another kilogram already. They reckon he's nearly caught up now. He's sleeping a bit better too, four hours at a time. He only woke once last night, which was great because I had an exam.'

She is aware that she's babbling, garbling on, filling up the empty silence down the line.

'An exam? How did it go?'

'Not bad. I think it went well. You know, for an exam.'

'You'll do well, Ella. You always do. And Tess? Is she better yet?'

'It doesn't quite work that way. Her eyes are open, and she's starting to respond more, so they think her chances are a lot better now.'

'How's her mum coping?'

'Fairly well, actually. She's amazing, she just keeps going, Louise. She's really tough like that. It's exhausting for her, though. I think it's easier now that Tess is out of intensive care, and I think it will be a lot better when she comes home.'

'Shit, it would be terrifying. It was bad enough when Connor was in the hospital. All those machines.'

'Louise used to be a nurse. It's not so bad for her.'

'I know what I was going to tell you.'

'What?'

'Remember Peter? Peter who flatted with us?'

'Of course I do.'

'He's just won a scholarship. Some flipping huge university

174

scholarship. It's worth thousands. He's going to the States for a year. It's some kind of specialist saxophone course.'

Nice, she thinks. Wouldn't that be nice.

'That's good news.'

'Yeah, he's stoked. Well, anyway, Ella, I'm ringing because . . . I'd like to see Connor.'

'That's okay. That would be good. When will you come around?'

'I was wondering if you would bring him here.'

'To your flat?'

'No, I'm staying at Mum's still.'

'Oh, I see.'

'And Mum would really love to see him too.'

She thinks of Andy's mother, and her flapping, fluttering ways, and almost says no outright.

'Um. Maybe?'

'What does that mean, "maybe"? Come on, Ella, yes or no? Yes would be the appropriate answer, in fact.'

'Well, how about you come and get him, and take him for the afternoon? Or for an hour or so. He might need a feed after that.'

'Exactly, he might need a feed. And he doesn't even know me, Ella. Look, can you help me out here? I'm only asking you to visit, not to bloody move in. And she's his *grandmother*, for Christ's sake. Can't you be a bit gracious, a bit generous for once?'

You're making me very angry, she thinks. You are so rude, she thinks. I might hang up on you now, she thinks.

'Ella?'

And what the fuck would you know anyway? she thinks. You're not the one up at four in the morning with him screaming. You're not the one walking around shattered.

'Ella, are you there?'

You're not the one changing his stinking shit and having your clothes vomited on.

175

'All right, Ella, I'm sorry. Sorry. I shouldn't have said that. I didn't mean to get angry.'

But then, I suppose you probably would do those things, she thinks, under different circumstances. You'd probably quite like to be vomited on, in fact.

'Okay,' she says quietly. 'How about Saturday afternoon? I'll bring him around. Will you be home?'

'Mum's away this Saturday, but next weekend would be good.'

'Next Saturday. We'll come over.'

'I'll come and pick you up.'

'We can get the bus.'

'No, I said I would get you. What, about two, say?'

'All right. Two o'clock. See you then.'

'See you. Oh, Ella, I know what I meant to ask.'

'What?'

'Can you tell what colour his eyes are yet?'

'Not exactly. Blue maybe. You'll have to see for yourself.'

Louise comes home and there's nothing left in the fridge for dinner so she orders a pizza. Then Jacob arrives home as well and they all sit around the table, and it's almost like a proper meal, like an occasion, except that they are all quiet. No one has anything to say.

'Have you got plans for tonight, Jacob?' asks Louise, but it's as though she's just asking the question for something to say, as though she isn't really interested at all.

'I'm going to a party. Barker's. It's his birthday.'

'You're getting on with him?'

'Hey? Oh, yeah, that. No, I think I got a bit worked up. He's a good guy, Barker. I might move back in.'

But Louise isn't listening to Jacob. She is flicking through the pages of a magazine.

Everything feels flat, and miserable; it's always flat and miserable now, and Ella feels she needs to do something, or

176

say something to make it better, to try to make the meal into more of an occasion.

'I had my first exam today.' She says this because Louise might be interested. Usually she wants to know about study, and how it's going. But Louise doesn't hear, or she doesn't answer.

'Was it okay?' Jacob asks.

'It was good. I mean, it's hard to tell, but I think I did okay.' She looks at Louise but she's immersed in her magazine.

'Now, see, this is interesting, this article recommends using smell, putting things that smell strong, or strongly familiar, near their nose. And using different materials and textures to stimulate touch.'

'What's the magazine?' Jacob asks.

'It's a head injury publication. From the States.'

They are away then, talking about the article, and really the exam is not important. She gets up from the table, rinses her plate and goes to her room, where Connor is sleeping in the cot, his arms flung out to either side.

At two and a half weeks Tess started moving her arms and legs, and had to be restrained because she started tearing at the IV tube in her arm. At three weeks she ate a spoonful of mashed banana, and sneezed, and thrashed around in her bed, furious, when a new and unfamiliar physiotherapist turned up. And now it is four weeks, and she is making all sorts of sounds, eating everything they give her. She is almost standing up alone, and she has signals for yes and no and when she needs to go to the bathroom.

But she hasn't smiled properly yet, and she can't speak; her left arm is tense and awkward and doesn't move easily, and her left pupil won't dilate. Each day Louise comes into her room and says loudly and brightly, Good morning, Tess, how are you, love? Each day she anticipates a reply, the first words.

In four weeks they have played her dozens of tapes and CDs, the same favourite tracks, over and over again. They have banged wooden blocks together in her ears; shone light into her eyes; stroked, tickled and pressed her face, her arms, and her feet; brought in garlic, perfume, bleach and freshly ground coffee to wave under her nose. Most of all they have talked, for hours. And this is the return on all those hours: to see her face shaping itself into vague expressions, her arms straining to move, her tongue pushing out whenever Louise asks loudly, Tess, show me your *tongue*.

You can see her in there now. You can see that it is the same person, battling and fighting, taking back possession of her mind and body, one little piece at a time. Louise doesn't think about the first black days any more. She finds it difficult to believe that she survived them. And she doesn't think about the old Tess, either – she won't let herself dwell for long on the single image that flicks up before her, time and time again: her tall, striding daughter coming into the kitchen first thing in the morning, wearing pink flannelette pyjamas and pulling her hair back up into a ponytail, rummaging in the fridge. She doesn't think about anything except this girl right here, with her inch of dark hair, and her mouth moving into new shapes, clasping to the therapist as she tries to walk on legs that bow and shake, and bend awkwardly.

They are working towards moving her to a rehabilitation ward. That's the next step. But it's not home, Louise thinks. They are saying that it could be two months or longer before Tess can come home, and this is frustrating because she knows it would be better there; she knows that once she's back in her own room, with her own things around her, with all the familiar smells of the house and the sound of the ocean at night, she will respond and get better. She's quite sure of it. But first Tess has to spend time in rehabilitation.

Kevin comes into the room with dripping hair, and shakes his jacket out, hanging it over the edge of the bed.

'Hi, Tess,' he says, 'you having a good day?'

Tess nods her head slowly up and down in response, and makes a low nasal sound.

'Hell, it's really pouring out there!' Louise says, annoyed, thinking of the load of washing she hung out this morning when it was clear and still.

'Yeah, it's a bit wet.'

'Do you need a towel? I'll go and find one.'

'Nah, she's right, Louise. Sit down.'

'Kevin, I was just telling Tess about the sheep.'

'The sheep?'

'Yeah, you know, your sheep.'

'My sheep?'

'Yeah, in your toilet.'

179

'Oh, the *sheep*. Bloody hell. Did you tell her about the markings?'

'No?'

'Yeah, she had this bleeding great fluorescent circle on her back. That's all I could see.'

'It was the middle of the night?' she prompts, thinking, *Come on*, tell her the story, she's listening.

'Yeah. I open the door, half awake, and it's almost pitch black. There's this great green spot shifting back and forth inside the dunny, and it's bleating.'

'You must have been terrified!'

'Didn't have time to think about it. She knocked me completely flat. About time I built an indoor toilet, I reckon.'

Tess *is* listening, and she's delighted. She's making an odd halting sound not far off laughter, and she's animated, her arms and fingers moving rapidly. Then suddenly both hands are shaking out in a purposeful gesture.

'Uh-oh,' Louise says. 'Toilet, Tess?'

Tess nods vigorously.

'Enough about toilets then,' Kevin says. 'I should shut up.'

'Could you help me with her?' Louise asks.

'Yeah. Sure.' He moves towards the wheelchair leaning up against the wall. 'This the right one?'

'Actually, no, we won't use it. We have to try and get her walking. We'll need to support her, one on each side. The therapist says she shouldn't use the wheelchair for short distances.'

'It could be a bit – urgent couldn't it?'

'Tess,' she turns towards the bed, 'do you want to try walking?'

The response is unequivocal. Tess makes a guarded sound, almost a growl, and shakes her head, pulling an expression somewhere between fury and distorted surprise.

'You really should try, honey. Maybe on the way back?'

If anything, she appears more upset this time.

'Up you go, Tess.' Kevin has opened up the wheelchair and pulled it close to the bed. 'On your feet.' He swings her legs confidently around, supporting her firmly around the waist and up into a standing position, and then helps lower her into the chair. The entire process takes seconds. Louise watches, astonished at his competence and the way he is handling Tess like this, without a trace of embarrassment or awkwardness.

'You'd better get a move on,' he says, spinning the chair around and passing her the handles.

Late at night she leaves the hospital and drives over to Margie's house. She wants to discuss the restaurant, because she's been worrying, somewhere at the back of her mind, about the finances.

'But what are you saying?' Margie asks, shuffling around the cushions on the couch. 'You can't come *back*, Louise, absolutely not. Tess is still taking up a hundred and ten per cent. You're not coming back for at least another month yet.'

'It's not sustainable,' Louise says, pouring herself out a second glass of wine.

'For me? Don't underestimate me! And Miriama is doing a fantastic job – she's been running all the morning shifts. It's busy, sure, but that's just the way it has to be at the moment. The girls all understand that.'

'No, I mean it's not sustainable financially. There's me on a full-time salary, and we're paying the girls to cover. It's been four weeks of double costs. Look, Margie, you can't pretend: I do the bloody accounts. I *know* we can't afford it.'

'Well, to be honest, I haven't even looked at the accounts since you last did them –'

'I can guarantee it'll be frightening.'

'Perhaps so, but it's necessary. What the hell else do you think you're going to live on?'

'I don't know. I don't know what I'm saying, Margie. Just

that it's going to be like this for some time yet, and the business can't afford it. That's all.'

'Well, then, I say we look at the accounts and we do the sums properly. Perhaps you want to cut your salary back to eighty per cent or something. Worst-case scenario. Maybe see if you're ready to do one shift a week. But Louise, your mental health is the most important thing. I think one way or another we carry it. If we go into the red for a few months we'll claw our way back next year.'

'Can we do that?'

'*Yes*, we can do that. Absolutely. Lou, you need to stop worrying about this. It's not your problem right now.'

Louise sighs and shuffles further down into the couch, enjoying the comfort of the wine, the warmth in her body.

'I appreciate it, Margie. Christ, I don't know how people with real employers cope.'

Margie giggles.

'It's just this ghastly sense of everything falling to pieces in the background. I haven't even paid the bills at home. I mean, I'm still driving around in your car.'

'It's fine. I told you, we're going to sell it anyway. But I take it your insurance has come through?'

'Yeah, thanks for doing that. I got a letter from the company last week. I'll go and have a spending spree sometime soon.'

'I'd better let young Chris know. He'll be relieved.'

'Oh, I didn't think to tell him. I was just speaking to him yesterday.'

'Did he come in to see Tess?'

'No. No, he hasn't done that yet. I don't quite know what's going on there. I didn't want to force the issue. He just called to see how she was.'

She had picked up the phone yesterday afternoon and been quite taken aback when it was Chris. She was unsure how to handle it. But he apologised immediately and directly. I'm sorry,

Louise, he said, I'm so sorry, and she felt a blaze of sympathy for him then, realising that he must have been waiting and suffering since it happened. It's all right, Chris, she said. Come and visit if you like. Yeah, he said, I might do that.

'Anyway, Louise,' Margie pours herself another, 'no need to worry about the bloody car, or bills, or any of that. Getting Tess better: that's absolutely all you can be expected to think about. That, and looking after yourself. Can't Jacob pick up some of the other stuff?'

'I guess he could. He's being fairly helpful. In a sporadic way. He's quite distracted, though. He's back to his writing. He stays up till the early hours and doesn't seem to do much else.'

'What about Ella then, couldn't she help out more?'

'I think she's trying. But the kitchen was left in a disgusting state the other night, and I have to admit that upset me. It was probably mainly Jacob's mess, but the fact is, neither of them cleaned it up.'

'You know what I think, Louise? I really think Ella needs to move out. She's not your responsibility, after all. She's a big girl, she can look after herself. Hasn't she got her own family?'

'She's got a father. Up north. Her mother died when she was young.'

'Well, see, Tess doesn't have a father. She's only got you. Look, Louise, you can't bloody save the world.'

'I'm not trying to. I *like* Ella. Generally. And Margie, I was there at the birth. I've never been at a birth. I mean, as an observer. It was astonishing.'

'I know. You talked about it for quite some time.'

'And when Connor came home I felt almost as though he was ours, it was like they were family, it was this exciting new part of our life, and Tess loved it, we both did. But then this happened –'

'Which changes the situation completely.'

'Which makes me think that I had Ella wrong. I really

thought she was close to Tess, but she hasn't shown much endurance with her at all. She's only seen Tess once in the past week.'

'Just tell her, Louise. Say it to her straight. She can find a flat. We could help her look.'

'You know what it's like with a new baby, let alone your first. And she's doing it all on her own – I've been there, Margie, and it's bloody hard work. I'm certainly not going to kick her out. I'm sure she's doing her best to help. And while Tess is still in hospital it's not too bad.'

'Louise, listen to yourself. You have not got the energy to deal with this. Would you rather I talked to her?'

'No, really. Connor's only six weeks old. It would be awful for her to have to leave. I don't *want* her to leave. I just want her to visit Tess. And talk. A bit more conversation would go a long way.'

'You're a crazy, generous woman, do you know that, Louise McMahon? And you worry me,' says Margie, shaking her head, and reaching for the bottle to top up the glasses.

'I shouldn't. I have to drive home.'

'Why don't you stay? We've got the spare room. I'll cook you a decent breakfast in the morning. Bacon, croissants, fresh orange juice.'

'Coffee?'

'Espresso even.'

'I'd love to.'

Crawling under the narrow cream duvet, with a vase of Margie's freshly cut roses on the bedside table, she feels herself breathing more slowly, her neck and back clicking, and relaxing, and she feels gratitude then for her strong, kind friend, for the wine, and the talk, and the spare room. *I need this,* she thinks. I'm going to need a little more of this, to get through.

She is almost asleep when she is flooded by a particular memory. She hasn't thought about it for years but the details are sharp and she can see the entire situation unfolding: Tess at two or three in the Botanical Gardens. Tess wearing a red corduroy pinafore, the one with the giraffe sewn onto the pocket. She remembers she was chatting with someone, a friend or another playground mother, and then turned around and saw Tess at some distance, climbing to the top of the high steep slide. She ran across the playground calling out Tess, Tess, stop, wait, but before she could get there Tess had made it to the top and pushed herself down, head first. The slide was far too steep, and slippery, and she went down fast, and out of control. Three-quarters of the way down there was a bump in the slide and she bashed her chin on the metal, leaving a thin trail of blood against the silver. It was there all week, the accusing mark on her chin, the little crust of hard scab, saying: *You didn't keep her safe.*

Louise flips on to her stomach and pulls the pillow over her head, tightening and releasing the muscles in her back, trying to relax. Her mind replays it again and again: the child skidding down, the red skirt, thin white legs kicking urgently, the small head bouncing against the hard, shiny surface. *You couldn't keep her safe.*

Sally has been off work for a week with a sinus infection. Chris has stayed in bed with her each day, keeping her company until after eleven, when he gets up to make her a lemon drink and bring her breakfast. He's gone to the supermarket for Panadol, tissues and magazines, he's done her washing, made hot curries for dinner to clear her nasal passages, rubbed Vicks into her back, and even wheeled the TV into the bedroom and sat up late watching videos with her, her head resting in his lap, playing with her hair and massaging her temples.

Finally this morning she woke up, sat up and said, 'Wow, I feel much better today.'

'That's good,' he said. 'That's great. So are you going to work?'

'Hmm,' she said, 'I'm not sure.'

He'd grabbed her waist and pulled her back towards him, and said, 'So, Sal, are you going to work, or are you going to stay here and have crazy sex with me all day?'

She'd giggled, and sat astride him, and said, 'Okay, babe, here's the deal: I'll stay if you call work for me, and plus, I get to choose the video tonight.'

'No,' he said, 'we'll go out. Look at you, you're all better.'

'Well,' she said reluctantly, 'but I shouldn't, not if I'm not going in to work.'

'No way,' he said. 'Enough of the geek attitude. Dinner in town tonight. A movie, and dinner. And you, sexy girl, you can choose both.'

Then he opened the curtains wide to the high trees and the day, and made love to her, and it's kept on in this same good way, all day long.

But she can't be completely better because now, in the late afternoon, she's fallen asleep again. He does the dishes, and walks out to the mailbox. There's something from the bank, and something for Sally, and a hand-addressed envelope for him. Coming back through the door he hears the phone ringing.

'Yo.'

'Good morning, I'd like to speak to Chris Ferguson.'

'I'm Chris.'

'Right. Hello there, Chris, it's David Fraser speaking from McArvey Small. You have an application in with us for one of our law clerk positions.'

'David. Hi. Yes, absolutely.'

'Chris, you have been shortlisted and we'd like to offer you an interview. Are you available Wednesday afternoon?'

He doesn't know whether he should wake Sally and tell her, or ring his mother first. He tries calling home but there's no one there. And Sally is still sleeping thickly, snoring through her blocked nose. Desperate to tell someone, to make it real – a spoken fact – he starts speaking aloud. Shortlisted, he says. Interview, he says. Wednesday. He walks to the front door, and back into the lounge, then turns and goes out into the garden where the sun is hot and bright.

McArvey Small – the application papers said that the company specialises in commercial work, tax, and mergers, with some litigation. Big enough, from what he's heard, to give him a shot at everything, but small enough that he'll get real work, real responsibility, from the beginning. But then, it's been so long now, it's hard to even think what the work would be like – he can hardly remember what it's all about. He starts to worry then that he won't be able to do it. He won't be able to answer the questions on Wednesday, let alone do the work afterwards. He thinks of the basic tasks, and of himself doing these tasks: using the library, finding references, forming an opinion. And clients, he thinks. Real work: I'd have to deal with clients.

He's suddenly scared shitless, because what if he's forgotten

187

everything, what if he misses it entirely, this one chance, turned up unexpectedly like this, on this good summer day, like an early Christmas present, like turning a corner at the end of a long black road? What if he misses it?

He starts to pace up and down the narrow path to the mailbox. No, he thinks, I won't miss it. I've got a good feeling. I think the timing is right.

He turns to head back into the house, planning to open up the cardboard box of books and notes stored underneath the bed, untouched since last year. He passes the letters lying by the phone where he left them, and picks them up to sort through. Something from the bank, which he puts on the windowsill, unopened. After Wednesday he might be able to sort everything out there, and a great many other things besides.

For instance, he thinks, it would get better with Sally, because she would say, See, Chris, I knew you were good enough; I told you it would happen. Sally would be delighted, and then it might be good between them all the time, just like this morning. He's thinking of Sally, and the way it was in bed this morning, as he rips open the other, unfamiliar looking letter. Black writing scrawls across the white unlined page.

To CHRIS FERGUSON:

You will open this letter and realise who it's from and then you're going to want to throw it away, or burn it.

You'll do almost anything to avoid reading this. That's the kind of guy you are, Chris. You can't face up to your own crap, and you can't handle me because I've known you longest of all, Chris, and I know exactly what you're like.

Why haven't you shown up to see her? Why haven't you spoken to us at all? We know why. It's because you're treacherous, and guilty. But even slimy lawyers get done in the end. (But then, you're not a lawyer, you're just unemployed, aren't you, Chris?)

I went out to the bay last week and surfed until dark. It was crowded, and there was this one guy, a grommet, who kept dropping in on me and everyone else as well. I kept thinking how much that guy was like you – always in the wrong place at the wrong time. Always coming in on someone else's territory and screwing up a perfectly good scenario.

You've screwed up more than my wave, Chris. You've done over my family, and my life. You think Sally won't know the truth. It's always the same lying denying behaviour from you. You will be left alone in the end. Everyone will turn away from you.

Jacob

He feels quite sick – nauseous, and a little as though he has been punched. Then he starts to feel angry. Jesus, he thinks, reading it again, becoming slowly worked up, slowly furious. *It isn't even true.* The loser, he thinks: he doesn't have a clue, because I *have* called, I've talked to Louise.

He doesn't want to read it again; he doesn't want to think about it any more at all. What he wants to do is go into the bedroom, wake Sally up, tell her about the job interview, and go into town for a movie and dinner. But it's there in his hand, the scrawled black writing on the plain white page, and he does want to throw the letter away then, because it's horrible, it's fucked up, and it's wrong. *Always coming in on someone else's territory.* What, Jacob, he thinks, like a dog? Are you like some fucking dog pissing on the corners of your land? *And does that make Tess your territory?*

He goes into the bedroom and carefully places the letter between the pages of Adams on Criminal Law, where Sally won't accidentally find it. Then he leans across her and kisses her on the forehead, and she wakes up and stretches, smiles at him.

189

Guess what, sexy girl, he says, and he tells her about the interview, and she jumps up, and they bounce on the bed together, shrieking and leaping around the room like children.

He wakes in the night, hot and groggy, flings the duvet back and lies with his eyes open, staring into the black room. He has been dreaming about Sally, and he reaches out and rests his hand on her head for reassurance.

She was sitting naked in a large chair, behind a desk, asking him complicated questions. He didn't know any of the answers. He was sitting there, silent, unable to talk, and all he wanted was for her to come over, come out from behind the table and take his clothes off too. He wanted her to stop talking, stop asking all these questions, rattling them off one after another. Sally asked: what if you were surfing, and there was a fat-arsed shark, what would you do in this situation, Mr Ferguson? Would you tell the truth? Sally was standing on the desk, wearing nothing, and then she was wearing a dark blue hat, peaked at the front. She asked: What if you were driving down the street, and somebody dropped in on the wave? Would you employ this person?

Then he was in the water, and she was sitting in his lap, unzipping his pants, and she had a camera, and blinked lights into his eyes: orange, then red, orange then red, orange then red, over and over again. He was in the water, his face was wet, his face was under the water, and he couldn't see, the light was up above, blurred into a single shade of red, blazing, until he woke up, hot, groggy and thirsty.

Ella gets the pram from the wardrobe and carries it into the hallway, but then thinks again and takes it back to the bedroom. They won't need it because they are only going to the house and back again; they shouldn't have to walk anywhere. She checks her watch. Andy said he would come at two, and it's quarter past already, so she sits down to wait on the couch, wearing her backpack full of spare nappies, cream, wipes, a hat and jersey. It is a hot, bright day and it feels like summer, but the weather has been changing and it could get cold, or windy.

'Are you going out?' Louise asks, coming into the lounge with a basket of laundry.

'Just for a while. I'll be back for dinner.'

'Oh, dinner . . . well, actually, I'm going to be out until quite late myself tonight. I'm seeing Margie about the accounts. But I think there's some chicken left over in the fridge, and some corn, and carrots. Jacob's out too, I think.' She looks up from folding the towels. 'An empty house again. Sorry, Ella.'

'Oh, that's fine. I just meant I'd be back about six, that's all. I didn't expect dinner. We're fine.'

'Are you going somewhere nice?'

'Not exactly. I'm taking Connor to meet his grandmother.'

Louise holds a pair of pants up in her hands, and starts scratching at a stain on the knee. 'Is that Andy's mother?'

'Yes.'

There is a brief pause. Louise puts the pants down on the chair and looks across at her, and she seems to be thinking.

'Of course. Andy's mother. Connor's grandmother. Sorry, I forgot.'

But I forget too, she thinks. About his other grandmother.

'Shall I get some milk while I'm out?' she asks.

'No. There's plenty left over at the restaurant.'

The doorbell rings and she stands carefully, balancing the baby on her shoulder.

'Good luck,' Louise calls after her.

The first thing Andy's mum says is, 'Ella, it's *great* to see you again.' She kisses her on the cheek, and then pushes past her, bending down beside Andy to look in the car seat. 'And hello!' she says, cupping her hand around his face. 'It's *very* lovely to meet you, little boy.'

'Mum, come on, out of the way,' Andy says, hoisting up the plastic seat. 'Let's go inside.'

Coming into the lounge she sees the low table loaded down with a cake, a plate of crackers and some kind of pale cheese, three yellow cups on matching saucers and a plunger of coffee.

'Come in, Ella darling,' Andy's mother says. 'Sit down, make yourself comfortable. Now, what can I get you? Would you like tea, or coffee?'

'Um, just a glass of cold water, please.'

'I've got some fresh orange juice? Or lemonade?'

'Oh, no, water's fine, honestly.'

'Yes, you're quite right, orange juice is no good at all when you're breastfeeding. I had terrible problems with my youngest – Jonathan – anything acidic and he'd be windy for hours. How is the feeding? You do look awfully tired, Ella. Are you eating well?'

That familiar feeling is rising up, immediately: the same angry feeling she always had with Andy, and his mother is standing there, standing right beside the car seat and looking down at her in that serious, concerned way, waiting for an answer.

'Hey, Mum, lay off, eh?' Andy says, smiling. 'She's just come in the door.'

'Look, he's waking up now,' she says, grateful that Connor

192

is stretching and batting his eyes open. 'Would you like to hold him?'

'Oh, but wouldn't I just!' Andy's mother says, moving over to the car seat. 'Here, let me get him out. Gosh, he's still very small, though, isn't he? Three weeks premature, Andy said?' But before Ella can respond she has lifted him up entirely, spun the green blanket around him, crooked him into her arm and started talking to him. 'Those eyelashes! Look, Andy, isn't he *exactly* like Jonathan?'

Andy stands beside his mother and they smile down at Connor with their heads leaning in together, and they look so alike, standing there like that. And he will probably look the same, she thinks, and then the angry feeling comes back. She knows she isn't being fair, and she knows she should try harder, but it has always made her feel like this – the perfect house, with the matching colours, and everything so pretty, and everything put away.

Connor starts to whimper, and she comes straight across and takes him, saying, 'I think he's hungry.' Then Andy and his mother step back, and look awkward.

'Where can I feed him?' she asks.

'Oh. Right. Sure. How about the bedroom?' His mother answers. 'Just down the hall and to the left.'

She stays in the bedroom for twenty minutes deciding what to do. She tries feeding him but he's not interested, which is hardly surprising as he only fed an hour ago. She checks his nappy, but that doesn't need changing either, so she walks around the room, jiggling him, and looking carefully at each of the six pastel paintings of various kinds of flower, and the photos of the two boys when they were small. There is a soft tap at the door.

'Hello?'

'Ella, it's me.' Andy's voice comes muffled through the wood. 'Can I come in?'

'Sure. Come in.'

He's surprised when he sees her, she can tell. He's surprised because she's standing up, and jiggling.

'He's finished. Just burping.'

'Of course. Just wanted to see if everything's okay.'

'Fine, yeah. We won't be long.'

'Sorry about Mum,' he says, sitting down on the bed. 'She can be a bit overbearing, I know. But she's excited. Honestly, she's spent the whole week talking about him, on the phone to the entire network, and hunting out the old photos of us. She's been waiting so long to see him.'

Well, that's not my fault, she thinks. You could have come around anytime. You could have brought her over.

'And Connor's her only grandchild. Ella, I think you need to understand that this is quite a big deal for us. In fact, it's a big deal for me.'

Yes, she thinks. Of course it is. I know that. Of course it is.

'There's something else, too.' He is sitting on the bed and looking straight at her, a serious look, and he won't turn away. He keeps trying to meet her eyes.

'I want us to talk about it properly. I think we need to sit down together and work out what we're going to do. Perhaps Mum could look after him for a couple of hours – it doesn't have to be today, but soon – and we can talk properly about it, the future, everything.'

That's reasonable, she thinks. That's a reasonable thing to ask. She kisses Connor's hand, and looks at the floor and doesn't say anything. There is a long pause, and she wants Connor to start crying, or to burp – anything at all to interrupt that concerned expression on Andy's face.

'Ella,' he says, 'I've been very patient.'

It's fair enough, she thinks. He just wants to talk about it. But he keeps going on, and she wants him to shut up now, just to be quiet for a minute so she can think clearly, and then she'll be able to say something.

'But I've been getting angry recently, and worried too. I think it's going to be damaging for Connor if you keep going down this path . . .'

What path? she thinks, suddenly furious. He's two bloody months old, Tess is in hospital with head injuries, and I'm simply surviving, that's all. There is no *path*.

'. . . and, well, sometimes I feel like you think you own him. Like he's your toy or something.'

Well fuck you, she thinks.

'I'll call you, Andy,' she says, gathering up the blanket from the bed. 'I'm going home.' He stays sitting, rigid, not moving.

'*Selfish*,' he hisses at her back as she walks down the hall and into the lounge, and awkwardly grabs up the car seat and her backpack with her one free hand. Then Andy's mother is on her feet and they are both following her down towards the door, but she doesn't look back until she is out the gate. She turns around and says, I will call you, Andy, and keeps walking down the street until she gets around the corner, when she stops to buckle him into the car seat. All the way to the bus stop it bangs hard against her knees and she wishes she had brought the pram.

They transfer Tess and everything in her room across to the rehabilitation ward, and within a week the new room has become a riot of colour and clutter. There are over forty cards strung up in rows across the windows and pinned all around the walls. Three mobiles hang from the ceiling: one with stars and moon, one with coloured glass animals, one with shells. Each week Louise buys a new bunch of flowers for her, and there is a particular place for these in the new room, right in the middle of the windowsill. At the moment there are five orange roses, and next to them an arrangement of shells and dried seaweed collected by Margie's son. All the puzzles, books, tapes and videos are stacked in the corner, and on the far wall, underneath the window, Louise has put up the posters from Tessa's work: perfect, bordered shots of the bush, thick with punga trees; mountains catching the early light; grey surf pounding on West Coast beaches.

Louise arrives early on a Tuesday morning and is surprised to find Kevin and Tess sitting together on the couch in the dayroom, watching television, with twin cups of steaming tea set out on the low table in front of them. The couch angles away from the door and neither of them notices her hovering at the back of the room. Tess looks beautiful from behind, her neat cropped hair revealing the fine tendons at the back of her neck. Kevin's head is just visible, his dark hair long and scruffy.

She is about to come rushing through and greet them both when Kevin starts speaking. Louise hangs back in the doorway because it's difficult to imagine what Kevin could be talking to Tess about, alone, in a situation like this. Of course it's not exactly the right thing to do, listening in like this, but she's curious, and decides that it's not entirely wrong either, because

196

it is a public space after all. She slides silently outside the room and leans up against the wall by the open door. The television is down low. There is no one else in the room and Kevin's words carry quite clearly out into the corridor.

Johnson, he says. That was the guy's name. Keith Johnson. We used to call him Shot.

Then Tess seems to ask something. She has started to speak now, in a low, whispering voice that you have to lean in close to catch. Kevin says, What's that? Oh, because you could count on him for a shot of scotch. I've no idea how he managed to get so much of it on board. Still had supplies after a fortnight. So, we were down in the great Southern Ocean, right, on the *Solomon*, a mid-size trawler – she's in pretty good nick.

Louise peeks around the corner and sees the back of Tessa's head nodding vigorously.

End of April. It's been two weeks, and we're about ready to head home . . . eh? what's that? Toothfish. Yeah, yeah, I said that. What? Oh, all right, Tess, give us a break. Look, a man's got to make a living, doesn't he?

It's quiet, and she strains to hear what Tess is saying but it's impossible to make it out above the low chatter of the cartoons.

Look, I'm just the bloody guy on the deck, all right? Not my call what we're fishing for, we just fucking do what we're told. Anyway, the purpose was scouting around more than fishing. Now, do you want to hear this or what?

Louise feels her face burn and wants to leap in and speak sternly to him because he shouldn't speak to Tess like that – he shouldn't shut her up. It's extremely important that she practises speaking, even if it is difficult to understand. But without being able to see his expression it's difficult to tell if he's actually annoyed or just having her on, and also, it would be embarrassing to step in now, and so she stays where she is, listening.

It's around negative fifteen, this particular day. That's

Celcius. Bit less in Fahrenheit. The scales meet at forty below. Fifteen's not a bad temperature. In a moderate wind it's fine as long as you're working. Your fingers'll go pretty quick, and breathing's a bit of a hassle. The air chaffs away at your lungs a bit. Breathing through your muff helps, but it crusts up pretty solid. You need to look out for your eyes, too. Shut them for too long and you can't open them – your bloody lashes freeze over. But on a fine day it's great out there. You've got a clear sky above you, you're busy on deck, you're in paradise.

So we're down past the Campbell Plateau, right, and we decide to head down further for a final couple of days. The captain reckons there's a goldmine out past the great Pacific Basin. We'd had a slow time of it and the holds were only half-full. That skipper was a greedy bugger. He didn't give a shit about zones and what have you. He was a fucking cowboy and he wasn't about to head home without a decent catch. Of course in hindsight it was a mad idea. We should never have been that far south in that bloody pipsqueak of a boat. She's a sixty-footer, the *Solomon*, and not really cut out for any kind of serious weather. But the skipper was dead on, because there was a shitload of fish down that way.

We slip past sixty south and it was all on. Twelve hours of the best fishing I've seen in my life. As I say, this guy's like a man possessed, and we keep pushing our luck. By the end of the day we must have been sitting pretty low in the water because we're taking seas aboard each time each time the rig comes up. It's not pleasant, I'll tell you, a foot of water at that temperature swilling around your ankles.

It's mid afternoon, we're changing shifts and the skipper picks what looks like a reasonable storm coming in from the west. The wind is going to be a challenge down there at the best of times, let alone with the kind of load we were carrying. Within half an hour we were recording forty, fifty knots. Now, that's one thing in the Strait but another thing altogether south of sixty with a full load. Pretty soon we started making ice. We're riding a high sea, the spray's kicking up and there's ice layering up on the rigging, so the skipper sends us out there with bloody sledgehammers to bash away at it, but the wind at that kind of temperature fucking kills you – there's no way you can stay out there more than a couple of minutes. Then even if you do get a decent whack in, the ice comes down in sheets, and of course the deck is slick, so the whole time you're trying to keep your head clear and your feet somewhere close to steady. We're starting on a bloody unhealthy lean and I can hear the skipper swearing his fucking head off because he's losing steering.

Louise slides her back down the wall and sits on the lino. A nurse passes and asks if there is a problem, and she smiles and shakes her head, waves her away. She's absorbed: she's never heard Kevin talk for this long.

It was quick, he says. Shot was down at the stern having a go at the big winch when the boat keeled hard and he slipped – got picked up by a wave and he was over. Couldn't have chosen a worse time for it. Fucking ten years of hauling gear and he goes overboard bloody chipping ice. It was touch and go for old Shot, I tell you. Survival time in the water down that way is about ten minutes flat, and that's it, kiddo, no second chances. I was up on deck at the time, up by the pilothouse, and heard the call. One of the boys got a line out to him straight away, and the skipper did a fucking incredible job of holding the ship in that kind of sea, but Shot was struggling to hold on. You could see him losing it. We rigged up a ladder and one of the crew went over to get him up the side.

When we finally got Shot up he was well and truly out to it. We spent the next four hours trying to get him back to some kind of temperature, besides trying to get out of the damned weather. Shot was fine in the end but I think he quit at sea after that. And the *Solomon* held up too, but I tell you,

I would never go back to the Southern Ocean in anything smaller than a fucking liner now. It's a different story on these freezer trawlers. Get down below on one of them and you could just about kid yourself you're on land. They've even got these dinky fucking personal heaters for each bunk. It's a whole new game these days, Tess.

Louise stands and quietly leaves. I'll come back later, she thinks. I'll go and get some jobs done. She takes the lift and heads back down to the main doors, feeling slightly disoriented, and drives down to the shops in the heavy morning traffic. The footpath is crowded with school kids, jostling one another and calling out, and occasionally making quick, darting movements in the direction of the road. A heavily loaded bus rumbles past on her left. She negotiates her way into the last available carpark outside the bank and steps out onto the street.

The teller asks her if she would like a receipt for her deposit. Yes, she says, thanks. She is dazed, thinking about Kevin's working life: how it unfolds far from shops, banks and streets, in places where these little complicated concerns are entirely irrelevant.

The sound cuts into her dream. He is crying, again, and Ella wakes immediately, staring into the black, with a thick buzz of tiredness singing in her ears. He keeps crying, louder and louder, and she flicks on the bedside lamp, picks him up and tries to feed him, but he turns his head away. His fists punch the air and he screams until his breath expires, his face starting to turn a mottled purple red.

Hush, now, she says, standing up, lifting him over her shoulder the way he likes. Hush, be quiet, Connor. Be quiet, you'll wake everyone up. Please, please, shush. She is pleading with him now. Louise is sleeping on the other side of the wall and it makes Ella anxious when he cries like this because Louise looks so tired at the moment.

She pulls on her socks and walks down the hallway into the kitchen. The green digits on the microwave blink in a steady rhythm – 5:20 – only two hours since he last went back to sleep. She puts the radio on low and starts singing to him, *I can't stand the rain, against my window, bringing back sweet memories.* She sings, and bounces, she changes position, flipping him around on to his stomach, and cradling him tight in her arms, and she offers him the breast again. But he tosses his head, furious, and he doesn't stop, he just cries, stopping only to take in a breath, then each new shriek reaches higher than the last. She can feel the muscles in her neck bracing, and tightening, and suddenly she wants to kick something, to kick hard; she wants to stamp her foot, she wants to run out the door and leave him here, leave him on the floor, and go and sleep alone in the garden shed. *Shut up!* she whispers at him. I am so tired, she thinks, I am just so tired. I don't know if I can do this any more. *But you have to*, she thinks. *You have to.*

———

201

When she wakes the door is open and someone is walking around. She opens her eyes to see Louise putting something down on her bed.

'Sorry,' Louise whispers. 'Didn't mean to wake you. Here's your mail.' She hands her a brown envelope, a yellow envelope and a small white package. Three things, all at once, all for her.

'What's the time?' Ella asks, sitting up.

'Nine o'clock. He's having a good sleep.' She nods towards the cot.

'It was a bad night, actually. I'm surprised you didn't hear him. He woke up five times. I just got him back down at six.'

'Oh, hell. You must be shattered. It's bit early for him to be teething, I guess.'

'Yeah. I can't think what it is.'

'Could be a bit of colic.'

Colic. What's colic?

'Colic. Right. What do you do for that?'

'You could try drops. I'll pick some up at the chemist this afternoon.'

'That would be great. Thanks.'

Louise leaves the room and she is alone with the mail, with the white package, and the yellow envelope, and the brown envelope. The white envelope has the little green university logo in the corner. *Results.* There is a phone line for results but she hasn't rung, and she hasn't been up to check the noticeboard either. Last year she called every second day, but this time there hasn't been space to think about it. And suddenly, here they are.

She doesn't know whether she should open the letter right now, immediately, or perhaps wash and dress, and make a cup of tea, and walk across the road, sit on the rocks overlooking the sea and open it there. Or open it now, still in bed, but make herself wait until she has opened the other mail first. She feels that there ought to be some small ritual befitting the situation, but nothing comes to mind.

She turns the package over in her hands and sees Auntie Jeanie's address on the back. It's soft and squishy and feels like clothes. The yellow envelope is from Dad, with his familiar bumpy handwriting. She rips into this quickly and slides out a card with a gleaming blue ball hung from a softly lit tree. Inside the card there is a cheque for twenty dollars. The writing in the card covers both sides and trails onto the back as well.

Dear Ellie

Well love Christmas already and can you believe it. And a special Christmas for you with the little one this time. We are thinking of you down there and hope it is going well with the baby growing. No doubt it's hard work for you, you will be such a good mum and I know your own mum will be looking down and proud. Perhaps you will come up in a few months when you are not so busy we would love to see you both. Your old cot is still in the shed. The baby could use it but I will give it a lick of paint, I think the spiders have had a good go at it, and the damp gets in there something chronic. Your Auntie Del asked me is Ellie going to keep up the swot next year, I would get worried for my girl with all of that and a family too. Well I will try and call you on Christmas Day again maybe Conner will have a kiss for his grandad to send down the phone. Margaret sends her love too she has started knitting a special outfit that we will send in the new year. Have a Merry Christmas. You will be the old Skinny Lizzie again now so make sure you eat well.

Love Dad

She reads the letter through twice, slowly. *Perhaps you will come up in a few months.* In fact, she was planning to make a short visit over Christmas, just for two or three days. Reading the letter, she sees now that this won't work, because it would be difficult to take Connor on the bus all the way up the island

– almost impossible in fact. Also, he wouldn't settle well in the strange house, and it would cost more than she can afford, and it simply doesn't seem like a good idea any more. It would be altogether better to stay here with the family. Perhaps they will let Tess come home, just for the day, and Andy will probably want to see Connor on Christmas Day, despite the argument, and that would be okay too. So, really, there will be a lot happening here, and it would be best not to go away after all. It will be a relief, in fact, not to have to bother.

The package from Auntie Jeanie hasn't got a letter in it, just a small white card that says:

Welcome to Conner
All the Best
Jean and Family

Inside there is a towelling stretch-and-grow, new, three woollen singlets that look well worn, and a knitted set with a hat and booties, in pale green with a white trim. He won't fit any of these yet but she hasn't got enough singlets for later so that's very useful. Even the hat will be useful, although it's a terrible colour. They remembered him, she thinks. They remembered us. She feels pleased, and a little confused, and thinks, Perhaps we should go home.

That leaves one letter. She picks it up from the bedspread, thin and plain between her fingers, with the clear little pocket showing her name. She puts it back down, runs her hands through her hair, and then opens it, unfolds it, and looks, and there they are in a row down the page: B+, B, B+, A. She is astonished, her chest thumping and her face hot, and she stands up on her bed and looks at the page again, lifts it up to her face and looks carefully, and they are still there, they really are, in fine grey print on the page. *Better than last year!* Despite everything. The B is for Plants and Algae of New Zealand and that's pretty good because she didn't think she'd pass that one, not after botching up the first assignment. Look, Connor! she calls out. Look, I've done it! He stays firmly asleep. Louise, she thinks, and she pulls on her jersey and runs into the hallway, calling, Louise, Louise! But there is a note on the dresser and she has already gone. That's all right, Ella thinks, I can tell her later. She boils the jug, because what she wants is a celebratory drink, and tea will have to do, although she'd prefer a glass of port.

The baby fusses and cries through the morning so she takes him out into the garden and sits under the thick cabbage tree, letting the shadows bounce and fall across his eyes until he becomes interested and starts to watch. At one o'clock he falls asleep and she makes herself tomato soup, heating it on the element until it boils right through and a curdle of orange forms across the top.

She pours the soup into a large coffee mug and sits down to eat, thickly buttering slices of bread. Jacob turns the stereo on loud in the lounge. He's still staying in Tessa's room, although he says he wants to move out and keeps talking about shifting back into the flat with his friend Andrew Barker.

He comes into the kitchen in blue boxer shorts and an old singlet that shows the fine, lean lines of muscle in his neck and arms. His hair is tufted up and his eyes bloodshot. He opens the fridge, takes out the bottle of apple juice and tips it back, gulping until it's empty.

'Fuck, I've got a headache,' he says.

She doesn't answer. She's not sure whether he is talking to her, and also, she never knows quite what to say to Jacob.

'There's jack shit to eat. Why is there never any bacon in this house?' He pulls the Weetbix box out of the pantry and puts four into a bowl, sprinkles spoonfuls of sugar over them, pours milk on top, and sits down opposite her.

'How's your day going?'

'Fine. Louise is still down with Tess. She left a note.'

'Yeah, I'm heading down soon. You can come if you want.

I've got the car. Mum walked.'

She hasn't seen Tess for over a week – not since before Saturday and the argument with Andy. And Tess is up and moving around now: she can walk, with support, and wash herself, and apparently she's starting to talk now, whole sentences, although Louise said her voice is strange, not her own – flat, and whispering. It would be good to see Tess today. And also, I can tell Louise about my marks, she thinks.

'I'll come down. But Connor won't wake for another couple of hours.'

'I'm going soon.'

Well, then, I can't come, can I, you jerk, she thinks.

'Maybe I'll go tomorrow instead.'

'Okay. Hey, did you get your results?'

'Yeah,' she says, looking at him, surprised. 'How did you know?'

'Barker just got his. Bloody geek, straight As. But he's doing sociology, so what do you expect? Piece of piss. They're so loose in that department, you could get a degree with a lobotomy. How'd you go?'

'Good. Not that good, though.'

'Well, you're doing all that science shit. Did you get them all?'

'Yeah, I did.'

'I don't know,' he says, leaning back in his chair. 'Don't know if I can stand another year of this. Not here anyway.'

She nods. If I had had another year to myself, she thinks, I could have done it: I could have finished.

'I might transfer next year, get offshore. The States is the place. Even Sydney would be better.'

'I suppose all universities have English.'

'Yeah. Some are better than others, though. Or else take a year off, go travelling. Head for Asia. Spend some time in a monastery. Give myself time to write. Ever heard of Sigiriya?'

'No.'

'Also known as Lion Rock. In Sri Lanka. Palace ruins, on top of a six-hundred-foot rock. So there's this huge mound of granite, right, and it's sheer, straight up from the valley floor.' Jacob starts brandishing his hands around, excited, demonstrating.

'And all these pilgrims used to go there, trying to get up to the top, heading for this holy Buddhist citadel, picking their way up on footholds worn into the rock. Except they keep falling off, smashing to their deaths. Eventually the British government put in this narrow metal staircase . . .'

She's trying to picture it in her head and she wants to ask, But what about the people that lived there, the original people, what did they eat, and how did they get food back up to the top of the rock if it was that difficult? But she doesn't ask these questions because Jacob is still talking.

'. . . then, at the top, there's these cave systems, with frescoes, and graffiti from a thousand years ago. I mean, shit, we simply haven't got a clue in this country about that kind of history.'

That's not true, she thinks, wanting to argue with him. What about Paikea; what about Porourangi? But she doesn't know enough – she's not sure of the facts, or the dates – so she doesn't argue with him, she doesn't say anything.

'. . . and the palace was built by this guy Kasyapa, right, famous for walling his old man, the king, into a stone tomb, alive. Why? He gets pissed off, because the old guy takes him up to a high point, and shows him a holy man, and tells him that's the sum total of his wealth. That's it, son. That's all you're getting. If you're wise, you'll understand. But all Kasyapa wants is the gold – he's corrupted, and so he's fucking untrustworthy. Nasty treacherous bastard. Comes to a bad end, though. As he deserves. Everyone leaves him. Even his elephant.'

'Would you go soon?' she asks, because she needs to say something.

If Jacob leaves, she thinks, it will just be me here, me and Louise, until Tess comes home. She imagines how pleasant that would be, having the house entirely to herself most of the day. How easy it would be here without Jacob's moods to contend with: his ferocious outbursts, and odd hours, and the way he either looks directly at you, as though he knows the intimate details of your thoughts, or else right through you, as though you don't exist at all. He is a disconcerting presence, and when she is alone here with him she always feels slightly on edge.

'It'd be fucking amazing,' he muses. 'Yeah, I'm thinking maybe that's what I do, just give it a break for a while. The thesis isn't going to go away. I can finish it anytime. But, you know, there are issues to sort out here first. There's a situation to deal with.'

He says this with strong emphasis, as though he wants her to ask questions, wants her to say, Oh, really, Jacob? When she doesn't say anything he crashes his seat forwards down onto the floor and starts eating again.

'Anyway,' he says through a mouthful of Weetbix, 'what about you? What are you going to do?'

Well, I'm not going to Asia, she thinks, or Sydney or the States. That's clear. It's about the only thing that is clear to her at the moment, because she isn't thinking about next year yet; she isn't even thinking about the summer, except that she will have to go on the benefit very soon, have to organise that this week, in fact, before the office closes for Christmas. Her student allowance stopped two weeks ago and her overdraft is near the limit.

She's dreading it, walking into that office, because she knows what they will think about a skinny brown girl with a baby on her hip, and she's dreading the way they will look at her, and the way they will curl their lips and tell her the rules, and the way that her name and her son's name will be entered into the system, turned into data for someone to punch into a keyboard somewhere for ten dollars an hour, and transformed later into statistics to be read out in social policy classes, and argued over in the newspaper. She imagines how they will look at her birth certificate when she's gone, and cock an eyebrow, and someone will lean across the desk and say, Another one from the East Coast, and it would be useless, completely futile, to try to explain, to say, But that's not me, that's not how it is. *This isn't what I came here for.*

Jacob is still looking at her, waiting for an answer.

'Keep going, I guess. Do one paper at least. I should be able to do that. I've pre-enrolled,' she says.

'Where will you live?'

'I don't know yet.' She quickly finishes eating her soup, realising that she will have to talk to Louise about this as well, because nothing is clear.

Connor settles down to sleep late in the evening. Once he has stopped sniffling and jerking she comes out into the lounge to find Louise there, sitting on the couch with a glass of wine and a book. *Now,* she thinks. *I should talk to her about this now.* And she sits down on the floor.

'Hi, Louise.'

'Hi.' Louise looks up from her book. 'Oh, hi, Ella.'

'How was Tess today?'

'Not bad. She slept a lot of the day.' There is something odd in Louise's voice, something sharp and hurried. That's all she says, that Tess slept a lot of the day, and then she turns back to her book. Well, Ella thinks, perhaps this isn't a good time. But I need to talk about it. I need to ask her what she thinks, about next year and everything, and if I don't talk to her tonight I might not see her for a few days. And I want some wine too. I could have some wine with her, to celebrate.

'I was wondering, Louise –'

'No, I'm sorry, Ella, I didn't get to the chemist today. I didn't have time.'

The drops, she thinks. She didn't get any.

'Oh, that doesn't matter. He's gone to sleep now. He might do better tonight, I think. He's worn himself out crying all day. Actually, I wanted to ask you about something else.'

'What's that?' Louise asks, but she doesn't look up from the page.

'Will it be okay for me and Connor to stay on here next year?'

Louise doesn't say anything, she keeps reading the book, but her face is turning slightly red and her jaw is moving, tensed.

Shit, she thinks. That's not how I meant to say it.

'Look, Ella.'

Louise puts the book down and stands up, and so she stands up too, because it feels really stupid, sitting on the floor when someone else is standing and talking to you.

'I've been meaning to talk to you about this for a while. I don't want you to misunderstand me – I was truly happy for you to come and stay with us.'

No, Ella thinks, let me say it again, let me try again.

'Connor is very important to all of us. And so are you. But we are having a crisis . . .'

'Oh, I know, I know, Louise, I didn't mean . . .'

'Tess has serious head injuries. Perhaps it's hard to understand how much strain this is putting on us.'

And she wants to interrupt again, she wants to say, No, Louise, I said it all wrong, that's not what I meant at all, please stop now.

'In the longer term I have to think about what we can manage.'

I'm being demanding, she thinks. *Louise thinks I'm too demanding. That's what she's saying.*

'The doctors think that Tess should be able to come home by the end of January. After that it's going to be a great deal of work, for me in particular, and realistically I think you might need to look into some other options, Ella. Even something temporary – just for a couple of months. Perhaps you could come back once we're a bit more settled.'

But she already understands exactly what is being said. And she does have other options, or she will make them, somehow, because she is not going to make demands.

'Sure. I'll start thinking about it,' she says, and turns to walk out of the room.

'Oh, hell.' Louise flops heavily back onto the couch. 'Ella. I want the best for you both, and if it wasn't for Tess it would be fine. But don't worry about it now. We can start thinking about this after Christmas. Let's just enjoy Christmas.'

Louise is looking at her anxiously.

'It's okay, Louise,' she says, 'really, it's fine,' and she's thinking how it hasn't been a pleasure for Louise at all, how they have been imposing, she and Connor, how they have been difficult, and in the way, at the worst time, when Louise has been dealing with the crisis. Then she wants to vanish, she wants to dissipate into the air, or fade quietly into the pattern of the wallpaper, but instead she goes into her room, where it is dark, and slides silently in under the covers, and listens for a while to the rise and fall of Connor's thick breathing, until she can think, clearly, about what to do next.

Chris is sitting outside on the grass, with an empty beer can and the phone beside him. He's about to go inside and get another when the phone rings. When he realises that it is David, from McArvey Small, he knows what he is going to hear. *I've got it*, he thinks, the idea coming to him clear and complete. A lawnmower starts up behind the fence so that he doesn't hear the actual words spoken, and he also doesn't hear the words that David says next. He walks into the hallway and David is saying, If you could return it to us by Tuesday, that would be great. Chris has to ask to have the information repeated. David explains that they will courier a contract around to his house this afternoon, and this seems the most impressive thing of all: the idea that papers will arrive for him, at his house, official papers, under urgency.

He calls his mother at work.

'Oh, Chris,' she says.

'Finally, Mum,' he says.

'Oh, Chris,' she says again, 'darling.'

'Shall we come up for dinner to celebrate?' he asks.

'Great,' she says. 'Good idea. I'm so pleased. Have you called your father?'

'No. I'll call him now.'

'Tell him to pick up a good wine on the way home. No, actually, I'll speak to him myself. When do you start?'

'The tenth of January.'

'And what's the salary?'

'Twenty-eight thousand.'

'Good grief, is that right? They're terrible to graduates, aren't they?'

'Mum, what are you talking about? It's a bloody fortune.'

'Well, that's right, it is. It's good. It's fantastic Chris.'

When he gets off the phone he makes a cup of coffee instead of opening a second beer and sits back out in the sun trying to calm himself, trying to put his ideas in order. Everything's going to change, he thinks. My whole life will be different. He imagines getting up at the same early time each day, shaving and putting on an expensive suit, catching the train in to work, and walking into a tall glass building, to his own chair, his own computer. I wonder if I get my own office? he thinks, and I wonder if it's anywhere near a gym? I might join a gym. Twenty-eight thousand, he thinks, the number repeating over and over in his mind. I'm going to save so much. We could buy a house. We could go overseas.

Thinking about all this, he decides that he is going to tell Sally everything. He's going to tell her exactly what happened with Tess, because it's hanging there still, unresolved, and this is the right time to resolve it. In fact he's always wanted to tell her. All along he wanted her to know, but the opportunity has never come up. And it has nothing to do with Jacob's letter, he thinks. He's simply decided that the time is right to tell her, now, at the same time as he tells her about the job. Because then it will all be okay: it will be resolved and clean between them, and they can start saving together for a house. We could even go on holiday, he thinks: we could go down south for a week before I start. I'll take out a loan, because I'll need one anyway, to buy a suit.

He suggests the holiday straight off, when she comes in the door that evening. Shall we go on holiday, Sally? he says. She puts her bag down and looks at him, interested but confused. And would you like to go shopping with me? What are you talking about, Chris? she asks, starting to grin. Well, I thought you could help me choose a suit, he says. For my job. No! she says. *You got it?*

He almost lets the other matter go. Sally showers, and he sits waiting on the bed, waiting for the clunking noise when she turns the tap off. He fiddles with the settings on his watch and practises a variety of sentences over and over in his head. *Hey, I should just clear something up.* Baby, before we leave, could I talk to you about something? *Sally, there's something I need to say.*

She comes out of the bathroom in a cloud of sweet scent, a towel tucked around her, and another wrapped around her hair. Stray drops of water cling to the skin on her shoulders. When he sees her like that he wants to take the towel off her, lay her down on the bed and stroke her breasts and legs. He doesn't want to have to talk about this at all.

'Hey,' she says, unravelling the towel from her head and shaking her hair out. 'What's the story? You look sad!'

'You think I'm sad?'

'Well, Mr Job, you certainly shouldn't be.'

'I'm not sad. But . . .'

She lets the towel around her body drop to the ground and he watches, distracted, as she steps one foot and then the other into her black cotton pants.

'. . . I need to talk to you.'

She fastens the catch on her bra and spins it around to the back, flicking the straps up onto her shoulders.

'Well – talk,' she says.

'When you're dressed.'

She's concerned now. She looks up, looks at him, concerned and confused, standing there in her bra and pants.

'Are you serious?'

'Yeah. I am.'

She pulls a cotton dress over her head, runs a handful of mousse through her hair, puts on a necklace, sprays perfume on her wrists and sits down beside him on the bed.

'Okay.'

'You know how I explained about Tess?'

'Yes,' she says, sounding guarded.

'I didn't just kiss her.'

'Oh,' she says.

'I slept with her.'

She stands up, and he can't look at her. 'You utter fuck,' she says.

She walks out of the bedroom and he sits there, waiting, and listening, but it is quite silent in the house. He cannot work out where she is or what she is doing. Eventually he comes out into the kitchen. Her car keys are gone from the hook and she has left a note on the table. *Gone to Fiona's. I'm leaving for the night,* she has written. *I'll contact you tomorrow. Don't try and call me.*

He has to decide what to do next because his parents are expecting them both for dinner in half an hour. He thinks perhaps he should go anyway, eat the roast dinner and cheesecake that his mother will have prepared, make up some explanation about Sally, and join in the toasts to himself and the new job. *Jesus Christ,* he thinks, what were you expecting, Chris? What the hell did you think she would do?

He imagines her arriving at Fiona's house, crying, yelling or raging, or perhaps still quite calm, setting down the facts, and he feels a bit ill then. He decides that he can't possibly go out because he won't be able to pretend, and thinks that instead he might just lie down in the bed, try to sleep, try to forget everything, until she calls him tomorrow. In other circumstances, he realises, and at other times, he would have called Jacob about now, to go drinking. I could get plastered, he thinks, opening the cupboard, looking for the bottle of vodka. I've got enough reasons to.

But then the phone rings. It's his mother, asking him to buy cream on the way up, and he says, Sure. Oh, and Mum, he says, Sally won't be able to come. That's a pity, she says. Your uncle and aunt are here. And would you bring up the contract? Your father would like to have a close look at it.

———

So he goes to his parents' house, and eats the pleasant meal at the table, set with the good wine glasses and the silver cutlery. If they notice that he is a little flat, a little less excited than might be expected, no one says anything. 'Where's Sally?' his brother Marcus asks as he passes a plate of beans across the table.

'She's got a meeting,' he says, quickly and easily. 'For work. She couldn't get out of it.'

'What's the news with Tess McMahon?' his mother asks.

'I spoke to Louise a couple of weeks ago,' he says. 'She's making some progress. I think it's slow.'

'You haven't seen her?' his brother asks.

'No,' he says, and then he can't understand why he doesn't tell them all, why he doesn't simply say, No, I haven't seen her at all, because her brother is furious with me, and screwed in the head.

Over boysenberry cheesecake his father talks about the various people he knows who work for McArvey Small. 'You should give this guy a ring, Chris,' he says, pulling out a business card with a small black and red logo in the corner. 'It won't hurt to find out a bit of background.'

Driving back along the motorway he imagines that perhaps Sally will have changed her mind, will have come home, and be resting in the bed, angry but ready to talk. Don't be so bloody ridiculous, he thinks. But still, he does believe that this will happen – eventually, perhaps not tomorrow, perhaps not even the day after, but eventually Sally will come back, and he will apologise properly, and it will be all right between them. He believes this because the signs are all there. It's clear in the fat glow of the moon, rising over the hill; clear in the individual notes of Vivaldi sounding out from the car speakers; clear in everything, all around him, that this is his time now, time for things to change, and the end of all the bullshit.

The signs seem so clear that when he arrives back at the

house and finds a letter pushed under the front door, a hand-delivered letter with nothing but 'Chris' written on a white envelope, and opening it finds inside another white page with black writing, he thinks that this must be an apology: Jacob, ashamed and embarrassed, writing to take back his mad words, his accusations. He reads it under the dim hallway light.

CHRIS

Alone in the night, what do you see? Your life is a story of cowardice and lies.

There are numerous examples. Like Marchant Ridge, when you gave up. You wouldn't go on to the hut, and then it was you crying like a baby in the rain, when the whole trip was your idea in the first place. You blamed everything on me, and that is entirely typical of you. Avoiding and denying.

But the fact remains that you are responsible. You nearly succeeded, but she's not dead. She may be walled up alive in her tomb, but she's still Tess, and she's going to come out of it, and tell everyone exactly how you tried to kill her, simply because you didn't want Sally to know the truth.

Louise knows you have no integrity. You're not fit to be considered anyone's friend. No one trusts you, Chris, no one. You are going to lose everything. As we have, but justice will be done. I'll leave you with some words from the master. For you to contemplate.

LIKE TO THE PONTIC SEA WHOSE ICY CURRENT AND COMPULSIVE COURSE NEVER FEELS THE RETIRING EBB, BUT KEEPS ON TO THE PROPONTIC AND THE HELLESPONT; EVEN SO MY BLOODY THOUGHTS, WITH VIOLENT PACE SHALL NEVER LOOK BACK, NEVER EBB TO HUMBLE LOVE TILL THAT A WIDE AND CAPABLE REVENGE SWALLOW THEM UP.

Jacob McMahon

He reads it again, and he is surprised at first, because it's not what he was expecting; and then it makes him laugh, because it's ridiculous; and then it makes him worried, because it's hard to figure out what's happening in Jacob's head – hard to tell, from this letter, whether he's connected to reality at all. Marchant Ridge, he thinks, why is he talking about Marchant Ridge? Jesus, it's not even true, he thinks, remembering the grey afternoon, his desire to go and visit Sally. He's full of shit. Marchant Ridge wasn't my idea.

He reads it one final time. The words glare up at him and seem ugly. He's not sure what the Shakespeare at the end is all about, although 'bloody thoughts' is clear, and so is 'revenge'. He's mad, he thinks. *He's barking fucking mad.*

The words linger in his head – they are insidious, and especially the part about Louise, because he can't help wondering now what Louise really does think, whether she is part of all this, whether she knows about these letters. But he can't believe that she would say these words, or let Jacob say them.

He turns the envelope over in his hand and it occurs to him that if he had stayed here, and not gone to his parents, he would have been at home when Jacob came around. He wonders whether Jacob knocked on the door when he came, or whether he would have knocked, had the lights been on. He tries to imagine what Jacob would have said to him, face to face. He imagines opening the door, picturing in turn Jacob punching him, knifing him, and coming in for a drink.

Later that night he understands clearly that the letter makes a particular, terrible accusation, about Tess, and about what happened in the car. Then he realises that he has to talk to Jacob about this, because it's getting out of hand and it has to be sorted out.

The tall guy in the group, the one with the orange striped shirt and the goatee, kicks the hackysack too hard and it veers left and out of the circle, smacking into the shoulder of a young girl walking past in a short pink skirt. Hey, sorry, the tall guy calls out, and the girl smiles, bends to pick up the sack, and tosses it back into the circle. Her friends look on and giggle.

Ella stretches her bare legs out across the bench and watches the little scene unfold, licking her pineapple ice-block and rocking the pram. It's busy in town for a Tuesday afternoon, busier than she would have expected. It's good to sit here in the sun, eating an ice-block and watching the people. The last of the lunch crowd ebbs away and the sun shifts to the far side of the street. It pours in, hot and glaring, through the high, open windows of the café above, and when she tilts her head back she can see them up there, pale faces wearing sunglasses, leaning out, chatting and smoking. Men in black suits pace quickly back to the office with their jackets flung over their shoulders, faces wet and red in the envelope of heat. After two o'clock Cuba Mall fills with students who sprawl in groups across the concrete, resting in the shade of occasional trees. Everyone has bare feet, and they all have metal rings in their faces and plastic beads on their wrists, twists of colour in their dreadlocked hair. They look like politics students, or philosophy students, or perhaps gender studies students, and there is no one familiar among them.

She finishes her ice-block and bunches her sweatshirt into a cushion, lying back on the bench and reaching out a foot to keep hold of the pram. She closes her eyes, letting the light break into a kaleidoscope of gold and black behind her lids. It is warm here on the bench, and comfortable, and she is fine.

There is nothing she needs right now because she has eaten, and Connor is sleeping soundly under the cool hood of the pram. We are fine, she thinks. We don't need to go anywhere right now.

Later she drifts down the street, back towards the main part of the mall. She wanders around the shelves in a second-hand bookshop, parking the pram in the corner and hunting through the science and nature section. There are stacked-up back issues of *National Geographic*, and dated bird-watching guides for the shore, the bush and the high country, but there is nothing of interest about marine biology.

The Farmers' window is decked out with trees and tinsel and snow, and a large black sign says *7 shopping days to go!* Inside, in the toy section, she finds an interesting rattle – transparent, and filled with tiny purple beads that sound like rain. There's a Tommy Tippee music player she'd like to get him too. It fixes onto the cot and has lights that turn in time to the music, like some kind of personal disco, but it's bulky and expensive, so she sticks with the rattle, which she will wrap, and then open, herself.

She looks in clothes shops as well. The air inside one shop is thick and sweet with incense and she feels giddy, quite separate from the street, detached in fact from the entire situation. She flicks though racks of saris in brilliant blue, gold and red, and gently touches the light tops and long skirts with gatherings of small bells around the waist. They are made of muslin, very fine muslin – material made to lift and billow in the slightest wind and let the warm air chase along the surface of the skin. These are delicate clothes, not the kind that she has ever bought, but she is suddenly tempted by a long full dress in a pattern of blue flowers. She wants to try it on, she wants to take it over to the counter and ask, but all the changing rooms seem to be full, and there isn't a size ten, and Connor is starting to stir in the pram. Well, I don't need a dress anyway, she thinks. This really isn't the time to buy a dress, and she leaves the shop and crosses the street to the music store, because in there you can pick an album and ask to listen to it. At the music shop she can sit perched on a stool feeding Connor, and in that way another hour will go past, simply, easily, and without having to spend any money at all.

At seven the sun starts to dip behind the tall buildings. She pulls her sweatshirt on and wraps Connor in a blanket. He is awake now, and irritable. She heads towards the movie theatres and the cheap kebab shop Tess took her to just a few days before the accident. They were friendly there, all the smiling girls behind the counter, and no one seemed to mind when the baby cried.

But when she gets there the restaurant is full, with a queue forming at the counter, and all the stools are taken where they had sat together at the long window bench.

Tess had held the baby, and they were laughing about Louise and the way she had, ridiculously, put away all small ingestible objects, mopped the kitchen floor – for the first time in a year, Tess reckoned – and removed the cat's plate to the porch, all in preparation for the baby coming home. I think Mum's expecting him to hit the ground running, Tess had said. She'll be enrolling him at gymnastics class within the month.

They talked about the birth that night as well. I can't figure out how Andy knew it was happening, Ella said, and then Tess admitted that she had looked up his number in the phone book and called him. What did you say to him? she asked, trying to sound calm, although she was furious and wanted to shake Tess, or stamp her foot, to make a scene. I told him you asked me to call, Tess replied. But I didn't, she said. I never said that! You talked about him, Tess said. You kept mentioning his name, all through the morning, and anyway, you were glad when he turned up.

That had made Ella angry and the night ended badly, with tension between them, and nothing further to say. She's wondered, once or twice, if it might have turned out differently without that argument – wondered whether Tess might have stayed home over the weekend and not gone to Chris's house, and not ended up in the car, driving along the Hutt Road in the early hours of Monday morning. This is not something she's talked about, not to anyone.

As she stands outside the restaurant with the smell of hot food seeping through the open door, her stomach growls and tightens. Connor's fussing starts to turn into an earnest, bewildered cry. He doesn't know where he is, and he doesn't know why it's getting dark, and cold, and he can't see her when he's lying down in the pram. I need to eat, she thinks, and we need to be inside. Pizza, McDonald's, anything. That's the first issue right now – eating and getting inside. Then she can face the second issue – where to stay tonight – but that's pretty much resolved. There is a backpackers' two streets up, and a room with a double bed costs thirty dollars. The man in the office had looked at her a little strangely when she'd inquired, confused by the pram and her small red backpack. We don't have cots, he said. I don't need one, she answered. He sleeps with me.

The cot is at Louise's along with all the boxes, packed and ready. She got up at six this morning and sorted everything out, then left a careful note on the bed. She'll go back for her stuff as soon as she gets a place, and she's got the evening newspaper in her bag, and a green pen. While she eats her chips and cheeseburger she's going to look through the ads for somewhere cheap, shared, and near to town, which will save money, because she won't have to get the bus any more. She has bought a new phone-card and once she gets to the backpackers' she'll start making some calls.

———

Coming out of McDonald's she sees someone she knows. It's definitely him – tall, wearing a black leather jacket, standing alone and watching the old man juggle tennis balls, the same man with the brown woollen hat who juggles every night, each time she comes through town.

It's Peter, her old flatmate. Peter, who lived with her and Andy, and then, later, just with her, alone. Peter would go out late practising saxophone most nights, and he would bring home one chicken pie and one apple pie from the service station and give her half of each. Andy had said Peter was going to America. She thought he would be there by now, but he's not, he's right here, standing and watching the tennis balls circle around in a perfect, uninterrupted rhythm.

'Peter!' she calls. He's searching the thin crowd, trying to work out where the voice comes from. She walks over, dragging the pram behind her. 'It's me. Ella.'

'No way! Ella! Oh, Ella, and a *baby*?' he says.

'You knew that!'

'Of course I did. Hey, come here,' he says, and gives her a hug. 'It's good to see you. So.' He bobs down to look in the pram. 'This is Connor?'

'How do you . . . ?' she starts to ask, but then she realises that Peter has talked to Andy, that Peter already knows about all of this. 'Yeah,' she says, 'yeah, this is Connor.'

'How old is he?' he asks, tickling at his ears.

'Almost three months.'

'So you've got it sussed by now, then?' He stands back up, smiling broadly at her.

'Well, no. There's a lot to it. But he's good. Hey, I heard your news.'

'About the scholarship?'

'Yeah, that's great – when do you head off?'

'Actually, I'm not sure. The scholarship only pays for half the cost of the course and I haven't been able to find the rest of the money. And plus, Lisa might not be able to work over there. Have you met Lisa?'

'No, I don't think so.'

'So it might not happen. I'm not thinking about it too much. But what about you, where are you staying these days?' he asks.

She feels her face turning red and she starts to scuff her foot urgently into the ground.

'I'm at . . . a friend's house, but I'm actually looking for a place at the moment.'

'It's not working out there?'

'No, it's not.'

'Found anything yet?'

'There's a couple of places up near varsity. I'm going to call tonight.'

'It would be tricky with a kid, wouldn't it? You'd need the place to be just right. Most people aren't going to want to flat with a baby, I guess. Has it been hard?'

'I haven't actually called anywhere yet. It might be, I suppose.'

She hadn't really considered that. It hasn't occurred to her until now that other people – normal, everyday flatmates – would consider a baby a liability, a problem. But of course they will. She might not find anywhere, not immediately; she might need to look for a place by herself instead, which would be easier but would cost far more.

'Hey, is it really bad where you are? Like, do you need a place straight away?'

She wants to say, Yes, I do, I need somewhere right now, but it's difficult, and embarrassing, and most of all she doesn't want to have to answer any questions about why it didn't work, about what exactly happened there, with Louise, last night. She's not entirely clear on it herself and she doesn't want to have to explain.

'Because we're going down south for Christmas – you could stay at our flat for a couple of weeks if you want, while you're looking.'

'Really?'

'Yeah, absolutely. We wanted to get a house-sitter anyway, but we never got organised. In fact, it's just around the corner from our old place. It's on Constable Street, number ninety-four.'

'Are you sure?'

'Of course. We're heading off early tomorrow, so you can move in straight away. We're away until the fifth. Stay the whole time if you like.'

'Wow, thanks Peter. That's fantastic.'

'I'll tell you what,' he says, fishing around in his pocket. 'I'll give you the back-door key now,' and he pulls at the keyring with his fingernail, spinning the key around and off, 'and then you can come whenever you're ready.'

'Is there anything I need to know?' she asks. 'Plants to water, anything like that?'

'Shit, no, Lisa hates plants. No, I don't think there's anything. But we'll leave a note. Ninety-four, just remember that. Ninety-four Constable Street.'

'God, I'm so glad I bumped into you. Thanks, really.'

'No problem. And it's great to see you, anyway. And great to meet the little guy.'

'Thanks. I'll leave you some money for the power and everything.'

'Sure, that'd be good.'

Peter is nodding, and turning his head, and he's ready to go now, ready to head off down the street.

'Well, see you later then. Have a good holiday.'

'Yeah, we will. See you, Ella.'

He kisses her on the cheek and starts walking away, but then stops, and turns back to face her.

'Hey, Ella,' he calls, 'you are okay for tonight, though, aren't you?'

'Oh, yes,' she answers quickly, 'we're fine for tonight.'

Walking into Ella's room, Louise thinks at first that the room is unusually tidy. Then she realises the cot isn't in the corner, the photograph and ornaments are gone from along the windowsill, and the plastic trolley of nappies, ointments and clothes is empty. She opens the wardrobe and finds empty hangers, a pile of cardboard boxes, stacked, and the foldaway cot packed up and leaning against it. What's going on? she thinks. Where are they?

There is a note on the bed, on a piece of paper torn out of a diary, and underneath it, four twenty-dollar notes.

Dear Louise

I understand how hard it is for you with Tess and her injuries. I have found us somewhere else to live. Thank you so much for having us to stay for all this time. Thanks also for all your help with Connor. The money is to cover food and bills for this week and also any toll calls I have made recently. I will pick up all my stuff shortly. I hope it doesn't take up too much space.

Yours truly, Ella.

She sits down hard on the bed and reads it again. If it weren't for the boxes stacked neatly in the wardrobe she would think that this was a joke – some complicated trick, or perhaps some kind of manipulation.

But everything is packed and it's quite clear: she's gone. With nothing owing, and with no apparent need for further explanation. Louise feels as though she has been looking out at a familiar view and has lifted her sunglasses onto her head, so that suddenly the faint yellow tinge isn't there any more, and the full, unmodulated colours of the landscape become visible.

Ella is someone who came to stay for a time, and now she has left. That's all the arrangement was about. She was simply a guest, who has decided to bring the visit to an abrupt end, and it's clear now that there is nothing important between them. *Not even the birth*, she thinks. Obviously Ella didn't think that was significant. None of it counted – those hours, her presence, the way Ella grabbed at her hands and called out.

At seven this morning, when she had got up and gone to the bathroom, Ella had brushed past her in the hallway, ready to go, with her jacket on and the baby buckled into the pram. You're off early, she'd said, surprised. Yes, Ella said, bye. She didn't say anything else, and Louise knew this was because of the difficult conversation they'd had last night. She had felt a little weary and irritated then, anticipating a week of sulking and avoidance. But not this. She wouldn't have expected an action quite so cold, so detached, from anyone, ever.

Does Jacob know? she wonders. But Jacob isn't home this morning; he doesn't seem to have come back last night at all. She considers the possibilities in turn: perhaps Ella has gone to Andy's, or to a friend's, or home to Gisborne. But she can't be in Gisborne, not if she's coming back later for her stuff. *I hope it doesn't take up too much space.* Nothing about, I'll see you, or I'll call you, just *I hope it doesn't take up too much space.* Perhaps she's found another kind-hearted sucker and turned up on their doorstep, as mysterious and alone as she was when she turned up here.

Louise feels ripped off, and furious, and she wants to go out and find Ella, and shake her, and say to her, *You stupid, stupid girl.* More than stupid, she thinks – she is being selfish, wickedly selfish in her self-effacing way.

And where is Connor in all this? she thinks. Ella's not considering him at all. He's less than three months old, and small: he can't be carted from one house to another, and what if she's camping on the floor somewhere, and where is he going to sleep tonight with no cot? She thinks of the baby, of his new, breaking smile, the precise lines of his nose, and eyes, the tight kick of his leg, the folds of his neck, and imagines him lying alone on the floor of a strange house. This makes her wild.

She's sitting there on Ella's bed, bewildered and furious, when she hears someone coming in the front door. This could be her, she thinks. She might have changed her mind.

'Yo. Ma! Are you home?' Jacob calls through the house. Not her.

'I'm in here,' she calls back.

Jacob comes in and his clothes seem bedraggled, dirty; his hair is a mess, he hasn't shaved and his eyes are bloodshot.

'You look terrible, Jacob! Where have you been?'

'Out.'

'All night?'

'Yeah, all night. I've got a lot on my mind. Walked up to the windmill. It was wild – it was such a clear night. You could see the South Island. What's that?' he asks, nodding his head towards the note in her hand.

'You walked all the way up to the windmill?' She is incredulous. It's at least a two-hour walk. Two hours each way. 'In the middle of the night? By yourself?'

'Yeah. I've got a lot on my mind, I told you. I had to walk. Gotta keep moving. I had a sleep at Barker's place for a couple of hours this morning. We just went out for coffee.' He fidgets with his hands as he talks, as if demonstrating his energy, his need for constant movement.

She looks at him, thinking about this, thinking about Ella too, considering how the world is full of strange and impulsive kids, acting on unintelligible impulses. But it concerns her when Jacob behaves like this, staying up all night, and it's particularly concerning today because he's been out alone and he has an

228

edge about him. He's extremely agitated and this makes her think there's something going on that she doesn't know about. At times she wants to ask him directly, Jacob, are you taking drugs?

'What's the letter?' he asks.

'It's from Ella. Do you know anything about this?' She hands it to him and he reads it quickly.

'She's buggered off!'

'Apparently so.'

'Just like that. She's fucking buggered off. What a loose unit.'

'So she didn't tell you, then?'

'Hell, no. I was just talking to her yesterday. She didn't say anything at all. She'd just got her exam results.'

Oh god, thinks Louise. She's failed her papers. She's failed her exams, and she's depressed, and now she's taken off, in god knows what state.

She tries to think through the events of yesterday. There was a long afternoon up at the hospital with Tess sitting in the wheelchair, in the sun, tugging at her green cotton sweatshirt and asking over and over again, Mum, is this my jersey?

Louise had really wanted Ella to come down yesterday, and bring the baby, because Tess had been asking about him all week, looking at his photograph pinned up on the wall: Can he walk, Mum? Does the baby talk? She had suggested to Jacob that he bring them both down in the car but Ella didn't come, so she and Jacob and Kevin spent the afternoon playing Scrabble, trying to get Tess to join in, repeating the name of each letter they used. But Tess couldn't remember the letters yesterday, she simply asked the same three questions over and over: Is this my jersey? When will I go back to work? Does the baby talk, Mum?

Then she'd come home exhausted, and there was Ella, and her question about next year. Well, she certainly knows how to pick her moments, she thinks grimly.

'I'm not sure what to do,' she says to Jacob.

'What to do? You don't have to do anything. She's split. That's her call. Shit, Ma, you got enough going on without worrying about this dizzy chick.'

'Tess is coming home for the weekend. How do I explain it to her?'

Perhaps Tess won't see the baby for months now. Perhaps she won't see him ever. Tess doesn't deserve this, she thinks, remembering her at Connor's birth, traipsing back and forth for hours, carrying hot towels. She has done so bloody much for that girl. But then, there's a great deal that Tess doesn't deserve; there's not a great deal of sense or justice in any of it.

'Just tell her the truth, Mum. Ella will have to explain it herself, eventually.'

'She's not going to understand. She's likely to get stroppy and misbehave. It could bring on a serious relapse if it's not the way she's expecting it to be on her first visit back.'

'She'll cope. She'll adapt.'

'God, I feel angry! Just leaving like this, the week before Christmas. What the hell was she thinking!'

'Mum, I really can't understand how you can be angry at Ella, and yet you let Chris off the hook.'

What are we talking about here? she thinks, surprised. Were we talking about Chris?

'I mean if anyone's had a detrimental effect on Tess it's that fucker.'

'Jacob, please don't speak like that. And I think you're confusing the issues here.'

'I'm not confused. I think there's only one unresolved issue, Ma, and it's about justice.' He stabs his finger in the air. His voice is raised, he's only a foot away from her, standing in the doorway, but he's yelling, he's spitting the words out.

'Jacob, what are you talking about? You are so worked up –'

'I'm talking about the truth. I'm talking about that fucker lying and denying.'

'This is getting out of hand, Jacob. You really need to let it go. I've spoken with Chris, I told you that. He's apologised, but it was an accident, and there's absolutely no purpose in going over it any more. How does it help Tess?'

How did we get here? she thinks. We were talking about Ella, we weren't talking about Chris at all.

'Fuck that!' Jacob yells. 'Don't you fucking get it?'

He steps in closer and she stays sitting on the bed. Her limbs won't move; they won't do anything at all. Jacob keeps coming forward, his face mottled red, staring at her.

'You're fucking *blind*, Mother. You just don't get it, do you?'

She can't speak. She's tiny. She wants to cover her head.

Jacob looks around. He's finding something to throw, she thinks, and she flinches. Then he leaves the room, slamming the door behind him.

She remembers: this happened; this is how it was.

Sitting propped up in the double bed, with the bedspread pulled around her. The bedspread speckled with dark red roses, and Jacob tucked in beside her. Reading a story about The Farm, and saying, Make the noise, Jacob. This is a sheep, what does the sheep say?

Hearing him come in downstairs, the thick clunk of the door hitting the lock, swearing as he takes his jacket off, starts up the stairs, trips, gets back up.

Hearing him come in, earlier than usual, drunker than usual, and about to find her here, with Jacob in the bed. Jacob is gripping her finger and he's frightened: he knows the clunk of the door as well, and he knows what will happen if he's in the bed. Jacob mustn't be in the bed, she thinks. He mustn't be in the bed because Jacob is not allowed in the bed with her, ever. That's the one thing he hates: Don't spoil the boy, Louise, that's what he says. He's drunker than usual, and Jacob is here, beside her, gripping her finger.

Realising, in the moment that his footsteps stop outside the door, that this time will be different, this time will be worse.

Move, Jacob, she whispers. Dad's home. Quick, get in the wardrobe, and he does move, scuttles low across the floor and pulls the shuttered door back against him, and she can hear him behind the door making soft whimpering noises. Stop it! she whispers. Jacob, be quiet!

He comes in, and says: You're still up.

She can't speak. She's tiny. She wants to cover her head. The baby starts crying in the cot. Don't cry, she thinks. Hush, Tessa, hush, please be quiet.

Little bitch, he says. Can't you shut her up?

He stands beside the bed and looks at her, and he's blind drunk. Little bitch, he says. Make her shut up.

When she gets out of the bed he hits her in the stomach.

When she tries to get back up he hits her in the face.

He moves towards the cot.

Don't touch her! she screams, and lunges at him, but the baby is under his arm, and wailing, screaming higher and louder.

I'll shut her up, he says.

Please, she says, trying to keep her voice steady and calm. Please give her to me.

He pulls back the curtains and opens the wide window.

You want me to shut her up? he says.

Please, she says, please.

He holds the baby out, flailing, in his hands. A cold gust blows in and she can hear the sound of a car starting up, and a rubbish bin clanking. The baby's hand, moving in wild circles, brushes up against the glass of the lower pane, making a small tap, tap.

Don't move. Don't speak. Don't breathe.

Whoops! he says, but he turns, and tosses the baby three feet across the room onto the bed, and laughs.

Shut her up, he says. Get her away.

She had waited downstairs for an hour. When Tessa was sleeping, and she could hear him breathing heavy and slow, she crawled from the doorway along the floor in the dark and opened the wardrobe door, bracing herself at the slight squeak. Jacob fell into her arms, stiff and gasping. We're going now, she whispered to him halfway down the stairs. *This time we're going.*

She stayed at the refuge for a week with ten other women, and kids everywhere, all of them playing up, and Jacob kicking and biting the other children, confused and traumatised.

The worker there, Joan, planned everything: organised accommodation, told her how to get on the benefit. Look, Louise, she said to her, sitting in the dingy office over a cup of tea, can you see how many women there are staying here? And this is just the tip of the iceberg. It's not something you've done wrong. It's not your failure. It's part of our society.

Talking to Joan was like unpicking stitching that had gone wrong, veered right away from the line and become bound up, with the threads wound over and around and going nowhere. She came to understand that there were patterns and routines to it, and understood too that although he had only begun to hit her in recent months, since Tess was born, it would have gone on, and swallowed up everything. She saw that potentially one of them would have been seriously harmed in the end, because it was all there, all the patterns, right from the beginning, except she didn't recognise them, and she didn't know how to change it.

Her father didn't see it that way. She told her mother on the phone. They talked for a while and her mother was restrained, but sympathetic. A week later her father wrote to her.

233

Dear Louise,

You are destroying your family and I implore you to reconsider. Your children face a future without their father if you take the drastic measures you propose, and I do not believe you appreciate the full consequence that will have upon their lives. Neither am I convinced that you have attempted to resolve these problems through mutual understanding and open discussion.

I believe that with good will, and patient, loving attitudes on both sides, early difficulties can be overcome, and surely, Louise, these troublesome times fade into insignificance in comparison to the joy of a stable, lasting marriage. This is particularly so when, as in your case, there are innocent little ones involved.

Your mother and I were witness to your wedding vows. We have always considered our own vows to be sacred – our highest duty – and would certainly have expected the same of you . . .

She refused to see them after the letter – didn't even contact Kevin, who was young then, only ten or eleven. Seven years ago Jacob found out that his uncle lived in Wellington and rang him up, quite out of the blue. He came around for a meal and they talked about fishing, and nursing, and the restaurant, and didn't talk about the family at all.

Mum died later that year, and against her better judgement Louise took the kids over on the ferry to the funeral. Her father delivered the eulogy, standing up in the small, packed church and talking for forty minutes about Colleen's commitment to the family, and the manner in which she always put others first. He didn't acknowledge Louise or the children – not in his speech, nor afterwards in the church hall. Several family friends smiled politely at her across the room, but, except for Kevin, no one approached her at all and so she left early, pulling the kids away from the mallowpuffs and pizza, whispering sharply to them that they would not go to the cemetery, but she would drive them out to the boulder bank instead.

It was a cold clear day and the three of them had walked for an hour, throwing rocks into the waves, and counting large tankers out on the horizon, and closer in small yachts keeling hard in the wind and tacking sharply in one direction and then the other.

After the refuge they had moved into a small flat, and she settled Jacob into playgroup. Later there was kindy and school, and after Tessa turned five she went back to work at the hospital, constantly juggling the schedule, always trying to plan ahead. She fed the children vitamin pills, and as many vegetables as she could force down them, because every time they got sick it was a disaster: it meant ringing around trying to find childcare, or calling in to the hospital at the last minute saying, I'm so sorry, there really is nothing else I can do.

She was alone – had few friends – and there really wasn't enough money, but she never thought of it at the time as being hard; it was simply hers, her own life, back in her hands, a matter for her to shape and form.

One day she saw his name in the death notices of the newspaper. Jacob had just turned nine. *Suddenly, due to accident*, it said. *Loved father of Siobhan, Jayden and Kara*. It didn't mention Jacob or Tessa. Even now she imagines these other faces – her children's unknown siblings – picturing them as three blond heads and wondering about their lives, feeling an unreasonable tug of responsibility and connection.

For weeks after, she was struck again and again by the realisation: we're safe. We're finally, completely safe. She cut out the small square of newsprint and kept it: as proof.

——

Louise sits on the bed in Ella's empty room with the light coming in hard at the window, and listens to Jacob thumping around the house. He slams the front door shut, and then she is alone in the house, and lies down.

How has it come to this? she thinks. *There is something terribly wrong with my son.* She thinks of Tess then, and her twisted face, and the way she can't speak properly, and how she can't walk more than three steps in a row, and for the first time the clear thought arrives: *It isn't fair.*

It is as though the little bridge she has built with her own hands has broken. She is right back where she started, on one side of the bank with an impossible chasm to cross. None of this is fair, she thinks. I didn't deserve this.

She thinks of the pottery wheel, her hands wet and cool in the clay, forming a bowl, and the way she would lose concentration for half a second, distracted by a classmate, or a song on the radio, and then the entire form would collapse, turn in upon itself, and she would have to take it off, smash it against the bench, knead it and start again.

Something is terribly wrong with Jacob, she thinks. And perhaps Tess is never going to get better. Lying there, on Ella's empty bed, it is difficult to understand why she continues: why she gets up each day, and pursues her little routine of care and attention; why she pushes against the natural decay of things, keeping it all alive and running – Tess, Ella, Jacob, the house, the restaurant, the silverbeet in the garden. Why am I doing this? she wonders, and all the cogs seem to spin down then to a jagged halt.

She doesn't sob, or swear, or rage, but simply rolls onto her stomach and gives herself over to an immense weariness. She realises that she may lie here, face down into the pillow, for some time. In fact, she feels as though she may never get up at all. Outside, there are seagulls cawing and a flurry of traffic on the road; there is the faint sound of neighbours talking on the patio, and the constant, repetitive beat of the waves. The sun rises higher and the room heats up, becoming a closed pocket of stale, unmoving air, and she does not move to open a window, or the door. She lies quite still, as blind and inconsequential as a stone on the beach.

Some time later the phone rings at the far end of the hall. She hears it and holds her breath, noticing a small instinctive burst of energy in her limbs, but it is not enough – she cannot move, or make a start – and so she lets it continue, lonely and persistent, until finally it stops, and the silence settles back over her like a blanket.

When she wakes it is late afternoon. She has slept for five or six hours. But still she doesn't move: she stays lying on her side, watching a web of high cloud disperse across the square of sky.

Another hour passes, and the colour of the sky changes minute by minute, until it is a full clear blue. Eventually she stands and stretches, pulls on her shoes, walks to the kitchen and pours a glass of water. She drinks it quickly, gasping for breath and feeling a slight spin in her head, the sensation of pressure around the sockets of her eyes.

Outside she crosses the road and starts along the shore, thinking of nothing except the motion of her limbs and the sun on her face. It is the height of the summer day and down by the water people are clambering along the rocks. They are points of colour caught in the brilliant light: a white T-shirt, an orange jacket, the bright red of a child's cotton jersey. Up on the road the toetoe bush is translucent, with the sun behind it. Each stem, and each pale head, thick with seed, curves around in a carefully balanced form.

She stands still on the footpath, watching the light move in bands across the flat plain at the edge of the headland, and listening to the faint calls of the children down on the rocks, and it starts to rise back up in her then, as an impossible, unreasonable faith: *Yes, it's worth it. It's worth continuing.* There are hours, or snatched minutes of solitude. There is the insistence of light and colour, and there is the odd sense of something good, something constant, that rises to meet her early in the morning, or late at night. Unfathomably, it is still here, more alive than ever now, when everything else is damaged and incomprehensible. It's like a secret life, she thinks. And it carries me.

The following day she goes to the café across the road from the hospital and buys the painting, the one she has contemplated over morning coffee for seven weeks. It costs her eight hundred dollars. She can't afford it: it will mean dipping into her small retirement fund. But she buys it anyway, signing the cheque with a flourish.

Back at home she puts it up over her bed and quickly touches the feather with her fingertip, and the small gold leaf stuck into the paint. The light catches at it: blue, gold and green. She stands back and notices the way the four squares balance one another. Each contains a single shape: a feather, a leaf, a mountain, a wave. The border around each square is a different colour. Two are dark, and the other two thinner and lighter, which gives the illusion of space, but it's the darker squares that she's fascinated by – the way the eye is drawn in and comes to rest at the centre.

Chris has started writing lists. This is his new discipline. He is doing this because his life is about to change. From the tenth of January he will have to be disciplined each day. He will have to get up early, and account for his time in six-minute blocks, so he is starting to practise discipline now, in these small ways.

Each morning he has written a different list, for three mornings now. Projects. Phone calls to make. And today, a list of Christmas presents. The most important item on this list is Sally's present. He doesn't know what it is, but he believes it's out there – the right gift, the single item that will make her understand that she can trust him, that it can all be fantastic again. He's spent an hour this morning mentally trawling through the options, and now he's ready to get in the car and head into town, start pacing up and down the long street of expensive shops, battling the crowd: bags, elbows and harassed sales girls at the till.

The right present could be clothes. It could be a dress, or a skirt, or some kind of top – like a jersey, only not a jersey. This could be the right thing, because it's what she is passionate about. But he's terrified of buying her clothes. He's never done it, not once in all the time they have been together. Figuring out the right size is only the first problem. He could look through her wardrobe for that, but then finding the right style – something that she would actually wear, that she would open up, lift out and adore – is very difficult. He wants her to say, It's perfect, in just the right tone. Already he feels defeated and is starting to consider a CD instead, or tickets to a concert, or perfume. There are many other ideas that seem to have a better chance of success. But if I could pull it off, he thinks, it would work, I know it would.

Getting the present to her could be a problem, because he doesn't know whether they will see each other on Christmas Day. In the three days that he has been writing lists, Sally has stayed at Fiona's. She has called him twice.

'So why the fuck didn't you tell me?' she asked.

'I meant to. I was scared.'

'That's pathetic, Chris.'

He didn't say anything at all then. There was nothing to say.

'Who else knows?' she asked.

'I think Jacob knows.'

'*You told Jacob?*'

'No. I think Tess told Jacob.'

She was silent for a long time. His brain whirred frantically, trying to get ahead, trying to work out what she was going to ask next.

'But how could Tess tell Jacob?' she asked, confused. '*After* the accident? She told him then?'

'It was the night before the accident, Sally. Tess came back. That's when I had to drive her home.'

She hung up.

The second time she called it went a little better.

'I'm at work,' she said. 'This has to be short.'

'How's it going?' he asked.

'Not bad. Megan's pissing me off. She's just ruined ten metres of fake fur.'

'Will you come home tonight?'

'No. Not yet. Maybe not at all. I don't know.'

He wanted to beg then – everything in him wanted to say, Please, Sally, please, please – but he kept control, he didn't let himself beg at all.

'I could meet you somewhere. For coffee. For lunch. We could talk about it.'

'I find it difficult to believe that all those times we talked about the accident . . .'

'I know. I know.'

'You were *lying*, the whole time. Do you have any idea how stupid I feel?'

'Don't feel stupid. I feel stupid.'

He thinks he can hear her blowing her nose. Someone is singing out of tune in the background.

'So anyway, what makes you think Jacob knows about this? Did he say something?'

'He's writing me screwy letters.'

'He's writing you letters?'

'He says I tried to kill Tess –'

'*What the fuck?*'

'– so that you wouldn't find out.'

'Chris?' she says.

'*Sally!*'

'What does he say in these letters?'

'Oh, that I'm a treacherous bastard, that I'm going to get done, that no one trusts me . . . general goodwill.'

'Sounds insane. Are you going to talk to him?'

'I probably should.'

'I'd say you have to. What a head case – oh! I didn't mean that. Bad choice of words.'

'I'm not sure how seriously to take it.'

'But it's kind of frightening, don't you think?'

'Yeah. It's awful. Yeah.' But not nearly as awful, he thinks, as you being away, and having to sit around on my own, writing lists, waiting for you, and not knowing what will happen next.

'I have to go,' she says.

'Okay. Call me again. Please, Sally?'

'Yeah. Bye, Chris.'

In fact he's been planning to call Jacob ever since the letter arrived. It's down on his list of phone calls to make: Jacob's name sitting there between the bank and his grandmother.

241

But one thing after another has come up and he simply hasn't got around to it. So he's taken aback when he's searching through the bedroom, tossing clothes around and trying to find his wallet, and Jacob calls him. He's even more surprised that Jacob wants to meet for a drink, wants to talk, tonight. Where? Chris asks. At the Breakwater, Jacob says. Just with you, or you and Louise? he asks. Just me, Jacob says. I want to talk to you alone.

When he puts the phone down he realises he is breathing fast, and he is sweating, and he can't remember now whether Jacob said eight o'clock or eight-thirty. He thinks of calling him back to check but decides not to, decides that it would be altogether easier to arrive at the restaurant at eight, order a strong drink, and wait if necessary. But I'm going for a surf first, he thinks.

The cold shocks him, in the usual way. He splashes into the water and pushes the board out, starts paddling, feeling the resistance in his limbs, the tingle on the skin of his fingers and toes. He ducks through the first breaking wave and this feels different than usual, because the helmet keeps his head quite dry, until he comes up, and water trickles in cold tight lines across his scalp. He dives down through the second wave and then he forgets the cold altogether, and his limbs are pushed by anticipation, the familiar impulse, the need to get out there faster, to start riding.

It's huge today, and, surprisingly, there's hardly anyone out. He paddles out the back and immediately a set comes in, and he catches it, stands, and rides all the way in, sinking to a slow finish a couple of metres from the beach.

He stays out for an hour, with the sun going down and the sky starting to fill with colour. The surf froths pink in the low light. The sets keep coming and he catches one wave after another; he's getting them all, eight and then nine fantastic rides, and he's starting to feel powerful, he is braced, and

242

triumphant, and a long way now from the grotty afternoon, the heat, and the frazzled shop assistants, away from the impossible garments that he didn't understand.

Eventually he had given up shopping for Sally and gone in to Surf 'n' Ski, bought himself a helmet, a surf magazine, a new rash vest and wax. He has spent a couple of hundred dollars today but he figures that he deserves it, because his life is going to change, and he can afford it now. He bought these items and now he feels that he has accomplished something.

The sounds muffle under the plastic shell and foam inner. He can't hear the gulls, and he can't hear the shouts of the other guys. What he can hear is his heart, and his breathing. With a helmet on he is pushing himself further, taking on waves that he would normally let pass. Paddling hard, with the roar of a wave twice his height coming up fast behind him, his chest thumps loud with fear and desire. But he catches it, and drops in, and he's there, riding it; he's carving to the right, and he's not coming off – he's going to make it all the way in.

This is me, he thinks, *this is mine*, and everything in him is competent and glorious. Everything else – the problem with Sally, the meeting with Jacob, having to buy a suit, and the incessant nagging questions about Tess – what does she look like? how damaged is she? – all of this seems small and far away, as irrelevant as the houses perched on the far hill, kept in their right proportion for the length of a long ride in to the beach.

When he trawls out of the water he is ready to meet Jacob. He rubs at his hair furiously and thinks: I'm going to deal with you. He is braced, and ready, because he's had the best session he's had for months, and he's decided he's not going to tolerate this crap any longer.

The restaurant is busy, with only the stools at the window empty. He scans the room but Jacob isn't here yet. It's eight

243

o'clock exactly, bang on dinner time. The three girls working tonight are moving as fast as they can, swinging out from the kitchen doors, carrying three loaded plates at a time. He can't see Margie anywhere, which is a relief. He's not sure exactly what will happen tonight and he'd rather there was no one around to see. If it starts getting heated, he thinks, I'll suggest we go outside. Casually. I'll suggest a walk.

He orders a beer and chips. He drinks quickly, suddenly hungry, thirsty and tired from the cold water. The chips arrive and he orders another beer, and starts planning what he's going to say. *Jacob, you're fucking deluded.* No, it's important not to provoke him. But he's going to say it straight, he's not going to stand for any bullshit. Jacob, let's be clear. There was a car crash. It was an accident. What happened with me and Tess is none of your business, and what happens between Sally and me is also none of your business. There are no secrets here. No one is confused except you. If you're so certain the world is set against you, go join the fucking Branch Davidians. That's a good line – the Branch Davidians.

The food is gone, it's well past eight-thirty, and Jacob still hasn't turned up. It's making him anxious now; it's making him edgy because he needs to have the conversation. He wants have it over with. He's fidgeting, and bored, and getting really irritated at Jacob. Arrogant prick, he thinks, what's he playing at? The surfing magazine he bought this morning is lying in the back of the car and he wants to read it.

He waits for one more minute, then circuits around the tables, checking and rechecking to make quite sure Jacob isn't there. He heads out the restaurant doors and over to the carpark. His car is at the far end. It's almost dark, but the grey light is still picking at the metal colours of the cars. He's turning the key in the lock when he hears the sound of a horn beeping and looks around.

There's a blue Mazda three cars down from him. Jacob is sitting in the driver's seat, looking over at him, not waving.

He takes the key out of the car door and walks over, slowly and casually. The window is down.

'Hey,' Jacob says.

'Hey.'

Chris stands there, unnerved, unsure what happens next.

'Do you want to come across the road?' he asks. 'Have a drink?'

'Nah. Nah, I don't.'

Jacob isn't looking at him. The seat is sloped right back and he's staring out to the water, his arms crossed over his chest.

'Okay. Okay. Well, do you want to talk out here, then?' Chris asks.

Jacob makes a vague noise and reaches over to unlock the passenger door. Chris slides into the seat and it's warm in the car, with the heater running and the stereo on low, the sound of Radiohead crooning. The horizon is a dirty rim of orange light straight out ahead. He sits beside Jacob, silent, and looking out at the ocean.

'So, whose car is this?' he asks.

'Mum's,' Jacob says. 'New.'

'Oh, right. Right.' You *idiot*, he thinks. Fucking stupid bloody question. But Jacob doesn't say anything else, just slowly runs both hands back through his hair, then recrosses them over his chest.

'How's the thesis coming along?' Chris asks, trying to think of something neutral, something safe.

'It's shit.'

'How's that?'

Jacob doesn't answer. He's silent, and small, slumped low in the seat. Okay then, so ask him, Chris thinks, just ask him.

'How's Tess?'

'Improving. Coming home. Sometime after Christmas.'

'Great! That's great news.'

'Yeah. Yeah, it is.'

Jacob sounds calm. Quite calm, and so, suddenly aware that he has been waiting for weeks to find out this information, Chris tries another question.

'Do they think she's going to recover? Like, completely?'

'Don't know. She's about seventy per cent at the moment, they reckon.'

'Seventy per cent,' Chris repeats, wondering about the other thirty, and just what parts of Tess that contains.

Jacob is silent. Clearly he is waiting. Clearly he is expecting Chris to start the conversation about the matter at hand. That's part of the whole unspoken deal here.

'Okay, well, Jacob . . . ah . . . about these letters.'

'The letters.'

'You, um, you're kind of making some pretty full-on statements. I've, ah, I've been quite concerned, actually, Jacob, and I, ah, I think we need to get a few things straight.'

'Shit. Forget the letters, man.'

Jacob's bluffing. He's playing some kind of game. Chris checks to ensure that he hasn't been locked into the car. He waits, tensed, ready to give back as good as he gets. Jacob doesn't speak.

'Forget the letters?' he asks after a while, and despite himself his voice breaks a little.

His brain scrambles to make sense of the situation, his arms and legs still wired, ready to move, to take action, but there is nothing here to respond to. It is very difficult to work out what's going on. The single immediate fact is that Jacob doesn't appear to be angry, he doesn't appear worked up at all. He's in a different state altogether. It's not clear what he should think, or what he should do next. It seems important to ask about the letters again. He wants to push Jacob for an explanation, an apology. After all, he's come here specifically to sort it out.

But Jacob is completely flat. The tape ends, and pops out, and the static hisses. Chris flips it and pushes it back in, practising sentences in his head: You've been saying crazy things, Jake. You owe me an apology.

But after a few minutes he decides to let it go, to let it all go, because the letters seem to come from another time, or another person. It's difficult to think that those crazy, violent words have anything to do with this guy here, slumping low and docile in his seat, slowly turning the windscreen wiper on, and off.

'It's not good with you, Jacob?' he eventually asks.

'Nah. Not good.'

They sit together and don't say anything. The orange horizon fades and it becomes completely dark. They sit there, and the other side of the tape plays through, and after a time Chris feels a warmth rising in his chest, and he thinks it is working out fine, because the letters aren't important after all. When it counts, when it's like this, Jacob needs him. Despite everything he needs Chris to sit here with him in the silence and be his mate, because Jacob gets like this at times, there's a pattern to it, and tonight is an example.

Ella is surprised to find the bus almost full, with old people travelling alone, and young couples, and large families up near the front, children bouncing in the seats and fiddling with new toys.

When she got on she placed her two dollar coin down in the little wooden hollow but the driver picked it up and gave it back to her. Free for Christmas, love, he said, it's all free today. There was an empty seat near the back and she propped Connor up on her lap and watched as people poured on at each stop, all these people heading out towards the coast. She's going out to the beach, to Houghton Bay, where she lived when she first came down to Wellington. It's a surfing beach, and there were always surfers out, even on the coldest days, and she remembers how she liked to watch them, bobbing in the waves like seals. They will spend the afternoon there, play in the sand, paddle, and eat sandwiches.

The sun has blazed all morning. At seven she woke to the baby crying and flicked on the radio, listening, while she fed him, to the announcer saying, Well, folks, looks like the best we've had in a decade. They lay together in the big bed and she stretched him out on her stomach, and laughed and chatted to him until he made his cooing sounds and smiled back at her. She got up and made breakfast, pouring herself a small bowl of Peter and Lisa's expensive muesli, and then it was time to give Connor his rattle, but it was a little too heavy for him to hold yet and he left it lying on the floor. She regretted not buying the music player then, and thought, briefly, about the full dress with the blue flowers as well.

Then it turned nine o'clock so she called Dad. He started telling her about how he'd been up since the crack of dawn because of the sheep and their facial eczema, which needed sorting out, Christmas Day or not. 'Maggie's put on a chicken,' he said, 'and the neighbours are coming across for a cold drink in the afternoon. We think we might put the deck-chairs out the front, on the driveway,' he said. 'Maggie's been planting pansies out there and they've come up a real treat. And how about the weather down there?' She told him about the still day and the blue sky. 'And are you having something nice for lunch with your friends?' he asked. Yes, Dad, she said, we're having ham, because it was far too complicated to explain.

When Dad said, 'Well, then, we'll see you soon, love, see you in the New Year,' she hung up, and didn't know what to do next. She thought about sorting through her boxes. All her gear is at Peter's now, because she picked it up by taxi from the house yesterday, late in the afternoon when she knew Louise would still be out. She left the key on the hallway dresser, and wondered whether she ought to leave another note.

But this morning she hadn't wanted to sort through her stuff so she sat on the floor for a while, watching Connor chew on the green butterfly. She sat on the soft maroon carpet, and then lay down looking up at the swirls on the cream ceiling, and bit gently at her lip. I could stay here, she thought; I could just stay lying here, looking at the ceiling all day long, and no one would even know. From that angle she could see the liquor bottles on top of the wall unit: the gin, and the Baileys, and the port.

That's when she realised they had to go out. She packed a bag with tomato sandwiches and a bottle of water and walked down to the shops to catch the bus.

At the beach there are children with kites, and inflatable rings, with new cricket sets and volleyball sets. A Dad and an older brother throw a ball between them, twenty metres across the sand, a strange ball with a tail, and it makes a shuddering, humming sound as it passes overhead. A small dog yaps and darts between the cricket and the volleyball, and mothers and aunts sit out under the shade of umbrellas and let the smallest children pour sand across their feet.

She finds a spot on the wooden slats outside the toilet block where there is shade. She puts a cap on the baby, and rubs sunscreen into his neck and arms and fat legs. She takes out the sandwiches, and flicks through a magazine she brought from the house. There is a story about a girl with leukemia, and she thinks then about Tess, and Louise, and Jacob, wondering whether they are at home sitting out in the garden, or up at the hospital. She wonders if Kevin is with them, and what they are eating, what they are talking about. I wonder if Tess will notice that we're not there, she thinks. But of course she won't, because Tess doesn't really recognise her at all yet, or she didn't the last time they went down to see her.

When she thinks about Tess she starts to feel sad, and a little angry, and a little confused, so she takes Connor down to the water and splashes his feet gently until he giggles. Is that nice? she asks him. Is that cool on your feet? She plunges him down, right up to his knees, but he is frightened and starts to cry. She walks in the shallow waves, splashing all the way along the shore and back again, carrying him on her hip, bending down to pick up the best shells, and noticing the thick trails of kelp out past the rocks. We could go for a walk, she thinks. That's what we'll do: start walking around the bays. She buckles him into the pram and pulls the hood across so he is shaded from the sun.

Coming around the point she sees a large group of people gathered in the distance, at the far end of the beach. They are focused on something in the centre of the tight cluster. Perhaps it's a barbecue, she thinks, but there is no smoke, and they are too close to the water. Perhaps it's a religious gathering. But there is no singing, and no one is lifting their hands in the air. The people are standing or sitting in small groups, looking, and pointing at something in the centre.

She walks towards the crowd, pushing the pram through the wet, solid sand near the water's edge. She realises that they are looking at some kind of animal – something washed up, stranded on the sand. Her heart starts beating a little faster because she's never seen a dolphin in the wild and it could be one – it's been known to happen out here on the south coast. Certainly, it's far too small to be a whale. Do they know what they're doing? she thinks, striding fast across the sand now. Has someone called DOC? The crowd is four or five deep and she can't see the shape; she can't make it out yet.

Approaching the fringes of the circle she catches a glimpse of the torso and it's clearly too fat to be a dolphin; it's the wrong shape altogether, and the wrong colour. Connor has fallen asleep so she leaves the pram out on the edge and ducks quickly to the front. A sea lion. More than that, a Hooker sea lion, unmistakably. *Phocarctos hookeri*. A small one, young, with its coat darkening to the brown-black colouring of the male. The DOC worker is already there, keeping the children back, and engaging in a serious conversation with a tall bearded man who must be a scientist. He will be excited, she thinks – there hasn't been a North Island stranding of a Hooker for years.

But it's not really a stranding, because they come inland, these ones, more than two kilometres. But he's alone, and young, separated from the herd. Creeping around the inside of the circle to try to view him from the other side she sees that he is cut, in long parallel grooves along his flank. The sand below is clumped, thick with black blood. He's dying, she thinks, but his eyes are open, and as she watches he raises his head and gives a sharp, angry bark. Behind her a child says, Mum, it sounds like a dog, not a lion. Why don't they call it a sea dog?

She remembers the pram and pushes her way back through the crowd. Connor is slumped into the side of the pram, unperturbed and unaware, and she jostles into a space where a couple just left and sits down. There's a clear view of the head from here – the black eyes, the frown line of whiskers. She notices the details: the markings on the back; the soft round snout; but particularly the odd movement of the front flipper, the left one, which shudders and lifts lightly, and then comes back down to rest in the sand.

After a time she notices also how the crowd is constantly shifting and changing. People come and join the circle, curious and excited, and some say, Wow, look at that, and stay for a minute, then turn and go. Others sit or crouch and watch for longer, and some of these take photos, and explain to their children. See, kids, they say, it's similar to a seal.

One or two of the men from the crowd approach the DOC worker, asking questions, nodding and rubbing at their faces. She'd like to go and ask some questions herself but he seems busy and she doesn't want to interrupt. She's guessing that they will wait for the high tide, to see if he swims out by himself. The small waves curl several feet away. Every now and then a strong surge rushes further up the sand and you can see him rocking forwards then, sniffing for it.

An hour on, Connor is still sound asleep. The sun slants low across the water and the blue sky deepens, dissipating into colour at the horizon. The water laps much closer to the sea lion's body now, but he's weaker, considerably so, his head flat on the sand, not moving.

She's started identifying people in the crowd. A few have been here the whole time: to her left, a woman in a yellow jersey who sketches in a spiral notebook in quick sharp lines, then flicks the page over and starts again; a man with a boy of six or seven resting between his knees; and an older couple, with cricket hats and sunglasses, who have laid out a small picnic between them. It is as though they share a secret, these ones who have stayed, as though there is a solidarity between them, a common cause. We're keeping watch, she thinks.

Sitting and watching the sea lion, flat and unmoving in the sand, with the crowd dwindling and the heat gone out of the day, a thick, blind sadness rises in her. It takes her by surprise and she doesn't have the energy to stand and move, to shake it off. The feeling has something to do with Tess, and an image of her lying immobile in her bed, the tubes and the bruises. And something to do with Louise. You're stupid, she thinks. Of course you feel like this. It's Christmas Day and you're spending it alone, because you had to move out. No, she thinks, that's not right. I chose to leave; I didn't have to.

She reaches for a stick caught under the wheel of the pram and starts to draw slow, full circles in the sand. I really don't want to think about this right now, she thinks. I could get really down. It's not going to do me any good sitting here moping.

And anyway, she thinks, it's not that bad. I can sort things out. Her exam results come briefly to mind and there is a small lift. And more important, there's Connor. She reaches up and runs her finger over his hand. There's him, and me. She nuzzles into his neck, kissing him, taking in his smell, and she wants to get him out of the pram and hold him for a while, warm and small against her chest. But he's sleeping solidly, oblivious.

It's overtaking her now, and the thought of her results can't stop it – even Connor's breathing and soft fuzz of black hair don't help. Shit, she thinks. No, I don't want to deal with this. As it overwhelms her she lies down on her stomach and rests her head in the crook of her elbow, biting hard at the inside of her lip. She tastes the trickle of salty blood.

I want to stay here. It's not a thought, it's an urge, and it's strong, and ridiculous. I want to stay here, I want to lie down beside him, all night. I want to lie here, and sink into the grey sand. I want to be underneath it all, where it's dark. The feeling is heavy in her stomach and limbs and she can't get up, can't shake it.

She thinks then of Dad and Mrs Loam, sitting out among the pansies making polite conversation with the neighbours. She thinks of the aunties, and her cousins further up the coast, but she can't imagine what they will be doing, because she hasn't spent Christmas with them since she was six. She thinks of Louise, Tess and Jacob, gathered in the lounge, with the tall palm tree decorated with red tinsel and cardboard angels, or perhaps up at the ward, underneath all the cards stung in rows across the bed. She thinks of Andy, too, and his mother, and his brother Jonathan, sitting up at the long dining-room table, eating with heavy silver cutlery off perfect white plates. She even thinks of Peter, and his girlfriend, somewhere in the South Island, in the mountains perhaps, or in the bush. She thinks of all these people, each face in turn flickering in front of her, illuminated brightly for a brief, brilliant second, and then the faces start to slip past in a little parade: start to move, circling around, the circles becoming faster, and wider, the same faces, around and around, spinning and moving away and blurring at the edges.

Then, after a while, she can only see one face, and it's Mum, in the kitchen. She is making biscuits at the bench in a blue apron, and looks up, pleased, or angry, or worried, and when she sees Mum's face she feels something buckle in her stomach. I'm going to lose it, she thinks. I have to leave – people will see me. She stands and pulls the pram up the beach towards the cutty grass on the bank.

Lying down in a little hollow, she thinks carefully and consciously for a time about her mother. The sand underneath her is warm from the day, and the cutty grass tickles her feet. What she sees now is that here, with the night shadows stretching out across the water, she is completely alone, that this has become the condition of her life.

Chris spends some time deliberating over the appropriate kind of flowers to buy. His grandmother was particular about flowers. She knew all the meanings, and if anyone gave her white lilies she would get quite upset because that meant death. It would be a terrible mistake to take lilies. The problem is that he doesn't even know the names of most of the flowers here, let alone what they mean. In the end he chooses roses – not red, obviously, but a mixed bunch: yellow, white and pink. Thanks, Jason, he says to the friendly guy at the checkout, who is wearing a name badge. Could you wrap them in some coloured paper?

He's trying to decide whether he should also take chocolate, juice or biscuits, so he pauses on the way out to look at the shelves. The main issue here is that he has no idea what she is eating, or whether she is eating at all. Jacob said she was seventy per cent better, which he assumes includes normal eating, and speaking – perhaps even walking. He knows this now, but in his worst moments he still imagines her in a wheelchair, with her head rolled forward, being fed with a spoon, and perhaps wearing some kind of hospital garment. He imagines that her face may have been mangled in the accident – he remembers there was a great deal of blood, and matted clots of hair – and is prepared for a broken nose, or other features somehow misaligned and distorted.

Each time he wonders about her face a single, uninvited image comes into his mind. It is Tess, leaning across him, the entire stretch of her from head to hips, and particularly her pale nipples, and the curve of muscle down over her stomach. It is sick, quite sick to think about her in this way now, and he feels disgusted with himself each time it happens.

———

255

Yesterday, after the heavy lunch, and tanked up on champagne and brandy sauce, his aunt, a school guidance counsellor by profession, cornered him in the kitchen and asked him a series of questions in a serious tone. Your mother says you've been quite flat since this accident happened, Chris. She says that even this new job hasn't got you excited. Frankly, I'm concerned. Do you think perhaps it would help to see someone professionally? No, he said, thank you. The worry, Chris, she continued, is that if you don't deal with your feelings about it now, it could well come back to trouble you in the future. It may start to affect all areas of your life – your relationships, your work, even your sleeping and eating. She leaned in closer and, almost in a whisper, asked, How are things with Sally?

He briefly considered talking to her honestly about all these matters. He would have liked to say, Well, I am going to see Tess tomorrow for the first time, and as far as Sally goes it's not clear whether she has left me or not. After all, his aunt was sloshed, and he was generally safe to say what he liked with her anyway. But there was the prospect of his father or younger brother walking in at any stage, overhearing and asking, What's this? What's happening? Everything's fine, he said, putting his hand out on his aunt's shoulder and smiling in what he hoped was a broad, reassuring way. Sally's spending Christmas with her family. It's easier for everyone that way. But thank you for asking. And he pressed her arm and slipped away to the dining room, carrying out a large platter of chocolates and cherries.

It's five days since he met with Jacob. Afterwards he'd wanted to go and see Tess immediately, the next morning, but Sally called first thing and asked him to come out for coffee and a discussion, and he didn't want to risk complicating that. It was his chance to give Sally the red leather bag, the one he'd found in a shop at the smart end of town: rectangular and lined, with a tricky clasp. It was his chance to be direct and vulnerable with her. But even though she adored the bag, transferring her cardigan and wallet into it immediately, she didn't say anything definite about coming back.

Then he decided he would visit Tess on Boxing Day, because it didn't seem considerate to turn up unexpectedly in the days immediately before Christmas. But in those five days he'd lost the urgency. He'd really rather wait now; he'd rather let it go until another time, when he's better prepared.

Getting into his car he thought of Louise – the way she looks when she gets angry, or disappointed. Then he briefly considered going back inside and ringing Sally, begging her to come to the hospital with him, but fortunately he realised straight away that this would be both stupid and unreasonable.

As he passes through the wide doors into the ward three impressions form: the sound of a loud television in the room to the right; the absence of people, staff or patients, in the corridor; and his stomach flipping over, making him desperate to leave. The last time he came to the hospital as a visitor he was fifteen and his grandfather was dying of a liver condition. On that occasion he had experienced an intense desire to run outside into the wind and all the way back home to the coast, where he could get in the water and let himself be tossed furiously around in the waves, and no longer have to watch his mother rubbing at his grandfather's slightly yellow feet, trying to keep the circulation going. Now, just inside the ward, he experiences the same urge, but then Margie is coming down the corridor towards him and it's too late to pretend he hasn't seen her.

'Chris!' Before he has time to work out what he's going to say, or how to hold his arms, Margie has him by the shoulders and is kissing him on the cheek. 'Good to see you.'

'Hi, Margie,' he says, feeling shy, but pleased, because he

hadn't expected her at all. Margie is someone you can always count on to make a situation comfortable. It's an extremely good sign, meeting her first.

'How was your Christmas?'

'Oh, it was fine, yeah, we had a big family do.'

'Up at your mum's?'

'Yeah. Loads of food, everyone falling asleep and so on. Except we haven't got any little kids in the family any more so it's not quite the same. I reckon I'd still rather get an Action Man kit than all these socks and music vouchers. But no, it was fine.'

'Nothing better than a good Christmas lunch and a snooze. Now, Chris, did you get my message? The insurance claim came through in the end, no problem.'

'Yeah. That was a relief. Although, of course, that's not the main thing. The money, I mean.'

'Well, it helps to have it sorted out. And I take it there was nothing further from the police – you said they came and questioned you?'

'Yeah, but I wasn't speeding, and like I told you, I crossed when the light was orange. I told the police that. I told them exactly how it happened. It seemed to be fine.'

'Good. That's good, Chris. All right, well –'

'Yeah. So . . .' He casts around, trying to think of a question to keep the conversation afloat, a way to avoid having to move on to the next stage. 'How's business going?'

'Reasonable, thanks. We're keeping our head above water. But, look, I'll let you get on and see Tess.' She gestures towards the room on the left. 'I must say, your timing's good. She woke up about an half an hour ago – she's full of beans today.'

'Right. Good. Um – is Louise in with her?' It's embarrassing to ask this, to have his fear made so transparent, but he needs to know: he simply cannot face going in with so many unknown quantities.

'Louise? No, she's headed down to the shops for a bit.

But she shouldn't be long. If you hang about for a bit you'll probably catch her.'

'Great. Thanks, Margie,' he says, and takes a confident step past her and on into the room.

At first he thinks her hair has been dyed, but then he realises that it is darker because it's so short. This completely changes the aspect of her face, the hair licking in dark flames around her neck and cheekbones. It makes her look years older, and he's taken aback, daunted, because this Tess is extremely sophisticated, dressed in a black polo-necked jersey and long skirt, sitting on the couch and flicking through the pages of a photograph album. He's stunned, and jubilant, and doesn't know what language to use, because she is here, whole, and more gorgeous than ever and it is quite simply as though nothing ever happened.

He had a dream once, in which he was hiding in a pile of firewood from Nazi soldiers, who clattered past in thick boots, waving long hooklike weapons in their hands – soldiers who wished to crucify him, and, obscurely, had a superhuman sense of smell. The troops had caught wind of his scent mere feet away from his face when he woke. He'd lain dazed for several minutes, astonished to find himself safe beneath his duvet, with the dawn and early morning sounds of the rubbish collection coming in at the window. The sense of relief, of some kind of universal grace and good fortune, had pervaded the entire day, and he hadn't been able to shake off a surreal sense of luck.

It is precisely this feeling that he has now as he sits down on the couch beside her.

'Hi Tess,' he says, and he wants to take her hand, or kiss her cheek, to make some small, warm gesture.

'Hi,' she replies in a flat way, and her expression is difficult to read.

Margie comes in behind him, and says, 'Tess, this is

Chris, you remember Chris? You haven't seen him for quite a while.'

'Yeah. I think so,' Tess says, but she's looking at Margie; she doesn't look directly at him. 'Chris was in the accident too?' she asks.

'Yeah,' Margie says quietly. 'He was. Perhaps he could talk to you about that.'

Well, thanks, Chris thinks, that's a bloody good place to start. He's perturbed and it's difficult to grasp, this Tess, so utterly familiar, despite the new get-up, perhaps not recognising him, not remembering. Exactly what does she remember?

An odd idea occurs to him then: if Tess doesn't remember anything, then what happened with her may not, in fact, have taken place. Perhaps I only wished it, he thinks. He considers the possibility that the concussion has affected his own mind and memory more than he realised. Perhaps I made it up? he thinks.

He is aware that he is playing a game with himself, but it's a very attractive game and he allows it to continue. If it never happened, he thinks, then the entire drama with Sally need never have taken place. Of course, there is Jacob to consider, and his accusations, but given the state of Jacob's mind his letters can't be taken as proof of anything. they were vague, and could have referred to almost anything, evidence only of Jacob's generalised sense of jealousy. Within moments Chris finds himself seriously willing to entertain this idea: *perhaps it never happened.*

'You were crying,' Tess says, and she's looking at him now. 'I made you cry.'

What is she talking about? Margie is awkward, looking about the room, unsure whether she ought to leave.

'I called you a loser,' she says. 'I was angry, and I said some terrible things to you while you were driving me home, and you got upset, you started crying. Then we crashed.'

No, he wants to say, I wasn't crying, exactly. I might have

been upset. That could be true. I could have been upset. I don't think I was crying.

'Did you go to the hospital too?' she asks, and he notices now that she speaks in a strange way. She sounds a little like a robot because her tone doesn't change.

'Yes, I did. I came in the ambulance with you.'

'Oh,' she says. 'I didn't know that.'

'I didn't have to stay, though. I only had a sprained wrist.'

'A sprained wrist from the accident.'

'Yeah.'

'And you're Chris? It's Chris, isn't it?'

'Yeah,' he says, 'that's right, I'm Chris.'

A nurse comes in with a wheelchair and says, 'I'm terribly sorry to break up the party. Tess, it's time for your physical therapy.'

'But I've got a visitor,' she says.

'I am sorry,' the nurse says, looking back and forth between Tess and Chris. 'You do need to have therapy now.'

'I hate therapy,' Tess says, and her face looks as though she should be yelling, but her voice doesn't change at all, 'and I have a visitor right now. This is, um –'

'Chris,' he says quickly, standing up and shaking the nurse's hand. 'I'm Chris.'

'– and we're talking. Actually, I hate therapy,' she says. 'I don't want to go today.'

The nurse hesitates. Margie crouches down low beside Tess.

'Why don't you go to the therapy session now, Tess,' she says, 'and I'll make sure Chris is here when you get back. That way you can talk in peace.' Margie looks across at him and he nods enthusiastically.

'Do you live nearby?' Tess looks at him.

'No,' he says. She doesn't remember where I live, he thinks, grappling with the idea. *She doesn't remember the flat.*

'Okay, well, you could have a cup of coffee at the cafeteria

261

if you want. I won't be very long. I'll see you soon, Chris.'

He watches the nurse help Tess into the wheelchair and wonders if he ought to help too, but he doesn't want to stuff anything up or get in the way. In any case, Tess looks like she knows exactly what she's doing. She seems comfortable and familiar with the manoeuvre, as though she's been practising for years.

Louise comes into the lounge carrying a plastic jug to water the plants. Tess is sitting up on the couch, with cushions behind her head and her arm flopping in the usual awkward way. She is watching television. It's *The Simpsons*, and she is laughing – a raspy, uneven laugh – and it makes her body shake. Look at her, Louise thinks. She gets it, she knows exactly what is going on. She watches for a while from the door. Tess laughs at all the right points, even seems to understand the subtle references to movies and politics. Is it funny, Tess? she asks, and Tess replies in her flat voice, Yeah, Homer's been fired.

She's better, Louise thinks, standing there with the jug of water in her hand. Really, she's practically better. She knows this isn't completely true because Tess still walks slowly, and not very far, and she can't run. She doesn't have good control of her left arm. Certainly she can't swim, play netball or drive. But she can write. Last week she left a little note for the kitchen staff on her breakfast tray, saying, *No eggs for me tomorrow please*, perfectly spelt, but the handwriting a little uneven. Her voice has little modulation. Often she forgets something said to her just a day, or an hour, before. She forgets people and names, forgets facts. She can't remember much of what has taken place in the time since the accident. Sometimes she asks the same question ten times in a row. But she can talk to you in depth about what she's seen on the news, or what you read out to her. She can read a little herself, but not for longer than ten minutes, and only when the print is large. She often gets tired, and exasperated, and shuts down, slamming her foot into the bed or against the wall. But then, Louise thinks, she had a temper before the accident; that could just be Tess.

Look at her, she thinks. It's been only two and a half months. I didn't think we'd get this far. But she'll get further,

263

she thinks, and she knows that although it has taken eleven weeks of unremitting effort to bring Tess to this point, the work will continue for many months yet. *She's going to get completely better.* She'd decided that, sitting in the visitors' room with Mr Kelly thirty hours after the accident, when nothing was certain at all, and she had no understanding of how difficult and immense it would be. But still, the sense of some kind of promise or pledge remains. *Tess is going to get completely better.*

They are sitting up at the table for lunch, just Tess and her, and Tess is doing her best to eat the ham sandwich without spilling tomato out the side, when the doorbell rings.

'Is it a visitor?' Tess asks, surprised by the noise.

'I'll see,' says Louise. 'You wait there.'

She opens the door and it's Ella, with the baby in the pram.

'Ella,' she says, astonished.

'Happy Christmas.' Ella hands her a box wrapped in silver paper, tied with a gold and blue bow. 'Sorry it's a week late.'

'I didn't expect to see you.'

'No.'

'Do you want to come in?'

'Yes, I'd love to. Can I?'

'Absolutely. Tess is here.'

When Tess sees them she says. 'Who's that Mum?'

'It's Ella,' Louise says. 'Remember Ella?'

Then Tess asks, 'Do you live here?'

'Um, well, I've moved,' Ella says.

'Is that Connor?' Tess asks.

'Yes,' Ella says.

'Mum, can I hold the baby?' Tess whispers.

Ella takes Connor out of the pram and puts him down in Tessa's lap, but she can't hold him up by herself because of her weak arm, so Louise supports him there. He kicks a little but he doesn't cry.

'He's small,' Tess says. 'I suppose he's not walking yet.'

'No,' Ella replies. 'He won't be walking for a long time.'

Louise makes coffee and opens the present. It's a biscuit selection so she unwraps the plastic immediately and offers them around.

Tess takes a gingernut. 'You like these ones don't you?' she says to Ella. 'These are your favourite.'

'Yeah,' Ella says. 'Yeah, you remembered – I'm a big gingernut fan.'

'But they're so damn hard,' Tess says. 'They really hurt my teeth.

'So,' Louise says, 'what's been happening with you two?'

'Well, I'm staying at a friend's house at the moment,' Ella says, and her face turns a little red.

'Oh. Is it working out there?'

'It's temporary. Actually, I'm looking for a flat. I wanted to ask you if . . . do you know anywhere around here? I really like it out here. I want . . . I'd like . . . it would be good to be nearby.'

'Are you sure, Ella? You're welcome to . . .'

But Louise doesn't finish the sentence, because Ella is shaking her head.

'Well, that would be great.' Louise says, looking at Tess. 'Wouldn't it be great if Ella lived near us?'

'I'd rather she lived right here.'

Louise looks at Ella, and Ella surprisingly doesn't flinch, doesn't look away at all, and then she is the first to speak.

'Tess, I have to move on. It was good staying here,' the words are directed at Tess, but she's looking at Louise, 'but we're ready for our own place now. You could come around, though, you could come around all the time.'

'We thought you might come back for Christmas actually. We had a stocking for Connor,' Louise says.

'I'm sorry. I should have called you.'

'That would have been good.'

'Sorry,' Ella says again. She's starting to look miserable.

'Here, have another.' Louise offers her the box again. 'We're eating at the restaurant tonight. Would you like to join us?'

'Yeah,' Ella says, 'that would be great.'

The best thing about coming down in the evening is enjoying the lampshades with the red grapes lit up, and glowing. They are Louise's favourite feature of the room, and every time she admires them she remembers how she spent an outrageous sum of money at the leadlight shop, at a time when they weren't sure whether they would even get the building – weren't sure that the restaurant would go ahead at all. But she bought the lampshades anyway, and it seems to her now that this was an important act of faith, because it all unfolded quite smoothly and according to plan after that.

Margie brings out a bottle of good red wine and starts pouring. What about you, Tess? she asks. I just want half, Tess says. I might get shaky. And Louise is surprised, and impressed, because she's read that it's unusual, this level of insight, this early on. She's watching Tess carefully because even though she had been excited all morning – asking what was on the menu, and who was coming – once they got in the car she became nervous.

The evening has been carefully planned. She made sure Tess had a long sleep in the afternoon, and they've come down late so as to miss the rush. There is no music playing, and Louise is going to take the order to the kitchen herself because it would be difficult for Tess to choose a meal with a waitress hovering over her. But even with these arrangements it's a busy public space, there are five people around the table, and there is a lot of stimulus to deal with. Tess is clearly uncertain and making a strenuous effort to do her best.

'And you, Jacob?' Margie offers.

266

'Yeah,' he says, sitting back in his seat. 'I'll have some.'

Margie sits down next to Ella and starts talking to her quietly, and Louise can't hear from the far end of the table exactly what is being said. Tess pulls on her arm. 'I need to go to the toilet,' she whispers.

'Sure,' she says, and she lets Tess stand up by herself, then takes her arm in order to negotiate a path through the tables.

When they come back Kevin has arrived. He kisses them both, pulls his chair up beside Tess and makes a little joke, saying that all he wants is fish and chips, because he's got to support his own industry. She notices Tess relax then, an almost visible softening in her body. Seeing this, she realises quite clearly that something unexpected has formed in the past two months – in all the hours that Kevin has spent with Tess, talking, or simply sitting there; in the endless rounds of Snakes and Ladders; in the way that he would help her stand and walk to the bathroom and back when she couldn't do it herself. She sees that Tess responds to Kevin quite differently than to anyone else, except perhaps Louise herself. Tess never really talked to Kevin before, she thinks. And certainly Kevin never talked to her.

'Kevin,' she says, leaning across Tess and speaking quietly, 'thanks.'

Kevin looks startled. 'What for?'

'Everything. All the time you've spent with us. With Tess. And for helping out – the lawns and the garden – you've taken on so much.'

'Well, that's fine Louise, except I can't say I've ever done your garden, much as I'd like to take the credit for it.'

'You haven't been mowing the lawns?'

'Nah, not me. Must be the fairies, Louise.'

'It must have been Jacob then?'

'Could have been.'

She looks across at Jacob who is not speaking to anyone, his face pale and sullen. Perhaps she has misread him. Perhaps this is part of his problem – the mood swings and instability – frustration at her failure to notice all his efforts, all the various ways he supports her. She feels a sick wave of regret.

'Jacob –' she asks, leaning over to the other side of the table, '– have you been taking care of the garden this entire time, and your mother hasn't even said thank you?'

'Nope.'

'Oh. You haven't?'

'No. Dunno what you're talking about.'

'Oh. Okay.'

Who then? *Ella*. It can only be Ella. It must have been her, doing this exhausting job all along, in between the baby, studying and everything. *And how much else has she been doing?* Louise flushes with shame. She is about to stand up and walk around the table to take Ella aside and say, I'm sorry Ella, I didn't realise, but Margie's suddenly up on her feet, pinging at a glass with her knife.

'I think a toast is needed –' she says.

A few people are turning around to look. *Oh no,* Louise thinks, Margie, no, don't bloody talk about her, don't draw attention to her. Tess could really lose it; she could become really stroppy, and physical, if she gets any more stressed.

'– in honour of someone we all love and appreciate –'

'Hear, hear,' Kevin says.

'– a fabulous business partner, cook and gardener, a mother of extraordinary devotion, and a kind friend to many. To Louise,' she says, and raises her glass, 'a remarkable woman.'

Everyone is on their feet, saying Cheers! Cheers! and they all come and kiss her, and pat her on the back, including Ella, who is a little awkward, and ends up kissing her on the ear.

The flat comes with a bed, whiteware, and an old couch: dirty pink, with stains, rips and pieces of foam coming out at the edges. It belongs to a friend of Margie's. It is just a few streets away from the restaurant and Louise's place: five minutes' walk or less. It has no view of the sea but you can still hear it. It's small, and it's not cheap – probably more than she can afford. But, Margie says, you can stay in contact here. You can see Tess more often, once she's home, and probably get a bit of local babysitting into the bargain. Yeah, Ella says, looking around at the chipped walls, the heavily stained carpet. Yeah, I'll take it.

Margie lends her a blue cotton rug to throw over the couch and then it looks great, almost as good as something from a magazine. Margie, Louise and Ella each carry a box into the flat. Louise walks through the house, from the bedroom to the small kitchen and dining area and back again.

'You could put up some posters,' she says. 'That would help.'

There is nothing else to shift, so they leave her to it.

'Come down for tea,' Louise says.

'I'll bring some juice,' she answers.

Once the cot is up, and Connor is sleeping, Ella unpacks her clothes first, hanging them carefully on the ten hangers borrowed from Louise's house. She takes out the photograph of Connor's hands and puts it up on the windowsill in the kitchen, which is sunny now, in the late afternoon.

Next, she unwraps the Greenpeace calendar that Louise gave her and puts it up on the bathroom wall. January is a photo of emperor penguins, hints on composting, and a month of blank squares. She has nothing to write down in January. I could go home, she thinks, for a holiday. But there is Mrs

Loam, and, really, she's not sure that she could stand it. It would be good to see Dad, but she would be trapped on the farm, and if Dad were working she'd be left alone all day with Margaret. I wonder if I could stay at Auntie Jeanie's, she thinks, and this strikes her as a new and entirely feasible idea. Yes, she thinks, with an unfamiliar sense of possibility: it would be good to stay with them. I could go for a while. I could go until varsity starts back.

Next door a woman is singing and banging in the kitchen. I should get a radio, Ella thinks. Smells of fish and cut grass come in at the open window.

Later, the phone rings with a shrill tone and she jumps. She had forgotten it was connected. It's Andy.

'How did you know my number?' she asks.

'Louise gave it to me,' he says. 'Is it a secret?'

'No,' she says.

'Mum wanted me to call you.'

'Oh.'

'She wants to invite you to a family lunch.'

'When?'

'I don't actually want you to come, to tell the truth. Not after last time. It's my great-aunt's ninetieth birthday. She's asked to see Connor. Would he be all right if I came and picked him up?'

'Yeah, sure. He'd be fine, for a while at least. An hour?'

'It's tomorrow. Short notice.'

'That's okay.'

'I'll come and get him at twelve.'

'All right.'

'See you, then.'

'Um, Andy . . .'

'What?'

'I could come. If you didn't mind. Then he could stay longer. It might be easier.'

'You want to come?'

'Well, I could. If it helps.'

Andy's mother has impeccable manners and greets her as though nothing has happened. She introduces her to everyone as 'Connor's mother' and this is a relief, because she was anticipating, at best, 'Andy's friend', with a sly wink.

She stands in the doorway to the lounge watching the old ladies lift their teacups with thin and shaking hands. There is a sudden flurry of activity, as if there has been a signal that she missed. Somebody carries the vase of roses away from the coffee table, and somebody else starts pulling the curtains closed as a hush spreads across the room. Andy's mother appears behind her with the cake. It is a large round cake, iced with white icing, and there are nine candles blazing on top. All around the edge is a band of fat cherubs playing golden trumpets, small wings forming on their baby bodies.

Sorry, Ella says, moving backwards and out of the way. As she steps back into the hall Andy is beside her, reaching out his arms to take Connor, so she passes the baby over and watches as he is carried across and placed in the aunt's lap, supported there by Andy. Connor's eyes grow wide in the low light, his attention held by the flickering candles.

He will want a photo of this later on, she thinks. I should have brought a camera. Up near the front a tall man has a camera slung over his arm but he's not taking any pictures. Ella makes a decision, and walks quickly across the room, reaching up to touch him lightly on the shoulder. Excuse me, she says, could you take a photo for me? The man smiles, and the flash blooms bright in the dark room. The singing starts, and then the candles are blown out and the curtains pulled back, and the old people wince and shelter their eyes from the sudden sun.

She sees then that Connor has been passed to Andy's

271

mother, and that she is tickling his stomach and making him giggle. She slips back out of the doorway and walks downstairs to the study, which is almost empty, except for a desk and a low bookshelf. She is looking for something, something in particular. She will take it with her upstairs, and later, when there are fewer people around, she will ask Andy if she can borrow it for a while. She wants to ask him this, as a favour.

Her finger runs along the row of spines until she finds it, and slides it out and lays it on the desk. Here, the tourist book about the Kaikoura coast. And here, the close-up shot of the blue whale: the silver, sulphurous underbelly, and one flipper, pitted with barnacles.